Courtney, E
Familiar Stranger

FAMILIAR STRANGER

By the same author

A MOUSE RAN UP MY NIGHTIE
FARES PLEASE
MY FEET ARE KILLING ME
THE PRICE OF LOVING
OVER THE BRIDGE

FAMILIAR STRANGER

by

Edith Courtney

SEVERN HOUSE PUBLISHERS

This first world edition published in Great Britain 1989 by
SEVERN HOUSE PUBLISHERS LTD of
35 Manor Road, Wallington, Surrey SM6 0BW

Simultaneously published in the U.S.A. and Canada 1989 by
SEVERN HOUSE PUBLISHERS INC, New York

British Library Cataloguing in Publication Data
Courtney, Edith
  Familiar stranger
  I. Title
  823'.914 [F]

  ISBN 0-7278-1750-7

Distributed in the U.S.A. by
Mercedes Distribution Centre Inc
62 Imlay Street, Brooklyn, New York 11231

Printed and bound in Great Britain
at THE UNIVERSITY PRESS CAMBRIDGE

Chapter One

Rhianna Morgan first fell in love with Rhodri Blackmore when she was nine years of age. She stood on the beach wearing a bathing costume her mother had made; it covered her sturdy body that was as straight and flat as a peg. Rhianna held a bucket and spade and her attention roved from the starfish in the bucket to the sea. There in the sea was Rhodri Blackmore – sixteen, very much a man, wearing the briefest yellow trunks, and revelling in the thrill of being towed across the bay on water skis.

He was an expert. He had told her so when she arranged to bump into him accidentally the other day. His pronouncement had not surprised her. She knew Rhodri Blackmore could do anything.

With the perkiness of nosey childhood she had asked him where he got that tan and he had laughed down at her replying, 'California.'

'California? Where's that?'

He had cuffed her yellow-gold head. 'In America. Maybe you'll go there one day.'

'Will you take me?'

'No fear. You'll have to be big enough to take yourself.'

She had gazed at him wide-eyed and believed him. Now she watched him triumphantly skimming, and an unrecognised feeling of resentment caught inside her. She wanted to be as good as Rhodri Blackmore. Better. One day she would go to America, emerge more important than any Blackmore and make him fall madly in love with her.

She put the bucket and spade down beside her mother, who sat on a rock amid the seaweed, then she went towards the jetty and waited for Rhodri to come back in. She saw him topple and sink three times and each time she yelled and

1

clapped her hands, 'Hooray!' as if he could hear her as he struggled for breath in deep water.

When he slewed in to the shallows she ran to meet him, not caring for the holiday makers standing or sitting in groups watching others being more active and entertaining.

'You fell in!' she called to him, her sturdy legs apart, her toes twiddling in the sand.

'Want to try it?' he yelled back, and thrust his fingers through his thick soaking curling hair. She helped tug the speed boat to shore and was fascinated by the movements of Rhodri's shoulder muscles; they moved like those of a jungle cat on television, his hips narrow with, she decided, a nice little bum.

One of his many friends was helping too. He had been steering the boat. 'Helloh!' he said to Rhianna, his brilliant black eyes sparkling with laughter.

She looked back at him suspiciously, thinking he looked like a film-star. 'Do you come from America?'

'No. I come from the Continent, but I always enjoy California.' He laughed his film-star laugh again and asked, 'Do you, too, like the California sunshine, heh?' He held out his right hand and Rhianna took it solemnly.

'How d'you do?' she enquired, then backed from him.

He looked at Rhodri, 'Your latest girlfriend, heh?'

'There's nothing latest about Rhianna, Carl,' Rhodri replied. 'She's become my shadow!'

Rhianna turned and ran away. She didn't want to hear him talk as if she were a nuisance. She wanted to be like his other girlfriends – those whom everyone knew he took home to The Turrets. They often came in sports cars and zoomed through the village, boys and girls sitting on the folded back hood, and every one of them laughing and being happy.

Rhianna had stopped being happy. At night she said her prayers, asking urgently that she grow up fast and marry Rhodri before someone else married him.

All summer she watched the tide times and learned to know when Rhodri Blackmore would be messing about in his boat. Now and again Carl Jurgan was with him, but Carl seemed to be visiting every country in the world and said he had never been to a proper school. He laughed at Rhianna and told her about America – Florida, Texas, Manhattan. She listened and knew that if some other girl married Rhodri she, Rhianna Morgan, would end up in Manhattan.

Once Carl bought her an ice-cream cornet and the three of them – Rhodri, Carl and Rhianna – sat in the bobbing, anchored speed boat licking their ice-creams, Rhianna's gaze fixed on Rhodri. Later she heard him tell Carl he felt he couldn't blink easily because little Rhianna was counting each one.

She denied it earnestly. 'I am not counting blinks,' she said, in her straightforward honest manner. 'I am loving you all the time.'

He looked astonished, then amused, then called out to Carl, 'Hi, she is definitely not like the others. She means it when she says she loves me!'

Carl smiled. 'You are a lucky fellow, are you not?' he said, and Rhianna nodded furiously because she thought Rhodri Blackmore indeed very lucky.

When Rhianna was twelve it snowed in time for Christmas. No one could truly believe it – never in living memory had South Wales had snow for Christmas. Indeed it was more usual for the sun to shine as though it were spring, keeping the snow at bay until February.

Rhianna ran to the little back garden of the cottage and held up her face and hands. 'Snow! Mummy. Snow!' she yelled.

Her mother gazed out through the kitchen window and waved. Rhianna waved back, glad her mother seemed so much happier these days; singing with the Ladies' Choir, trotting to the shops with more vigour.

She came running back into the house and Will Pepper was there, thick set and looking more so because of the heavy tweeds he wore. Today he also wore brown leather gaiters.

'You're all dressed up,' Rhianna commented.

3

'Aye,' he said, standing with his back to the fire like she vaguely remembered her father doing. 'Your mother says it's up to me to tell you.' '

Rhianna stared at him, sensing something dramatic, and her mother went to stand beside him, one hand in her apron pocket, the other going around him.

Will Pepper stuck out his chest. 'Well, your mother and me are to be married on Boxing day.' He waited while Rhianna looked at her mother for verification, then he said, 'The Colonel has honoured us by allowing us to hold our party in his great hall in the evening.'

Rhianna stared from him to her mother and tried to think this one out. Then she shook her head wonderingly. 'You can't be getting married,' she told Will Pepper. 'Mum is married to my Dad.'

'Ah,' said Will Pepper, and leaned forward, putting an earth stained finger under her chin. 'But your Dad is dead, isn't he? Dead and gone.'

Rhianna jerked from him, her face flaming. 'You said you were her friend!'

'I am her friend,' he returned, and turned to the woman leaning against him. 'Aren't I?'

Mrs Morgan looked at her young daughter. 'Rhianna darling,' she tried, 'I have found the last years very lonely –'

'You had me!'

'Yes, dear,' came the quiet reply. 'I did, didn't I? And thank you,' but then she looked into Will Pepper's eyes and it was as if Rhianna wasn't there at all.

She left them and went down to the beach. The tide was out, small boats were packed close on the quay, and seagulls screeched for food. Flakes of snow settled on her bare golden-coloured head and she wondered if it would get so cold that the sea would freeze all over and she would be able to walk to America. She gazed towards the Devon hills, imagining that the great continent was somewhere just beyond them. 'I'll be famous,' she vowed. 'I'll show them. Let everyone go away like Rhodri and Carl, or get married like Mum. I don't care.' She flung out her arms dramatically and shouted at the sky with her legs set stolidly apart. 'I don't care. I don't! I don't!' Then she sat on the sea wall, feeling the damp come through the skirt of her coat, her heart half saying she wouldn't mind getting pneumonia and dying.

She enjoyed a self-pitying snuffle and thought how the sea looked empty and lonely without yachts or speed boats; just miles and miles of grey wetness. She decided her mother was a meany, going behind her back, pretending to be friends with Will Pepper and now she was going to marry him. Marry him? Would Will Pepper have to come and live with them? One of Rhodri Blackmore's father's servants, a farm bailiff, come to live in her house!

Snobbery rose slowly in Rhianna Morgan as she got up from her wet seat, slapping the cold away with swinging arms. It had become even more necessary that she attain great importance. She had to prove she was equal to Rhodri Blackmore and better by far than Will Pepper.

She skipped thoughtfully back over the road and up the hill. Will Pepper was still there, sitting in Dad's chair drinking coffee.

'You said you're going to have a party at The Turrets?' she demanded suspiciously, her head tilted.

Her mother laughed and gave her a hug, 'Oh Rhianna, you're a good girl. You'll be staying up late that night. Isn't the Colonel good to his staff?'

'Will Rhodri be there?'

'I should think so.' Mrs Morgan looked at Will Pepper, and he nodded.

'Aye, he'll most likely be there.' And Rhianna went up to her room, hugging herself and already forgiving her mother in the light of this new wonder.

As she went she heard her mother say, 'Does the boy like it up at Oxford?'

'He's a boy no longer,' Will Pepper said. 'And I can't think why he's reading classics. Be better if he was learning to look after his father's estate.'

Rhianna went to the piano-shaped musical box standing on her washing stand beside the big china bowl and jug. She lifted the musical box and kissed it. Rhodri and Carl had given it to her last October, because neither would be here

5

again for weeks. Well, the weeks were passing; soon it would be Christmas and Rhodri would be with his father at The Turrets. Maybe Carl would come too.

Oooh, she flung herself onto her back on the bed. It would be a wonderful party. Then, with a sudden thought, she jumped off the bed again and ran to the top of the stairs.

'Mum! Will you make me a new frock?'

'Yes, dear. Decide what you want. We'll go into Swansea tomorrow and get material.'

'Oh yes, let's!' Rhianna called enthusiastically, hearing her mother's quiet voice as she turned.

'She has taken it well, hasn't she? She'll go far. She's a brilliant child when she puts her mind to it.'

'Ought to be on the stage,' said Will Pepper.

'Good gracious. I don't know if she can act.'

'Not acting I was thinking about,' said Will Pepper. 'She's one that likes attention and showing off.'

'Oh, Will,' came Mother's laugh. 'Don't tell me you're jealous of my only child.' Then there was silence, so Rhianna went back to her room to find pencil and paper and design her own frock for the wedding party.

It was not long before she heard Will Pepper leaving and she ran to the little window to watch him. Yes, his shot gun was on the passenger seat, and he got into the Land Rover as though being Colonel Blackmore's farm bailiff was the highest any man could get. Mary Johnson, who lived across the road, ran and stretched up to him. Rhianna saw them laugh together, then Mary hurried away.

Rhianna stuck out her tongue at the retreating Land Rover then went back to her drawing, concentrating on a frock that would make her look older, with tiny massed frills where a bust should be. But at the back of her mind a decision was forming: she would definitely be an actress, as Will had said. She might even be a film star. Not only would she go to America and become famous and important, but she would also become rich. Rhodri Blackmore would be swept off his feet, then, crawling on his knees, he would beg her to marry him. She would be very kind and love him for ever.

The latter part of the subconscious dream slowly became conscious and she stopped to think about it, a smile playing all over her face. Rhodri had lots of girls – he still brought them home and waved to Rhianna when he drove past her in the village. They were unimportant, she decided.

Then, looking at her design again, she wondered which dream meant the most to her, really and truly – marry Rhodri or become famous and rich in Manhattan?

Mrs Morgan sat up most of the night making a dress for herself and another for Rhianna. Rhianna insisted hers was blue and shiny. It had to be, because that was the way she always saw Rhodri's eyes – blue and shiny.

'When he sees me, Mum, he has to fall in love with me. Right then.' She clutched anxious hopeful fingers to the left side of her chest and looked dramatically at her mother.

Mrs Morgan concentrated on using the old treadle sewing machine. 'If you leave me alone you can have your dress in half a mo'.'

'Can I have a wide belt with it?'

'You've got a wide belt with it.'

'It has to show up my waist. It's no good having frills at the top but no waist in the middle.'

Mrs Morgan smiled and obliged. The dress was all Rhianna had requested and finally it was shaken out and handed to her.

Will Pepper came in, smelling of wood and dank trees, of dead leaves and earth. 'You making things for her again? I've never come across such a spoiled kid.'

'I'm not spoiled.'

'You're downright cheeky!'

Rhianna clutched the frock to her and ran upstairs.

Mrs Morgan left the machine and went to the kitchen, 'Your dinner is ready. In the oven.'

He ate heartily and Rhianna stood before the dressing table mirror upstairs and preened. She tugged the belt in so tightly she had to breathe out and try not to breathe in again until she was dizzy, but the blue was right, the frills were right, her shape all over was right. The only flaw was the pair of twelve-year-old legs sticking out at the bottom. She fretted over them for a while, but then twirled and laughed, enjoying her reflection. She lifted her hair and examined her face, practising expressions; all to be used for the innocent enticement of Rhodri Blackmore.

Christmas day was as nothing to Rhianna that year. What was chicken and Christmas pudding when tomorrow she might be in Rhodri's arms? She sighed deeply as she tipped the jug of deep yellow custard and watched some of the contents land in her dish.

'Good stuff.' Will Pepper grinned as he took the jug from her. 'Leave some for other people, greedy guts!'

She didn't speak to him. He could bath twice a day but still seem unclean to her. For a moment she considered why. She didn't like him, she concluded. She simply did not like him. Sometimes, horror of horrors, he touched her.

The yellow slithering custard reminded her of his touch, slippery in spite of the rough dryness of his skin and, yes, she decided, yellow. She stole a glance at his hands. They were not yellow. They were a very healthy hard, scrubbed red, but they always felt yellow. Definitely, they felt yellow and slippery.

She spooned the custard off the pudding, ate enough to pretend it was all she had ever wanted for Christmas, then left most of it.

She would never like Will Pepper.

The wedding went well. Everyone was so kind. Mrs Morgan became Mrs Pepper and was overwhelmed by it all.

'Will!' She gazed into his face, 'I have rarely known such kindness.'

'Keep your finger in the right hole, my dearest,' returned Will Pepper, and Rhianna disliked him more.

The wedding cars were packed as they drove to The Turrets. Over the coast road and down into the valley, where gardens were bordered with lanterns and the house glowed with light, the faint cloth of snow making all Whesley

8

Vale look like a wedding cake.

Rhianna tilted her head a lot while in the same room as Will Pepper and he often looked at her suspiciously, but she felt utterly beautiful and waited in the great hall to dazzle Rhodri Blackmore.

The Colonel had gone so far as to hire a small band. 'My gift to you, Mrs Pepper,' he said graciously, his big nose more pink than ever before, and Rhianna saw her mother blush and glide into Will Pepper's arms.

Will looked strange, no longer in heavy tweeds. His shoes were black and shiny and new, and his feet could glide skilfully across the floor. Rhianna sat beside a potted palm and tried not to let her scowls show on her face. Will Pepper was acting again, worse than ever. Being smarmy to her mother. Why was it only she who could see it?

Rhianna smiled, inclined her head at anyone who acknowledged her and said no, she didn't mind sitting alone, she preferred it, actually, if they would excuse her. So they did, wandering away and leaving her looking like a waif peeping through the palm tree leaves, watching the doorway.

Time went on. Rhianna suspected her mother was just a little tipsy while Will Pepper was becoming more and more expansive, especially when he and Mother did the tango. The music came to a stop and Will Pepper stood and clapped like everyone else, but his voice was calling, 'What about a push, heh? Let's have a push.'

Rhianna had no idea what an apache was, but when she saw it she put both hands to her face and hoped Rhodri would not walk in now. Will Pepper was doing a sort of tango with Mother but he was holding her back, almost to the floor, and acting as though he was terribly cross with her. At one moment she slid on the floor on her back and Rhianna jumped to her feet, but her mother was laughing, so Rhianna sat down again looking more lost than ever.

She moved from the potted palm and went nearer the doors. She smiled at a girl who had vacated a seat and said hello to all her neighbours, most of them knowing her from birth. It was mortifying that they should see her mother on the floor, but Mary Johnson came over to her, laughing.

'Isn't it lovely, Ree-anna,' she said, 'to see your mother enjoying herself again, poor woman. Will is doing her such a lot of good.'

Rhianna thought about it before replying, 'They're both acting.'

'Of course,' rejoined Mary Johnson. 'It's their night, isn't it? And we all act most of the time, don't we then?'

Rhianna stared at her and saw a sadness in Mary Johnson's eyes. Mary had never married and was, so Mum had once remarked, past it now. Yet, Rhianna thought, she had seen Mary laughing happily with Will Pepper.

Rhianna sat for almost three hours waiting for Rhodri to appear, and during that time she learned that if you sit quietly no one knows you are there after a while. No matter how kind they are, they forget about you.

Unless Rhodri came quickly she would be a star in America. Better than being a wife and having to wash dishes all the time.

Rhodri came at almost midnight and, because he wasn't looking backwards, didn't see her. She watched him make a bee-line for a tall woman who was every bit of twenty-two years of age, yet had her hair down her back.

Rhianna's scowl stopped being secret. It came onto her face and her chin drooped with dismay. She watched Rhodri and the tall woman dance. She watched their feet and not once did either of them step on the other's toes.

Rhianna hated them both.

The Colonel, with his grey hair sliding sideways off his bald crown, came to the centre of the hall and announced a Paul Jones.

Everyone but Rhianna got up to dance. The music jigged, everyone danced around in two big circles. When the music stopped every woman took the man who had stopped before her. Rhianna knew no one was noticing her. She was completely forgotten.

She stood up in the blue dress that was to have worked a miracle for her and she walked decidedly towards the dancers. She waited until the music stopped and everyone formed two rings again. As they re-began the dance Rhianna went to the centre. She danced alone, holding up her arms with fingers and thumbs placed so. In her mind she became a ballerina, centre stage – the only person who mattered.

She sensed being noticed, at first causing amusement and giggles, but she ignored them, a sensation of triumph building up inside her.

She twirled prettily on her toes and saw Rhodri Blackmore smile. Without ado she twirled towards him then curtseyed low. Rhodri stepped to her and took her in his arms.

For Rhianna Morgan it was heaven. She stretched both arms up about his neck and let him waft her about the floor.

'Do you like my frock?'

'I love it.'

'I love you too. My frock's the colour of your eyes.'

She gazed up at him, silently commanding his eyes to look into hers, and they did. Her voice was innocent as she asked, 'Isn't Carl here tonight?'

'No. He's in San Moritz. Ski-ing.'

'How lovely,' she said, in her best grown up voice. 'I shall do that when I'm a famous actress.'

'You should join a drama group,' he said. 'That's where to start.'

So, once the Christmas holidays were over, Rhianna took the bus into Swansea and she joined a drama group.

Every weekend during the rest of her twelfth year, and right through to her fourteenth, she asked Will Pepper, 'Can I come to work with you in the morning? I'm willing to help.'

At first he scoffed, 'It's no good you coming; Rhodri isn't there. You'll never set eyes on him.' But then he just said, 'No!' Later on it became, 'Can't you get your damn kid to wash her ears out? I've said no.'

So her meetings with Rhodri Blackmore were confined to summer when he was often with his own sophisticated friends, people like the tall woman – who must be more than

11

twenty-two by now, yet she still wore her hair dangling down her back.

Rhianna learned things about this woman; her name was Fay Hanson and she was, as she put it to a companion in the coffee shop, gah-gah about darling Rhodri.

Rhianna's future was shaping up as God, or Fate, planned.

Chapter Two

'Hi Rhodri! Will you buy a ticket?'

'What for?'

'Our latest play.'

'No. I have other things to do. Sorry and all that. Ask Carl. He'll buy one.'

'Carl! You'll come and see me act won't you?'

It had been a good summer. Now the tourists had left, though the village was not yet prepared for the biting winds that would shoot up the hills and whistle around curving narrow streets.

'It's not until the end of this month.' Rhianna glowered at Rhodri. 'I had a dozen to sell and I only have two left. Now everybody says either they've bought already or they don't like plays.'

'Rhianna,' Carl slung his towel over his shoulder, his hair tight with sea water against his scalp, his body goose-pimpled, 'I will buy two tickets, so? And if our friend is too miserable to accompany me I shall take a lady.'

'What lady?' Rhodri half grinned at him. 'I didn't know you knew any.'

'Ah,' Carl inclined his head as if this was a great secret. 'I shall ask the beautiful Fay Hanson to allow me the honour. Together she and I will see the even more beautiful Rhianna Morgan in this, her greatest hour.'

Rhianna laughed. 'She won't come!' She looked at Rhodri again. 'I could get another ticket for you.'

Then she regretted saying it because Rhodri nodded. 'You can get me two, too.' He gave her his special smile, the one that said he liked her and wished to indulge her. 'We'll make up a party. I'll get one of the girls to come with me.'

There. Another two tickets sold.' He looked smug, unaware of Rhianna's dismay.

'We will clap for you,' Carl promised. 'And we will shout encore.'

'Not only that,' Rhodri laughed. 'We will boo everyone else.'

Rhianna looked from one to the other, sensing they were teasing, but not knowing how or why. She said a little peevishly, though she smiled, 'This is to be my big night. I have the big part.'

Carl took the two tickets she offered and handed over the money, concentrating on re-clipping his wallet with cold fingers. 'What is this play, heh? What name is it?'

'*Heaven Is All This*.'

Both men burst in to loud laughter, bending backwards, laughing towards each other, 'And you are to be the star?'

'I am,' returned Rhianna indignantly, and Rhodri sighed and shook his head.

'Rhianna,' he said, and for the first time *ever* she heard a gentle sigh in her name, 'there cannot be another like you.'

She waited, something magical happening inside her as she stared into his sky-blue, brilliant eyes, the eyes that seemed to be able to see into her and around her as no other eyes had ever done. She saw a type of wonder dawning in them, then he asked softly. 'How old were you last birthday?'

'Fourteen.' She couldn't understand why she felt terribly shy of Rhodri Blackmore; it had never happened before.

'You make me feel an old man, Rhianna,' and the sigh had gone from her name.

'You aren't old!'

'He is most old,' Carl laughed, 'with another birthday coming so soon.' Rhodri shouldered him into silence.

'I'll have the tickets for you tomorrow.' Rhianna promised. 'Will you be here with the boat?'

Rhodri paused to think about it. 'Yes,' he said at last. 'About half-past-two.'

Rhianna's smile was brilliant as she gave a little hop prior to running away.

14

Carl called after her. 'Hi! You never had a date before?'
She turned to look at him, her run interrupted, 'Date?'

'You do not understand? Your great dream – he has dated you.'

'No!' Rhodri called, and Rhianna's gaze shot to him, drowning in the eyes that were not blue any longer but very dark, and the sudden hope followed by disappointment was clear on her face. Rhodri shrugged, 'Oh all right. Be here with the tickets at half-past-two. I'll take you for a spin somewhere.'

Rhianna felt sick and happy and awful and wonderful. 'In your car?'

'If that's what you'd like.'

'Oh, yes please.' Her lips were apart, her feet astride in the same childish way, yet she smiled at Carl because he was looking at her as if she were a woman.

She turned and sauntered away. No, she told herself, I must not run. Children run; I am a woman.

She didn't look back. She felt sure Rhodri was watching her with critical eyes, seeing her legs, her bottom, her waist, the back of her neck. Rhodri must be truly seeing her and, oh he must think her beautiful, and sophisticated.

Once out of sight of the beach Rhianna kicked up her heels and moved as if on wings. The hill to the cottage seemed a hill no longer and she went in through the doorway with such gusto the door banged back, hitting the wall. Her mother came running from the kitchen, a bowl of cake mix tucked under one arm, a wooden spoon in the other. 'What is it? What's happened?'

'I have a date!' Rhianna cried. 'Rhodri Blackmore asked me out.'

Her mother stood as if vexed then backed into the room, Rhianna following her. 'Mum, aren't you thrilled? I have. Just him and me. We're going in his car, the open topped one.'

'He's too old for you. And you're trying to get above your class.'

'He's perfect for me.'

The mixing bowl was put on the table, but the wooden

15

spoon was waving in the air. 'Rhianna, you are still a child, a schoolgirl, with too many big ideas. You are far too young to be going out on your own with men. Especially rich ones.'

'You don't like Rhodri?'

'Nobody doesn't like Rhodri. Everybody likes the whole family – what's left of it – but he has a reputation with the girls.'

Rhianna pecked her mother's cheek. 'He'll be good with me. I trust him to the ends of the earth.' And she turned for the staircase and ran up to her room. She needed something special to wear, something that would make Rhodri realise she was a woman.

'Rhianna!' her mother called. 'Don't go making yourself look like a tart. He likes a bit of class.'

Rhianna nodded. A bit of class – what did a bit of class look like?

Next day she went to the sea wall wearing casual grey slacks and a sweater that had a tiger prowling across her chest. Her hair glowed with health and golden lights, her face was pink with happiness, though her heart thumped hard with a sort of fear. Rhodri might not turn up, Rhodri might decide he didn't like her and would never date her again.

But he was there, waiting, the car like a long scarlet bomb and she didn't wait for him to open the door. She jumped in beside him, panting, a schoolgirl loaded with excitement.

Rhodri didn't waste time. Rhianna suspected his aim was to drive her somewhere, then drive her back as fast as possible. The car roared across the common and Rhianna held onto her ears as if afraid her head was about to be off.

'There,' he said, as the car cruised into a car park at the end of a narrow peninsular. 'How did you enjoy it?'

'Marvellous! But I felt like you'd forgotten I was here at all.'

'Forget you?' He reversed the car into a grassy space. 'Impossible.' But Rhianna knew he had forgotten her. Those remarkable eyes of his with their thick, dark, curling lashes had watched the road all the way. He had been exhilarated by speed on the road the same as on skis, thrilled

16

by his own dexterity in manoeuvring through narrow winding hedge-bound lanes.

She accused, 'You didn't need me with you at all. You would have been just as happy on your own.'

He turned off the engine and looked into her indignant face. 'Rhianna! Just what do you expect of me? I'm buying tickets for your play, I arrange to spend time with you this afternoon, and now you sit there getting all dramatic.'

'Well, thank you anyway,' she murmured. 'I would like you to bring me again. Next year. When I'll be fifteen.'

He gaped at her. 'What difference does your age make?'

'My mother says you are too old for me.'

'God a'mighty! Tell her I'll soon be twenty-one and she is invited to my celebration. You can come as well, if you care.'

Rhianna let out a long low groan of pleasure. 'I didn't think you'd ask. Not me.'

He nodded importantly. 'This time I'll dance with you, so don't go making an ass of yourself.'

She nodded and laughed, remembering the last time she had danced in Rhodri's presence. In unexpected shyness she looked away, towards the cliffs and saw great, coloured wings gliding silently from their top-most crags.

'Oh look,' she exclaimed. 'Hang-gliders!'

Rhodri got out of the car and, taking off his jacket, slung it over the back of his seat.

'Aren't you afraid it'll be nicked?'

'Here? Not likely.' She jerked her head at what she considered to be his innocent belief and he said crisply, 'Will you be there to sing happy birthday or won't you?'

'I shall ask my mother.' She left the car, her attention bobbing from Rhodri to the wings that soared out over the arc of Golden Beach far below. 'What about Will Pepper?'

'Do you like him?'

'No.'

'Then we have something in common.'

She felt stung. Was that all she and Rhodri had? She hurried from him, pretending to be more intent on the fliers than on him and realised Rhodri was right. He was wealthy,

17

set to inherit a fine home and a prosperous business. She was hoping for a grant to go to university and might inherit a fisherman's cottage, which, rumour had it, had once been inhabited by smugglers and wreckers.

Suddenly it seemed imperative to do better than anyone else. Not only on a stage where the play was put on for two nights in the village, but in everything. She had to become equal to Rhodri Blackmore. Hopefully even surpass him.

The impulse gathered strength and Rhianna Morgan hurried to the group of young men fiddling with harness and wings on the cliff top. Up here the wind was steady, blowing her hair back off her face, so she lifted her gaze into it.

She spotted Carl and called his name, surprised and pleased. 'I didn't know you were here!'

'So you are delighted with me, heh? Because I pop up when you do not expect me?'

'You know I am.' She clasped her hands together in rapture. 'Are you going to fly? Can I come with you?'

'You are joking, Rhianna.'

'No.' Her face was serious. 'I have always wanted to try.'

Carl shrugged. 'It is too dangerous. How could I explain to Rhodri if you fell, heh? He does not understand, but he has the great affection for you. If I did not fall us both he would break my neck, and I do fall us both I will break my neck.' He laughed engagingly at her. 'Carl cannot win. Oh no, no!'

Rhianna laughed. 'Rhodri doesn't even know I'm alive. Please take me up, Carl. Please.'

'I cannot, *chérie*. There is not the room on my craft.'

'Then borrow one. There, that one. He must be an instructor, look he has a two seater! Please Carl. He is your friend. Must be. Do ask him.'

Carl's face pointed into the wind, the grounded aircrafts of his companions making little flapping and scudding sounds against the sheep cropped grass. Then he called, 'Hi there, Thomas. My friend here wants to travel with me to the moon. You have a twin craft . . .'

Thomas grinned knowingly. 'It's dicky.'

'Oh no,' Rhianna cried. 'I have watched hang-gliding so

often, I know what to do. Please? You have a crash helmet to loan me. I'll be all right, I promise!'

Both young men stared at her, not wanting to disbelieve, then both nodded, moving their arms as if relinquishing all responsibility.

'You will be my passenger, you understand?' Carl insisted, and Rhodri stood frowning, his blue eyes pulled into glinting slits as she allowed herself to be strapped up.

Rhianna flashed a smile at Rhodri and he turned his back on her. She would have had utter faith in Rhodri if he had taken her up but now she transferred that faith to Carl; his fingers busy about her, buckles and belts, the sense of excitement rising, other young men and women coming to watch the preparations, to eye her with amusement.

Then came the moment of leaving land – that trembling moment of ecstasy and fear, the shuddering of the wings, the momentary unbalance until Carl positioned his body, then the utter silence and the glory of being almost as good as God, gliding stealthily above the beach, gradually downwards, yet blissfully tranquil, and all the time, Carl was in charge.

'Keep still *chérie*,' he said softly. 'Do not move even your beautiful nose, or Rhodri will have the broken heart for ever.'

She wanted to laugh at such a silly threat, but a glance at Carl's face told her to do as he bade her and allow him to concentrate.

The wind caught them and they swirled, an air pocket swooped them low, then raised them again and Rhianna laughed. She hoped that somewhere behind her Rhodri was on the cliff top, watching, admiring.

She and Carl came down in what seemed something of a rush, the hard sand coming up to meet them. Then she toppled and cried out with the suddenness of it, the wings dragging her along the line of cockle shells, scratching, cutting into her ankles. Carl yanked her to her feet, breathing hard and laughing, his normal, happy self.

'That was good, heh, Rhianna? You like to be like the bird?'

'Yes, oh yes. It's so exhilarating!' Carl eased his helmet off and Rhianna flung her arms about his neck, 'Carl! You are wonderful! Wonderful! So clever at everything!'

Carl pushed her from him, his face darkening. 'Hi you are in trouble, *chérie*. Your dream is to become the nightmare *pronto*.'

She turned and Rhodri was striding along the beach, covering it fast, his face like thunder. She tried to unbuckle herself, her hands getting tangled with Carl's. She had an urge to get away, escape before Rhodri caught up with her. He wasn't proud of her at all. There was no sign of admiration in him.

'You blasted little idiot!' he bellowed as he drew closer. 'And you, Carl, want your head read! Since when have you gone around taking schoolgirls on stupid trips like that?'

'My friend, Rhianna is very intelligent. She knew she had to sit and wait for it to be over.'

'She did not know what to do. I saw what was happening up there. You could have both been blasted well killed, and all because of an empty-headed schoolgirl twit!'

Rhianna squared up to him. 'And what about you coming across the common at eighty miles an hour? You could have had me killed too.'

'There,' Carl put in, smiling. 'We are both so much enamoured of the twit that we wish to kill her. Is that not right?'

Rhodri glared from Carl to Rhianna, then grabbed her arm and marched her away. 'You are in my charge,' he announced, 'and you stay that way until I get you back to your mother!'

He took her up the cliff path, climbing quickly, Rhianna panting but as lithe as he. They reached the car.

'Get in.'

Silently she did so and sat with her hands in her lap, dismayed that nothing ever went as she wished.

'I brought sandwiches,' Rhodri said, 'and a flask of tea. We might as well have our picnic then drive back.'

Rhianna gazed up at him. 'You brought sandwiches?'

He nodded, blue eyes accusing, 'Why not?'

Happiness was welling in Rhianna again, 'I thought, I mean, I imagined you'd drive me here, drive me back then think your duty done.'

'Duty?'

'I'm terribly sorry. Really.'

'You have an odd way of looking at life, Rhianna. You give a damn for no one but yourself!' He poked around his feet, under the seat, then beside it. 'Is there a package under your seat?'

'No.'

'Strange. I put them near to hand. I'm sure I did.'

She stared into his eyes, seeing her reflection. She wanted to laugh but was afraid to. 'Were they with your jacket?' she asked. 'You put that over the back of your seat and it's half slid under you.'

He stared back into the merriment of her face and slowly realised where the sandwiches were. 'In my pocket.'

She nodded and he lifted himself gently, pulling the bottom half of his jacket from under him, groping in the pocket and pulling out the squashed bag.

She giggled, 'You sat on them,' and all the tension, the excitement of the last half an hour exploded inside her. She collapsed deeper into her seat and gave vent to laugher. 'Oh Rhodri Blackmore. You big twit. You sat on them!'

He looked at the mangled food between his hands, 'D'you still want one?'

She nodded and leaned towards him. He opened the bag, dislodged a sandwich that was bent and dented and handed it to her. Then he stretched out an arm around her. 'You were in real danger up there.'

She felt the smoothness of his shirt against her cheek and snuggled closer, biting the battered sandwich. 'Is it chicken or turkey?'

'Turkey.' They munched together, and he said quietly, 'We've been pals for a long time, Rhianna. I should hate to lose you now. Whesley wouldn't be the same without you.'

Rhianna closed her eyes. Had anyone in the whole of creation ever been as happy?

*

21

The village gossips were agog. They knew they should have expected it, but they hadn't. They met each other during their window shopping, they showed each other the glossy photograph in the local glossy magazine – it was printed by the little man around the corner so the contents had to be true, but no matter how many times they looked they still found it amazing. Yet there it was: *'The engagement is announced between Miss Rhianna Morgan, only daughter of the late Mr and Mrs Peter Morgan of Fisherman's Cottages, Whesley, to Mr Rhodri Blackmore, only son of Colonel and the late Mrs Blackmore of The Turrets, Whesley Vale.'*

The photograph of Rhianna was not that of a schoolgirl. It was of a nineteen-year-old who had learned as much as was possible in the village arts and drama classes about improving oneself. Stage make up and artistic lighting had helped the photographer beyond his wildest dreams. He had produced a photograph that made Rhianna look a relative of royalty.

She had acquired gloss. It was still a temporary thing. She could switch it on while it often switched itself off, but the photograph looked permanent. The villagers were surprised, proud and a little befuddled. The fact the engagement was also announced in *The Times* was lost on them. For all in Whesley, this was the picture, the magazine that counted.

Rhianna walked with her golden-coloured head high. At college she had gained distinction in art and design. She was to be a rich man's wife. And she adored him. She also tried to possess him.

Rhodri smiled and acknowledged the congratulations of those outside his circle of friends and the wise cracks of those within it.

Carl Jurgan flew from Zurich for the engagement party.

Rhianna had a gown made. Sapphire blue to match her sapphire ring.

On the night of the celebration she stood before her mirror and told herself she should be happy, delirious. She wasn't. She wished her mother was alive. She wished her

22

step-father wasn't merely a farm hand for the man she was promised to. She told herself she was an unutterable snob. She told herself she had made her choice; Rhodri or stardom in America. It was Rhodri. She should be happy. She *would* be happy.

The Daimler came for her from The Turrets right on time, and she tried not to shudder as Will Pepper got into the seat beside her. She did not like the smell of the man, and had objected to the eighteen months spent in the house with him since her mother died.

As the car moved away curtains of cottages both sides moved surreptitiously. Will sat back, uncomfortable in dark suit, collar and tie.

'Well,' he said, 'You've done well for yourself. Bagging a rich man.'

'I didn't choose him because he was born wealthy,' Rhianna returned testily. 'I happen to be deeply in love with him.'

'Oh aye,' said Will Pepper, and grinned knowingly.

She made the Daimler stop on the crest of Emlyn Hill so she could gaze down into the valley, and her heart filled with pride that The Turrets could look so magical on this summer night, the dying sun streaking the sky with pink and gold, the trees on the hills as thickly green and patterned as a bed of new parsley. Young deer would be born among them. Will would protect the beavers.

She smoothed the white fur wrap about her shoulders and was glad it was nylon. She smiled at Will. 'It looks as if the Colonel has at last got himself a new Welsh Dragon.'

Will looked towards the battlements of the ancient great house nestling below and beyond and nodded. 'Aye, he reckoned the Union Jack will last another year or two if next winter's gales go easy, but the Welsh flag had to be special for his future daughter-in-law.' Will's knowing look became a smirk, and Rhianna switched her attention from him impatiently.

The chauffer glanced at her in the driving mirror and she jerked her head. He accepted the unspoken instruction and drove on to where the portico of the house cast shadows, and a lone blackbird paused in song until the car became silent.

Will escorted Rhianna to the door with an air of already being related to it, and Jarvis, the butler, twitched his nostrils slightly as if he, like Rhianna, could smell pine trees and dank moss on Will Pepper.

Music floated from every pore of the old building and Rhodri was waiting, striding to meet her, his blue eyes brilliant, approving of her, his hands held out.

Rhianna's heart skipped beats and she wanted to bury herself in him, wrap herself to him, and keep him from all else but her own all-enslaving adoration.

He was an assured man of twenty-five, already in his father's business, at ease in the board room and well versed in the art of stocks and shares, of take-over bids and making money while gaining power. Rhodri Blackmore looked a wealthy, influential, handsome man.

His arm went about her and the kiss was shorter than she needed, but the wrap had to be thrown to Jarvis and she was swept further into the house. There were glittering chandeliers, the gleam of silver-ware, opulence and success. Rhianna drank it in. She adored it.

As if he had been watching for her, Carl came forward, looking even more like a film-star than ever – smoothly dark, with a wicked expression as he bent graciously to kiss the back of her hand.

Rhianna felt good, important. Tonight she was the star. Tonight everyone knew Rhodri was hers and hers alone.

The Colonel came to meet her, puffing and blowing, not as young as he had been, putting on weight and glad his son had chosen a healthy, good-looker to help carry on the family name.

'What's your opinion of the orchestra?' he asked. 'Chose it m'self.'

'Very nice, thank you.' Rhianna smiled into the face that was like a map of red veins.

'I – er – thought you wouldn't mind a few waltzes, what? Bit old-fashioned, I know, but many here tonight are old-fashioned.'

24

'Of course.' Rhianna smiled, and knew she continued to please him.

Rhodri took her into his arms and danced her close, her head against his cheek. All was bliss until she learned he had promised the next dance to someone else.

She pouted. 'You're engaged to me now. You aren't supposed to dance with other girls!'

'Darling. An engagement doesn't mean you've put a bit and blinkers on me. I still appreciate other beautiful women.'

The other beautiful woman was at his side, claiming her dance, and he swept her away, her full, floor-length skirt swishing out, partly wrapping itself about his legs.

Jealousy and mortification swamped Rhianna. She stood alone, feeling discarded.

Carl came, lifted her chin and smiled into her face, 'Ah, come *chérie*, where is the happiness heh?'

'You saw what he did, Carl? He just left me!'

'Do you expect him to change because he put a ring on your pretty finger, heh?'

'But we belong to each other now.'

'So?'

'He should stay by me.'

'All the night? Then I could not dance with you. Come, let us drink. Perhaps then your ill-temper will disappear.'

'I am not ill-tempered!'

'True, true. I am wrong to say such things. You are nervous. For so long you eat out your heart for him and then he dance with another. How cruel.'

Rhianna laughed then. Only Carl could tease so effectively, and they danced and swirled and laughed more.

Peeping over Carl's shoulder Rhianna watched Rhodri, watched him laugh with other girls, watched other girls raise their manicured, lady-born hands to touch him – one even let her fingers stray to his chin and the bile rose in Rhianna until she felt sick. *He was hers.* She should be courted publicly. Did he think that because he had placed a sapphire on her peasantry finger that he was now foot loose and fancy free?

25

Later she saw Rhodri's blue gaze searching and she wanted to giggle childishly. He was missing her. Rhodri was looking for her. Serve him right. He should not have left her in the first place. He should hold her against him to open every dance. Wasn't this an old-fashioned evening? Then old-fashioned manners should prevail.

She hid from him, watching him stride around the floor, watching him avoiding girls and old ladies who beamed at him with sparkling faces, as if they wished they were young enough to enmesh the most eligible bachelor in the vicinity.

She saw him go to the bar and Fay Hanson was there. Fay in a gown so skimpy from the hips up that it had no back and very little front. It was purple and, vile colour that it was, looked good on her. Fay moved in a slinky, seductive manner. Rhianna hated her more than ever. Will Pepper was getting Fay a drink; Will Pepper was putting his arm about Fay.

'It's a known thing,' Rhianna humphed from behind the white plaster copy of the *Venus De Milo*, 'that she is anyone's as long as it wears trousers.'

Then Fay Hanson slank towards Rhodri. Fay entwined her smooth bare arms about Rhodri's neck and nuzzled her cat-like body to him. Rhianna gasped. Rhodri laughed, patted Fay's rump then danced with her.

Rhianna came out of hiding and went in search of Carl. She couldn't find him. She searched other rooms, the library, even the five bathrooms. She contemplated searching the gardens with their swinging fairy lights, their myriad colours and swaying, cuddling couples. She wanted Carl. Now. She needed to flaunt him before Rhodri. Make Rhodri know how it feels to be jealous.

She came back to the great hall and Rhodri had disappeared too.

She took a glass of wine and strolled around, greeting people as if this had been all arranged: Rhianna Morgan being gracious to people; Rhianna Morgan looking beautiful.

She reached the end of the hall where the great glass doors stood open and the north star shone vividly. Rhianna realised she had wandered around the hall three times.

People were looking oddly at her. She backed out, through the doors and stood silently, her heart hammering because she couldn't cope. Her mother should have been here. If only her mother hadn't died. If only she had someone to turn to, someone to talk to, someone close.

She leaned against the wall and the outline of a man was near the balustrade. *Rhodri. With a woman.* A tall, slender woman in a purple gown that left very little of her body to imagination.

Rhianna wanted to shriek but her throat tightened, her hands clasped and she felt the sapphire in her ring. How dare Rhodri Blackmore give her a ring then cavort on the terrace with Fay Hanson?

She heard Fay give a little moan. She heard Rhodri breathe, 'It's all right. Sssh. I won't tell a soul. Come with me, just come with me.' Then Fay was in his arms, the tall trees rustling beyond them, whispering suspicions to Rhianna.

Rhianna hunched her shoulders, startlingly aware of her peasant background, a farm bailiff for a step-father, seeing the heir to The Turrets making a fool out of her.

Oh, to hell with them! To hell with all of them!

Without a sound escaping from her, tears of inferiority and horror coursed down her face. How dare he? The whole village would know. Fay would tell. Fay would brag.

Rhodri half turned and saw her. 'Rhianna!' There was no sigh in his voice, only the startled sound of a man embarrassed, then Rhianna was running back to the hall. Tell them herself! Let them all know! The engagement was over. She would retain her pride even if she lost everything else.

She stood on the dais that led to the glass doors and tore the sapphire from her finger. 'I hate him!' She screamed, on stage again, playing a part, the injured heroine, victim of a disloyal hero.

The orchestra stopped playing; people stopped dancing to stare, to wonder; the ring flew over their heads, the blue sapphire shimmering in the chandeliered light, and fell with a small tinkle.

Rhianna saw Will Pepper's face, shocked, furious. She saw the Colonel, bewildered, stuttering silently, and she realised she had done wrong. Once more she had caused a scene. Rhodri would hate it.

Shaking, scarlet faced, she ran, pushing among the crowds, blinded by tears and shame. 'He's out there!' she stormed at the Colonel in the vain hope of making someone understand. 'With Fay Hanson. I saw them. *Cuddling!*' Then she was snatching her white nylon wrap and flying down the steps, screaming as she went, 'He's out there now. On the terrace. With another woman!'

It was almost two miles to home, most of it in utter blackness, trees either side, owls calling, suddenly swooshing from branches above her. She sobbed until she could sob no more, the run became a walk and, when she finally got to the cottage, she washed her face and went straight to bed.

The sheets were cool, the pillow soft against her cheek. Her fury spent. Rhodri would forgive her if he loved her. She would forgive his philandering. Tomorrow he would call. He would bring flowers and the ring. He would hold her and she would kiss him.

Tomorrow would be paradise just for two.

Will Pepper was disgusted. He shouted up the stairs as he came in much later. 'If your mother knew she'd turn in her grave! Her wonderful daughter chucking away the chance to be lady of the manor. Where's the whisky bottle?'

Rhianna yelled back, 'You finished it last night.' Then got out of bed and put on her dressing-gown. She came downstairs.

'Where in hell have you hidden it?' Will demanded.

'D'you want a cup of tea?'

'Have you telephoned young master Rhodri?'

'No.'

'You'll lose him. He's a gentleman and he'll want no truck with a big-headed show off with no manners!'

'He did ask me to marry him.'

'And now he's got another chance to think it over. You telephone him, my girl, now, or you'll never set eyes on him

28

again. You insulted the man, in front of all his guests. Them Blackmore's got more pride even than they got money.'

'He loves me.'

'Not after tonight he doesn't. You telephone him and be apologetic, then he might condescend to forgive, though I can't see a man brought up like him forgetting a thing like that.'

Rhianna walked past the telephone on the way back to bed, then she lay awake listening for it to ring. Surely Rhodri would phone and explain what he was doing on the balcony with Fay Hanson. Surely he would understand his fiancée's fury at what was supposed to be her important night?

It was daylight before she fell asleep and she refused to go out next day. She dreaded seeing Rhodri driving around; God forbid, with Fay Hanson beside him.

Will prepared for work, grumbling. 'Those Blackmores have been good to us. Good to the whole village. My job depends on them. Then you go and fling it in their faces.' He tucked his food box under his arm and went to the door. 'End up marrying who ever'll have you, you will, and consider yourself lucky. What with your airy fairy ideas of fame and fortune and bloody big head.'

A week past and Rhianna had to nip to the shops. She wore a scarf that covered the lower half of her face. She prayed silently that gossip about that night had cooled, that another scandal had gripped the village, and she acknowledged no one. No one acknowledged her.

Indignation and fury fought inside her. People should understand Rhodri's place was beside her, not holding Fay Hanson out in the darkness of a summer night.

She hated the whole world, but hated herself most. She knew it was inverted pride preventing her going to see Rhodri, to explain. She told herself it was also Rhodri's stubborn pride that prevented him contacting her, but soon he would. Soon he was bound to.

A few days later she paused to look at the gown shop on the corner of the main road. The window was wide, the models skinny, taking up little room, so she could see beyond them; all through the carpeted shop to the little space beyond where rows of curtains told the world that was the place for fitting. There, wearing a bridal gown, with a flowing veil and a tiara of diamonds and orange blossom, stood Fay Hanson.

Will Pepper came in for tea, in a hurry, needing to be back on duty for the night. 'Poachers!' he said tersely. 'Young Rhodri told us to get after them.'

'He hasn't bothered before.'

'He hasn't been ratty like this before. Those blue eyes of his are full of nastiness and no wonder. Look at this.'

Will struggled to release the latest copy of the local glossy magazine from his jacket pocket, then flung it to the table. It was curled and grubby where other gardeners and workmen had thumbed and gawped. Rhianna picked it up quickly.

What had been in last week's magazine she didn't know and didn't care, but this one shook her. *Rhodri Blackmore was engaged to Miss Fay Hanson, only daughter of His Honour Judge George Hanson* . . .

That night Rhianna packed a suitcase, made sure her Post Office savings book was in her handbag, left a note for Will Pepper and slipped away from South Wales.

A month later she was employed as nanny to the two small children of an opera singer, known professionally as Madam Elina.

If anyone in Whesley cared about Rhianna's whereabouts she didn't know because she received neither letters nor callers. The past had gone. She was in London where the main theatres and opportunities were. She was set on the journey to Manhattan.

Madam Elina was large with big rings on her big fingers, and a big bust that rose and fell with the greatest control each early afternoon as she practised her scales. She also sang 'Meee meee meee' on the same note as long as a single breath would last while she searched in the refrigerator or had a pedicure and manicure. Rhianna learned that Madam's heart was also big and Madam believed that all who had ambition should dedicate their lives to that one aim.

'Rhianna,' she said in her beautiful contralto voice. 'You appear to be doing nothing with your free time.'

'I do a lot with the Palace Players Group.'

'And you act four times a year.' Madam gave one of her great dramatic sighs. 'I have counted. You have been with me over two years and appeared in eight plays that no one bothered to see. I have sung here, in Milan, Toronto and Paris. You are wasting your life.'

'I attend auditions.'

'Pah! Go to Drury Lane. Ask for something to do when you aren't cuddling my babies.'

'Drury Lane?'

'Any theatre you like. Try them all. Ask for the stage manager, help paint the scenery, make a point of meeting those who can help you on the way. Pull your finger out or you'll miss the boat.'

So Rhianna tramped the streets and rode buses waiting for the chance to help a stage manager. When the chance came she took it and spent her free time working at it for love and hope.

For another year Madam nodded and commented that the world was hard and cruel but that Rhianna would learn the hard way. Then came the moment when Rhianna cried a little over the children and accepted a large box of chocolates off Madam. She, Rhianna, had a full time job as assistant stage manager.

'Ah well,' moaned Madam, as she tried fixing a velvet red rose to the shoulder of her black lace gown, 'at least you have gained a green card. Now you are free to act, but don't be surprised if you never appear on stage in the West End.'

Rhianna thanked her, moved into an attic that had been advertised as a studio flat, and waited for the next break.

It came when she landed a part in a performance staged in a small theatre near Luton. It was opening night and the clear evening sky suddenly became crammed with dirty black clouds. Those clouds dropped torrential rain; thunder made the hall quiver and lightning made pink faces turn ashen.

31

Rhianna held the stage, her acting ability at its best, the part ideal for the nervous quiver in her voice. 'Woe is me, oh, woe is me!'

Laurence Paget dived into the hall to avoid a soaking. Luxuriously white haired and bespectacled he suspected there might be bugs in the seats, but he wasn't going to risk pneumonia in this damned forsaken country. Why in hell he undertook to produce a play in England in the first place he couldn't make out.

Rhianna's sense of the dramatic kept him awake. Her confidence, her personality came across the other seats to him and, instead of sleeping, he watched her and became fascinated. She had what it takes. He could make something of her – and he found her very attractive.

Afterwards he went behind stage and Rhianna noticed the handsome, lean face wearing the clean gloss of success as he approached her.

'Hi!' he said. His hair waved and shone in the hard lighting, his suit was well cut, of expensive cloth. 'Would you care to take dinner with me?'

That dinner led to many other dinners, and picnics and laughter.

'Well well,' the stage manager mused when Rhianna finally told him she was leaving to work with Laurence Paget's company. 'So Fate used a thunder storm to send you a fully fledged producer who knew what he wanted when he saw it. Talk about the luck of the Welsh!'

Rhianna did any task Laurence asked of her. At first she made tea, waiting on him and showing no signs of impatience. She listened to others, mimicking all that made the famous so. She made no quibble when Laurence advised elocution lessons, under his direction, nor did she demure when she was requested to help the wardrobe mistress.

And all the time Laurence Paget noted and approved. He promoted her to bit parts and, by the time his contract in Britain was up, his protégée, Rhianna Morgan, was understudying. She had become a fully-fledged member of the company and was included in its tour of America.

Chapter Three

Rhianna's first sight of New York almost blinded her to the Statue of Liberty. She had done it. Got here!

Laurence Paget stood beside her on the deck of the liner, his attention on her, her pleasure also his.

'Oh Laurence, you are brilliant bringing the company this way, by sea, instead of flying. What made you think of it?'

'You.'

'Me?'

'I wanted to see your face as you watched America rise up out of the Atlantic and throw you its challenge.'

'It would be just as thrilling from a plane.'

'Too fast. Much too fast. From clouds to top of skyscrapers in seconds. We had the time and we all deserved the break. Needed the rest. Lynsey's looking a heap better and raring to go.'

Rhianna nuzzled against him. 'I hope she appreciates you as much as I do, leading lady or not.'

'Remember that when your turn comes to be our star.'

Rhianna laughed, but thought of all the hours, the weeks, the months she had spent obeying him – walking, sitting, turning with a monstrous book on her head – how she had sat and practised before her mirror enunciating such things as 'the rain in Spain falls mainly on the plains'. How often, too, she had resented standing in the wings watching Lynsey Webb get all the glory.

'I don't think Lynsey is terribly good as Miss Fairfax,' she said thoughtfully.

'All understudies think that way. Have you ever wished she drops dead?'

'No.' Rhianna lowered her head so he couldn't read her face. 'But I have wished she'd break a leg or join another company.'

33

'Your chance will come.' Laurence stood easily, watching the America waterfront draw nearer, hearing the wash of water about the hull.

'What if the play flops before that?'

'A risk we all take.' He half smiled. 'Warren wasn't too keen to cough up for Oscar Wilde in New York. Too stuffy he said, old-fashioned.'

'Too English.'

'Yea. Something like that.'

'So Lynsey had better be good.'

'Lynsey had better be more than good. Warren wants his investment back with a big profit.'

'What does he look like?'

'A multi-millionaire with a belly protruding over his trouser belt. Sloppy, you'd most likely call him.'

Rhianna shrugged. 'What money does for some men.'

'A lot of the stuff in this case.'

'Makes you want to spit.'

'You said that in true lady-like fashion.'

Rhianna laughed, accepting the tone of rebuke, and Laurence touched her face as if to soothe after his remark. 'You wait till I take you to the observatory on top of the Empire State Building down-town. A hundred and two stories. Can you skate?'

'You already know. I told you. No, I can't skate. You promised to teach me. In Central Park.'

When, later, she walked around Manhattan Rhianna kept her head high. Looking down was disturbing – there was only the pavement called a sidewalk – but when she looked up she saw magic. Buildings standing in spite of gravity, and her knowing millions of people were encased between their numerous floors. It was proof positive of men's achievements. Men with foresight and ambition. Rhianna liked that.

After the play's first night, which was not sold out, Rhianna sat in Lynsey Webb's dressing room and gently wrapped Lynsey Webb's quilted gold silk cape about her.

'Thoughts of Manhattan scared the life out of me at first,' she said softly. 'The realisation of it, not the place itself. D'you understand?'

Lynsey finished fastening her suspenders and examined her legs. 'No. And I, for one, don't intend staying here for the rest of my days either. Hollywood might be as dead as the dodo to some people, but I'd be flaming cross if I got to heaven without working there.'

'Hollywood?' Rhianna echoed, while her eyes noted the way Lynsey held herself, the long, white neck, the utterly flat tummy. 'You have everything you could possibly want here! Fame, fortune, men.'

'Men!' scoffed Lynsey. 'Have you seen my old man lately? He's mooning around with a face like a moron.'

'He doesn't like New York?'

'He knew damn well I loved my job when he married me. Now he has to get on with it.' Lynsey stretched her leg and examined the back seam of her stocking. 'Suspect I'll have to have a varicose vein op soon. Oh blast! Why on earth doesn't someone hurry up and invent anti-aging?'

Rhianna smiled. She liked the idea of Lynsey aging. The faster the better. 'Your husband adores you!' She tried to ease her conscience. 'You don't know how lucky you are.'

'I've worked damned hard to get this bit of success and I'm determined to hang on to it.' Lynsey wagged a finger at Rhianna as if warning her off.

'Terry's pleased for you.' Rhianna urged. 'His eyes pop out of his head every time they see you.'

'Terry wants a wife, but he married me. Didn't he?'

'Yes.' Rhianna was puzzled. 'So?'

'Wives have children and make cocoa at bed-time.' Lynsey leaned closer to Rhianna, her hands fumbling with the back clips of her bra. 'Here, for God's sake help me or he'll be storming in because I'm taking so long. Can you imagine me pregnant?' She turned so Rhianna could fix her bra. 'It wouldn't be my veins I'd be thinking about then, it would be the depth of water under Brooklyn Bridge.'

'Lynsey! You mustn't say things like that! You have so much!'

'And I want more. Now, before I'm completely senile and depending on cement in the wrinkles to get work.'

'Well, of course —'

'There is no way I can give all this up and start breeding. I can get drunk on applause and I'd like to be drunk permanently.'

Rhianna listened, understanding but resenting.

'Did you see that picture of Garbo in the paper the other day? God, my heart went out to her. All that precious beauty and talent gone. Puff!' Lynsey shrugged her small breasts more comfortably into the bra.

'What if Terry leaves you?'

Lynsey climbed into a scarlet dress and waited for Rhianna to zip up the back. 'He won't leave me. I am good in bed. Could have made a successful profession out of it.'

'But you love him?'

'Of course I do. With all his tantrums these last weeks I'd have kicked him out long ago if it wasn't for that.'

Rhianna watched Lynsey peer closely into the mirror, smoothing her brows and touching up her lipstick. 'Your beauty will last until you're a hundred and ten. It's pure English rose.'

'Is that all?' Lynsey laughed. 'Think of the stardom one could earn if one remained young, well, an attractive age anyway, until two hundred.'

She laughed at Rhianna, her eyes large, the scarlet dress tight. 'Now, if you don't mind I'll slip into that cape you're busy fondling. It is mine. I earned it!'

Rhianna jerked to obey, and Laurence Paget's voice boomed down the corridor outside, 'Rhianna! Are we eating tonight or am I on a fast?'

'We're eating!' she called back, and Lynsey gave her a meaningful look.

'Keep in there. No babies to worry about. Maybe he doesn't know how, but he'll prove useful some day.'

Rhianna tossed her golden-coloured head and let Lynsey precede her to the door, 'If you keep your word and jump off Brooklyn Bridge he might give me your part,' she said.

'Might,' retorted Lynsey, 'but I'm not the jumping kind.

Been a fighter all my life.' And she strode off, pulling on long white cotton gloves, symbols of the part she played on stage: Miss Fairfax in *The Importance of Being Earnest*.

Rhianna sighed and watched the elegance, the poise, the confidence of the star. 'I can do it too,' she told herself, her hands fisted to her sides, 'I can. I can. I must. I will.'

Laurence Paget came briskly around the corner, his spectacles glinting as ever. Sometimes she wondered how he could see through them; surely the million lights of New York reflected on them and dazzled him.

'Come on, baby, get a move on. My stomach thinks my throat's cut.'

She laughed, ever remembering he was her bread and butter now and might be her diamonds later, 'Where are you taking me?'

'Fancy dancing?'

'Love it.' Sometimes she wondered why he never saw through her willingness to accompany him. As he held her coat for her she said, 'There must be a million girls envying me tonight.'

'Five million,' he replied, and Rhianna wondered if he had ever taken a girl to bed.

His car was at the kerb but he ignored it. Rhianna didn't question him. She knew it was faster to walk. He slipped an arm about her, but it was not a movement of *amour*, it was a persuasive and unspoken request to get moving. Her high heels tap-tapped on the sidewalk and people turned to stare at her.

'I ought to be wearing Lynsey's red dress and silk cape,' she murmured. 'Give them something to look at.'

'Keep trying.' He was intent on his journey forward.

'If we're going dancing I ought to wear something with a bit more room in the skirt.'

'O.K. We'll pop into the apartment. The night is young.'

Rhianna didn't look at her watch. She knew it was near midnight.

He said, 'There's some folk I want you to meet. They've got influence. Will give you a load of publicity.'

'You mean they'll tell the world I'm still an understudy.'

'I mean they'll tell the world you come from a little place called Wales in England –'

'Joined onto England.'

'O.K. Joined onto England, and you got the same accent as Burton. He came from a couple of miles from you.'

'And that gives me star quality?'

'It gives you what folk like. You gotta get that over to them. That you got what they like.'

She took him up to her apartment and he stood in the centre of the room waiting for her. A letter was on the glass-topped table. He could see the grass-green coloured carpet under and all around it.

'You got more mail from home today?'

'Mmm.'

'Doesn't look like you opened it.'

'I'm not interested in Whesley any more. It died for me seven years ago.'

'Maybe the letter's important.'

'It says my father's ill.'

'Your father? Hey, how d'you know if you haven't opened it?'

'All the previous letters said so.'

'Yea?'

'He wants to see me, talk to me.'

She came swiftly from the bedroom, clipping a diamond bracelet about her wrist. 'Do I look up and coming enough for you?'

'You've got those shadows under your eyes again. You want to get rid of them. People will think they're my fault.' He laughed without humour and Rhianna let him slip her coat over her shoulders.

'It's true. One day I'll tell the world you own me like a robot. Someone to walk beside you and look good.'

'Not a robot, baby, a Ming vase, and I'm working on you all the time.'

She took a deep breath and picked up the envelope, opening it and quickly reading the letter.

'Yes, it's from Mary Johnson. She's a neighbour of my father's. Thinks I should fly over and listen to him.'

Laurence made for the door, then waited for her. 'Go on Saturday if you want to, but make darn certain you're back here by Tuesday.'

She snuggled against him, both her arms wrapped about his. 'I can quite understand why young girls fall for older men. They're not only better looking but they're kinder too – more understanding.'

He hugged her grip closer to his body and a sort of joy swept through Rhianna. Everything in her world seemed right. The path to success stretched before her, the lights of New York calling her onwards, blazening encouragement, and this man was a God-sent gift.

On Thursday she watched *The Importance of Being Earnest* from the wings and saw Lynsey at her best, fit as a fiddle and loving every second of the audience's applause.

Afterwards Rhianna told Lynsey about Mary Johnson's letter. 'Laurence has said I can go.'

Lynsey looked surprised, 'I'd say you'd best hang on. What if I faint or something?'

'You faint? I doubt you've ever fainted in your life.'

'O.K. I'm fine, and there's a dozen others could step into my shoes. Why should I worry about you missing a chance, heh? Deep down inside me I hate your guts, and the guts of every young one on the way up, but if anyone's going to wear my shoes I'd rather it was you.'

'Are you really scared of fainting?'

Lynsey spread her hands palms up. 'Think about it. What happens if I do get over-tired and pass out? Someone else comes to take over and they like the feel of being Miss Fairfax. What happens to me? You aren't the only chick Laurence has his eye on.'

'I am the favourite.'

Lynsey looked thoughtful, then: 'I shan't pass out. It took years of slog to get here and I'm staying. Go on. Hold your papa's hand, tell him you're a dutiful daughter and love him dearly, then come back and save me from some other young upstart so eager to step into my shoes she'd trip me downstairs.'

Rhianna shuddered, 'You're in the oddest mood, you've given me the shivers.'

'As long as I don't give you your big chance things are fine. Right?'

'Right.'

But Rhianna didn't fly to Will Pepper. The thought of him led to thoughts of Rhodri Blackmore and that was uncomfortable. She also wanted to stay in Manhattan, just in case Lynsey fainted or tripped down the stairs.

She talked to herself in bed during the early hours, imitating Lynsey's elocutioned voice. 'I've spent years getting where I am and I'm not risking losing it. I belong here, acclaim and fame await me. Money, the lot.'

On Saturday evening she was in the wings as usual, watching Lynsey, one part of her admiring the star's professionalism, the other part hating it, wanting to step onto stage herself and say those gentle words, 'Dear, dear Earnest . . .'

On Sunday Rhianna left her bed about noon, stretched and got into her robe. She tied the belt then smoothed her hands down over her hips, luxuriating in the sensuous feel of pink satin about her: Laurence's last gift. She mused fleetingly on the oddness of the man. He never made a pass at her. Some time she must ask him straight out.

Now she crossed to the window and drew back the heavy curtains. Across the road a man stood, so far down he looked distorted, but her heart leapt and for a second she felt sick. She hurried away, wondering why, when she was thinking of Laurence, should she have seen a stranger and thought it was Rhodri Blackmore?

She went to the kitchenette, impatient with herself. She was tired. Everyone was tired on a Sunday. It was the only day of the week they could allow themselves tiredness. She drank strong, black coffee and thought of Whesley. The sun was shining. If she went to the window again and craned her head upwards she would be able to see the sky. Back home spring would be alive, golden yellow in gorse bushes and baby creatures seeing the woods for the first time. Maybe the tide was coming in. Rhodri might be on the beach already.

She made a little choking sound and laughed at herself, scathingly. 'A young girl's fancy, and all that, turns to thoughts of love . . .' She made more coffee then went back to the window. Down below the traffic wasn't moving; everyone was honking horns. It seemed that all New York wanted to get out of town.

She scolded herself for her self-pity, then went to the telephone and dialled Laurence's number.

'Wondered if you'd be up yet,' he said. 'How d'you feel?' He sounded as though he had been on his exercise bike all morning.

'Fine.' She couldn't tell him of her longing for Whesley, the aching for The Turrets with yellow faced primroses dotting the valley, of bluebells amid the trees, scenting the air like nothing Chanel had ever brought onto the market. 'I thought I'd invite the company round this evening. Have a bit of a get-together.'

'Get-together? What in hell is that?'

'We talk, yarn, maybe sing a bit.' She paused as a thought came to her. 'Can you play the piano?'

'Sure,' he said. 'Play anything. Mother wanted me to be in an orchestra.'

'About eight tonight, then.'

'About eight,' he echoed and rang off.

Rhianna phoned Lynsey. 'Laurence is coming around tonight for a sing-song, how about you bringing Terry? Didn't you say he plays the mouth organ?'

Lynsey laughed loudly, 'That was years ago. When we were kids.'

'You mean you met him when you were kids?'

'Didn't you meet anyone special when you were a kid?'

Rhianna's heart made that dreadful leap again. Rhodri was there, in her mind, and there were miles and miles of sea between him and her.

Rhianna got dressed up for the occasion. She felt confused. She wanted to stay here, but all the time there was this instinctive call back to Wales.

The crowd arrived in the apartment about nine o'clock that evening and everyone was glittery. She had invited the entire company so the small bar in the corner of the room was kept busy, mostly with people helping themselves. Talk was of success. No one ever mentioned failure. Terry Webb looked handsome in a careless way. He wore a tee-shirt and jeans. Lynsey kept walking away from him and he kept wandering after her, neither of them talking much.

Rhianna overheard Laurence say to a group about him as he gently swished his brandy glass. 'Had our time cut out, I can tell you, getting Broadway to accept Wilde. But they've heard about him now and we're only starting. The future is all there, in the palm of our hand. Just stick with it. That's what we have to do. Stick with it.'

Rhianna offered dishes of small-bites and eventually got Laurence to the piano. He surprised her by not being as inhibited in his playing as she expected, and he could syncopate merrily.

Good humour grew in every part of the apartment except, Rhianna thought as she gazed around, the bedroom. There the coats, the furs, were piled on easy chairs and there she might have a quiet moment.

She touched Laurence's shoulder and bent to his ear, 'Going to powder my nose.'

He nodded and she hurried away, sure no one's evening would be spoiled by her short absence. She opened the bedroom door and the blessed darkness met her. She went inside, then paused. Someone was in here. Her finger pressed the light switch. She squinted in the flash of illumination then quickly switched the light off again. Not daring to breath she slid out of the room and softly closed the door behind her.

Her eyes were huge with surprise. She hadn't even noticed Lynsey and Terry were no longer with the merry-makers. They were there, in her bedroom, making love.

Rhianna went to the kitchen and put the kettle on. A coffee seemed more suitable than yet another drink. The surprise had left her shaking. The memory of Lynsey's face as her head lay back on the pillow was vivid; Lynsey might not want Terry's baby, but there was no doubt she enjoyed his love making.

Rhianna sat on a high stool. She had known Lynsey the elegant, Lynsey the subtle, determined. Now she knew Lynsey the lover, her long beautiful legs folded across the small of her husband's back.

'Love,' Rhianna thought. 'That was not lust, that was love. Rapture.' She wanted to cry, as if she had suddenly discovered something previously unknown to her. Yet she had once lain like that with Rhodri, loving, knowing he was as one with her, utterly giving and taking, secure in undreamed of trust and security.

She wondered how much of her surprise at seeing Lynsey's rapturous face had been burned by jealousy, knowing that mutual loving is soul swamping, a million times warmer, lovelier, than being on stage pretending to be someone you aren't.

She shook herself irritably. She was being maudlin, stupid. In minutes Lynsey and Terry would be separate again, quarrelling, getting on with life. Who could imagine a whole career ruined for the sake of moments on a bed? Yet that is what she would be doing if she returned to Whesley.

She drank her coffee then went back to her guests, certain she had retained her air of sophistication, yet seeing them all here, together, gave her a momentary feeling of loving them all. They were chunks of her existence.

'Where's Lynsey?' someone called, and Lynsey replied lazily as she came from the bathroom, *soignée* and cool looking, undisturbed in clothing or manner.

'Did your better half bring his mouth organ?'

'I brought it,' Terry called and followed Lynsey. Everyone set up a slow hand clap, shouting at Terry not to keep them waiting, and Rhianna wondered if she had dreamed the scene in her bedroom.

' "Yellow submarine!" ' someone called. 'Play a Yellow Submarine!' 'Oh no!' someone else called. 'That's old hat!'

The telephone rang. Laurence was sitting nearest to it and lifted the receiver, listened then gestured to Rhianna. 'You,' he mouthed. 'From home.'

43

Rhianna stepped over feet, legs and supine bodies and took the receiver from him. 'Hello?'

'Ree-anna. That you?'

Rhianna's heart sank. 'Yes, Mary.'

'You recognised me then. Now how did you know it was me?'

'Your voice, Mary.'

'That's right then. I'm sorry to trouble you like this and I'm not sure about this phoning all that way –' Her voice rose slightly as if the waves of the Atlantic were trying to wash the past nearer. 'Rhee-anna? You still there are you?'

'Yes, Mary.'

'Well now then, I told Will you are busy being famous over there, but he is ill, Rhee-anna. Very poorly, and he keeps asking for you. If you could just come. Only for an hour or so, though you know you can come and stay any time. This is your home now, isn't it?'

There was the noise of the room about Rhianna, her colleagues beginning to talk between themselves. Terry trying notes on the mouth organ, Laurence laughing softly.

'Rhee-anna,' Mary's cry rose. 'It is urgent. Please be a good girl now, just this once.'

'I'm terribly busy, Mary. I can't always get time off. I have to be here for every show –' She glanced at Lynsey and knew Lynsey was feeling contented, satisfied.

Mary shouted, 'Rhee-anna!'

'All right!' Rhianna called back. 'I'll speak to the producer. Yes, I promise. Good-bye now. Good-bye Mary.' She put the phone down and her brain wouldn't work. Mary, the parochial neighbour, had telephoned transatlantic. Maybe Mary did really think she should return home. Rhianna turned to Laurence and he was watching her, his face uplifted, his shining mass of pure white hair slightly untidy. He raised his brows in question and she shrugged, silently saying, 'I'm sorry, I'll have to go.'

A few days later she was on the plane to Britain, her inside swirling with trepidation.

Chapter Four

Rhianna was immune to the admiration on the taxi driver's face as she climbed into his cab and said, 'Will you take me to Fisherman's Ridge, Whesley, please?'

'You American?' he asked, and she shook her head, unaware the rain made her styled up hair look a darker golden.

'No. I'm only working there.' She sat back in the cracked Rexine seat as he set the cab in motion, swerving expertly out of the station yard and into the mass of traffic.

He jerked his head, curiosity as well as admiration still apparent as he glanced at her in the mirror. 'Bet you're glad to be home,' he tried, then, when she didn't reply, he sighed as if wondering why the beauties always got away, and concentrated on driving her to Whesley as fast as possible.

Rhianna watched Swansea unfold about her, the wet streets more picturesque than she remembered, the people grey and huddled beneath their precariously blowing umbrellas. Wales, she thought, the odd bit stuck onto Britain that catches most rain.

She had travelled thousands of miles to get here, and now it was something of a shock, the familiarity of the High Street, down through Wind Street, where Oliver Cromwell once stalked, edging the docks area, then curving on to the Mumbles Road, passing new buildings, and the old; the gas works, the prison, the great, white County Hall.

The wind came in spasms, gusting from openings to the beach. She could see the Bristol Channel, angry, fighting to possess the land, and she reflected that all nature seemed to be fighting to possess. She was trying it with stardom; she had tried it with Rhodri Blackmore. Yet with clenched fists tight to her sides she had longed for him to see beyond the

45

tantrums, to see the insecure girl who thought it necessary to own him.

She felt curdled inside now as Whesley drew nearer, she could hear his deep voice warning bitterly, 'Rhianna, you behave like a three-year-old. Next time you create a scene over nothing it will be the end for us. I mean it.' She hadn't believed him. She had believed that actresses were allowed to have tantrums.

Now the mixture of excitement and dread made her want to stop the driver, not go to Whesley, return to New York, to her ambitious life that was an adventure; fame or failure.

The taxi changed lanes on the dual carriageway. Driving was difficult, the rain coming in sudden onslaughts that blocked all vision. She felt isolated, no Laurence, no Lynsey, no involvement with anyone.

She tried re-assuring herself. She had matured since she last travelled this road seven years ago. She had learned that actresses don't have tantrums – there is always a more amenable actress ready to take their place – and no producer, not even Laurence, had the tolerance Rhodri had shown.

She drew the front of her white trench coat closer about her long legs, and unthinkingly gave her belt a tighter tug. It was like waiting to go on stage, but worse, because she now had to stick it out for, at least, a few days. She had to go up to Will Pepper's bedroom and pretend to forgive him for marrying her mother; forgive him for changing Mrs Morgan to Mrs Pepper.

It was on the grave stone: *Here lies Jean Pepper . . .*

Rhianna put her hand to her face, squeezing her thumb and forefinger to the inner corners of her eyes in case the tears should roll. She should not have come home. She should have been honest and told Mary Johnson she couldn't.

The taxi covered the six miles in record time, then slowed.

'Here?' The driver gestured to the corner.

'Please.' She didn't want him stopping outside the terraced cottage door, didn't want her arrival announced to neighbours or passers by. She wanted to climb that hill and

46

go alone into the white washed place of nostalgia.

She paid him off and he drove away. Rhianna stood in the rain, listening to the sea on the other side of the road, noticing the yachts pulled up onto the jetty, and the wind threatened to blow her breath away.

She walked the few yards to the foot of the hill, then looked up it.

Her step-father was dead!

Stunned, she stood there, watching them carrying the coffin from that black painted doorway, six men, all in black overcoats, and the hearse waiting.

She put down her suitcase; it was too heavy to carry when in a hurry. She left it against the dark stone wall, and began rushing up the hill.

Maybe it wasn't her step-father. Maybe he had taken a lodger. Maybe Mary Johnson had moved in with him. Remembering his arm about Fay Hanson, his arm about many women, increased Rhianna's horror of the separation covering the last years. She had gone to find fame and fortune; all she had really found was more ambitious people and an inability to write to anyone she had left behind.

Now the hearse with its roof of flowers seemed to symbolise the whole of those years. They were dead and gone. Rhianna had come home too late.

The hearse drew away as she reached it, and she recognised the woman who hurried from the doorway towards her.

'Rhee-anna? Is it you?' Mary was stifling tears.

'Yes Mary. Is it Dad? Is he dead?' How silly some questions were.

'I'm sorry, love . . . But I wouldn't have phoned, not all the way to America if it hadn't been serious.' The wind buffetted both women, flinging Mary's black dress so it clung to her, showing the fullness of her body.

'You didn't say he was dying! You didn't say –'

'He wasn't then. You were a long time coming!'

Rhianna blinked the rain from her face. 'I couldn't get a flight.' But she knew she could, if she had tried.

'You had better come in. Wait for them to come back.'

'No!' Rhianna remembered, with the same knife thrust of jealousy, her mother's love for the man in the coffin, the way her eyes shone and her face sparkled the day they married at the registry office. 'I want to go with them!'

'It's gentlemen·only!'

'I'm going to the cemetery!'

'No, love!' It was a wail. 'He didn't want to be buried. He told me. He said he deserved cremation.'

The hearse went past, then cars. The last car was just pulling out from the kerb and Rhianna yanked the rear door open. 'Thank you, Mary!' she shouted, and squinted into the driving rain. 'I left my suitcase down the bottom!'

Mary disappeared from view as the cascading of weather filled Rhiannas' ears, and she collapsed into the soft leather seat.

Shock made her close her eyes, to sit, stiff and cold. She felt concussed, like an illness, and the car, swishing back along the Mumbles Road was going faster than funerals should, because this one didn't want to hold up other traffic.

A male voice said with indignant etiquette, 'Good morning,' and Rhianna turned her head as if asleep, only half realising she had invaded another's privacy.

Rhodri Blackmore! She was sitting barely eighteen inches from Rhodri Blackmore.

He heard her sudden intake of breath and smiled derisively. 'So people have taken to cadging lifts at funerals now.' He didn't look at her. He concentrated ahead, as if to emphasise she was unwelcome. She couldn't speak. There was an interminable silence while she stared at him. Seven years! And her heart was saying she still loved him!

She must be off her head. The knowledge hit her like a sledge hammer and she had to cough to avoid choking. The unexpected tenderness and longing for him was overwhelming. She wanted him to behave as if she had come home to stay, to greet her with laughter and kisses.

Instead, a frightening coldness emanated from him as assuredly as from the open door of a freezer. 'Isn't it usual – ' his deep voice vibrated ' – to, at least, introduce oneself when thumbing a lift?'

Thumbing a lift? The sarcasm of the man. No surprise on seeing her. No wry comment about long-time-no-see or any other trite remark.

She gazed at the familiar square head, the thick black curling hair, the clean classic cut of the profile. She couldn't avoid an awareness of subdued magnetism; it was like a great shadow filling the car, and she couldn't say, 'It's me. Rhianna.'

She felt he was accusing her by not looking at her. He must have seen her talk with Mary Johnson. He must know it was she who opened the door of his car and barged in. How dare he humble her further by demanding an introduction, as if she were a complete stranger.

She tried to sit further into the corner, looking around, noting the old silk pull-ropes, the sticking out ears of the chauffeur. This was the grey Daimler from the Blackmore estate, a vintage job the old Colonel adored and, of all the cars in the cortège, this was the one she had entered un-announced and uninvited.

Rhianna tightened her lips rebelliously. To say now, 'It's me', would surely bring verbal vitriol on her head. Rhodri Blackmore would never forgive the girl who flung his engagement ring away in public barely a week after he had given it to her.

The agonising nausea came like a cramp at the memory of that dreadful evening – her in that special blue dress with the rosebuds she had so carefully sewn about the toe-touching skirt; her, Rhianna Morgan, finding her fiancé on the terrace with Fay Hanson. Had she really been so unsophisticated that she had screamed before everyone, those who danced and those who didn't, that he was faithless, that because he was rich he thought he could do as he liked? Shame now made her blush, to wish yet again that she hadn't come home at all.

She told herself the ring had come off too easily, if only it had stuck. If only . . . If only . . .

She had written home only once, from grimy digs in London. Will Pepper had written back telling her little except he was still Farm Manager at The Turrets. There had been no further contact other than the odd picture postcard, the usual Christmas card, but no letters, no visits.

Now the man sitting beside her spoke again, exasperated. 'I suggest you kindly explain.' But he still didn't look at her.

Rain lashed the windows, the gale force wind hit the side of the car and, in spite of its weight, she felt the Daimler shudder.

She wanted a cup of tea. She wanted to cry. She wanted to be welcomed by Rhodri, wanted his arms held out so she could melt into them, be enfolded in their warmth. God, she wanted to be anywhere but here. She wished she wasn't wearing the white trench coat over a cream coloured suit. The white boots looked ostentatious. She wasn't dressed for a funeral.

He said impatiently, 'Am I joined by someone who is deaf?'

Rhianna's answer was a whisper. 'It's me, Rhodri.'

'Me?' He turned then, and his eyes were tightly closed, as if they were determined never to open, never wanted to see the world or the things in it again.

His long slim hand lifted and moved towards her, sensing, the fingers spread. The tips touched her thigh, then her waist. They traipsed sensually over the curve of her breast, and she didn't move. She felt paralysed. He was blind! Rhodri was blind.

It was when he touched her throat, her ear, that Rhianna felt the greatest shock. His cold skin against hers.

'A woman,' he said unemotionally, and when she uttered no sound he went on, oddly brusque, 'You must forgive my manner of approaching you. People object to being touched, and I object to touching them, but in this instance I consider it a necessary evil. Who are you? Why are you in my car?'

Rhianna stared at the square jaw, at the lips that used to quirk with laugher but were now turned down with disapproval.

'Rhodri!' It was less of a whisper. 'What happened?'

Stupefaction then disbelief filled his face. His mouth

50

quivered as if afraid to ask, but she said quietly, 'Yes, it is me. Rhianna.'

He spoke her name as he had often done, with the Rh sounding like a sigh, the breeze rustling leaves in the rose garden in October. 'It can't be! Not Rhianna!' and his hand lifted again, paused, then the backs of his fingers caressed her rain wet cheek before returning to their place on his knee. It was as if memory had been suspended, and only the tenderness of the moment remained.

Suddenly, as if in tune with the flash of lightning that came from across the sea, he snarled, 'Get out! Get out of this car!' and the hand that had wanted to caress was thumping the chauffeur's back. 'Stop! Stop at once!'

Rhianna jerked the handle of the door. 'I'll go! I'll go!' Was it her voice calling? So high, so querulous. 'Make him stop. Make your chauffeur stop!'

The car pulled in to the left, easing to the kerb, and other cars swished past, their occupants craning to see through rain swept windows.

Rhianna was gasping. She opened the door and the wind caught her, any sound whipping from her lips. She was on the pavement, the weather surging at her, tears of bewilderment and dismay running down her face.

This was the homecoming she had dreaded, but never, in all her agonised thoughts, had she expected it to be as bad as this.

If only her mother had not died. If only she had kept the sapphire ring on her finger. Dear God. If only – if only –

The car moved away and Rhianna leaned against the railings of the playing fields behind her. She clung to them, glad of anything steady in a wild buffetting nightmare. She couldn't walk. She had no will left to try anything but stand and let all that had happened wash over her.

Then the car came back, reversing slowly, and the rear door opened. The command was shouted. 'Rhianna!' and she ignored it. To hell with him and his Daimler. She was not going to the funeral. She was going to stay by the railings; they were firm, they were secure.

'Rhianna!' His voice came over the sounds of the gale.

51

'Get in here. Fast.' She could see him, in his black overcoat, using an ebony cane, trying to find his way out. Her brain said he could stumble, fall, and her feet moved. They carried her to the car and in to the deep comfortable seat.

'Shut the blasted door,' he said, and the chauffeur was there, bending to the wind, closing it for her.

She was shivering, soaked. Was she the elegant person who had strolled onto the tarmac the other side of the Atlantic, coming home to see her sick step-father? My dad, she called him. It sounded better; as if she had someone in Wales who cared about her.

She huddled in the corner, not looking at Rhodri Blackmore, while he gazed sightlessly ahead, ignoring her, though she could hear his breathing and guessed how furious he was with her.

The wheels hissed on the wetness of road, the wind howled and there was no sign of the storm easing, but inside the back of the car was a terrible stillness. Two people who had once loved, now each pretending the other wasn't there.

It seemed like eternity until they finally reached the chapel. Rhianna didn't move. The chauffeur opened the opposite door and Rhodri lifted his face to the sky, as if glad of the wind and rain. He took the ebony cane as if he hated it, and he stepped out – tall, broad shouldered, a man who had been brought up to inherit authority.

Rhianna watched him walk away. No one offered him help. No one approached him, yet the men huddled beneath the boughs of a great tree gazed at him with what was akin to awe. Rhianna reflected that once they would have given an arm to be invited to The Turrets. Was it possible blindness had made Rhodri so unsociable that others learned to leave him alone?

Rhianna wondered when the blindness had come. Had it been a sudden thing, or something that had been creeping up on him even as he kissed her, his breath warm against her cheek, his lips sighing, 'Rhianna . . .'?

There were no women in the cortège, so she waited until all the men had gone into the small square building, then she followed. The chauffeur said nothing, but sat in his front seat, stiff, like a totem pole, his ears sticking out either side his blue-grey peaked cap. When she eventually climbed out, he drove into the shelter of the elm trees to wait.

Rhianna sat in the back pew of the chapel and listened to the service. 'Goodbye, Dad. You meant well. Mum loved you. Pity I didn't understand her need of you. Pity she didn't understand my desperate need of her. Goodbye, Dad . . .'

When she came out of the chapel the sun was making a weak white effort, and for a moment she stood gazing up at the doubtfulness of it. Was there a bus she could catch? Maybe a phone booth where she could call a taxi?

She was aware of no reason for saying goodbye to Rhodri. He would be relieved she had gone, and his chauffeur would inform him.

She walked fast to the gates, hearing car doors opening and closing behind her, engines purring into life.

Another funeral was coming in and she waited, in respect for it to pass. Then the grey Daimler was beside her, the back door opening, and that commanding voice saying, 'Rhianna. In here.'

She saw him lean forward and speak to the chauffeur, then the uniformed man was getting out, not as tall as she had thought, thick set and pug nosed. He came to Rhianna smiling, an ugly man in a nice way.

'Join him,' he said. 'He's lonely. It can't do any harm.' Then he held the door open and waited.

Rhianna hesitated. She wondered if the chauffeur meant she couldn't do any more harm than had been done already, and when he moved his head in an inviting gesture, she climbed obediently back into the comparative warmth.

Rhodri didn't turn to her. He made no move at all. It was as if he was no longer aware of her, but she was aware of him. She tried to convince herself it was a purely chemical reaction. It wasn't love. Not after all this time. Puppy love didn't last from nine to twenty-six.

They had gone almost three miles before she felt she had to break the silence, had to speak, say something, anything. She said, 'Thank you, Rhodri.'

'You invited yourself,' he returned tonelessly. 'I merely allowed you to finish the journey.'

She gulped awkwardly. 'Of course.'

The rain really had stopped and the wind was easing. Rhianna looked at the Bristol Channel; it had been a surging mass of gun metal grey, now it was streaked with silver shivers.

She said, 'I didn't know Will Pepper was dead.'

'Someone must have told you.'

'I didn't know about your blindness either.'

He didn't flinch. 'You really have been out of touch.'

'When did it happen?'

'My blindness? Just over six months ago.' Then his lips became less downward at the corners, as if he was indulging in some sort of secret smile. 'Is it possible we are still birds of a feather, Rhianna?' Her name was a sigh. 'Other people are afraid to mention it. One can talk about scabies or leprosy, but not about blindness.'

'Do you want to talk about it?'

'No.' He was abrasive again. 'I want you to remember it.'

She wanted to take his face in her hands and kiss away the pain she saw there, but his abrasiveness was real, his shoulders set, his hands tight about the top of the ebony cane.

She said more calmly than she felt, 'At the moment I'm rather glad you can't see. I must be looking my worst.'

'Your hair is all loose?'

'How did you guess?' There was a slight easing of tension.

'You never liked the restriction of hats, and if you had it pinned to the top of your head when you started out the wind would have blown it free.'

Almost silently she laughed, pleased he remembered. 'It's dangling like long rats' tails.'

'Then you haven't had it cut?'

'No.'

His head moved slightly, as if in unconscious approval, and Rhianna felt another surge of pleasure.

She said conversationally, 'Things have obviously been

happening to you.'

'And to you, surely,' he said subversively. 'I understand your experience with the Whesley Dramatic Society stood you in good stead.'

'It helped,' Rhianna said, remembering. 'But I was a long time getting a job once I arrived in London.'

'You are doing well now?'

'I was lucky,' she said. 'I was an Assistant Stage Manager for a few years.'

'A.S.M.' Rhodri said, and laughter, teasing, were almost in his voice.

'Don't you scoff,' she chided gently. 'The whole company has a run on Broadway. And I'm an understudy.'

'Fame!' Rhodri derided familiarly. 'There was a time you'd have scorned an understudy.'

Rhianna looked from him, rows of tall houses were rushing past as they neared Whesley. 'There was a time I would have scorned *The Importance of Being Earnest.*'

'Is that what you're with?' He was incredulous, on the verge of enjoying himself, and Rhianna bristled.

'I agree it's not *Joan of Arc,*' she retorted, 'but just getting *The Importance of Being Earnest* to America was something. They're not mad about Wilde out there.'

'And you did that?' Now he was scathing.

'No. The producer did. He has friends.'

'Aaah,' Rhodri breathed, as if all was explained. 'The producer did.'

Rhianna glared at him. There had been a deliberate insinuation in his words. 'I'm a good actress,' she railed. 'Laurence wouldn't bother with me if I wasn't.'

'Laurence?' Rhodri said, in deregatory tones. 'So his name is Laurence.'

The cars turned the corner in the village and began to climb the hill.

Furiously Rhianna prepared to leave the Daimler, but as the cottage came into view, trepidation swamped her. She felt like a visitor about to enter a strange house, not a daughter coming home.

Rhodri didn't move. She turned to him, 'You'll come in,

55

of course.' She couldn't prevent the tremor in her voice. 'Everyone else seems to be. Mary probably prepared for them.'

'She's on the doorstep?' Rhodri twitched his head slightly, guessing.

'Yes. She's a bit plumper now than I remembered, but otherwise the same.'

'Wearing a pinny?'

Rhianna's fury died. 'As a matter of fact she is. It's black with purple things, like pansies, all over it.'

'Pansies,' he echoed. 'I had forgotten pansies.'

'Little things,' Rhianna said, and put out her hand. Her fingers caught his sleeve. 'A cup of tea,' she promised, 'Good, strong, black stuff.'

'No thank you.' He withdrew his arm as if objecting to her familiarity.

'You came to the funeral. Why not for a cup of tea?'

'Coming to the funeral was a gesture. To let Mary know I hold no umbrage. Entering the house would be a different matter.'

'Umbrage?' Rhianna was mystified. 'Why should you hold umbrage?'

He moved the cane; it hit the door and irritation crossed his face. 'Rhianna, I am not the man you knew. Never will be again!'

She remembered how he used to look, the whole of him a true Welshman's colouring – black, strong hair, summer-sky blue eyes fringed with thick, dark lashes, and skin that absorbed the sunlight then turned to dark golden.

'Go in,' he said. 'Have a cup of tea. You must be in need of it.' He hesitated, 'And we will not meet again.'

She stood on the pavement, bent towards him, her voice quietly dismayed, 'You can't be still holding that scene against me! It was dreadful. I was selfish –'

'Which scene?' His voice deepened, cutting, and when she didn't reply immediately, he repeated, 'Answer me! Which scene?'

'Forget it,' she returned lightly. 'I remember something you seem to have forgotten.'

'Rhianna,' he responded grimly. 'When a person can't see they are thrown back on their thoughts. There is nothing to distract the mind. I remember all the scenes. You created dozens, and to hell with anyone else's feelings.'

She flushed, ashamed and embarrassed, aware of the chauffeur sitting ramrod straight, pretending to be deaf, but she couldn't let Rhodri go, not like this – him blind, and her bereft.

She bent further into the car, speaking slowly, 'Then you will remember how we drank hot tea together. When we were both young and silly. Maybe now, on my home-coming, it will do no harm to do the same thing again.'

'Goodbye.' He ordered the chauffeur to move away, but against her will Rhianna cried out.

'No! Wait! Rhodri. No one spoke to me at the chapel. I can't walk into this cottage, be among these people. Not on my own.'

Her voice trailed away as she realised she was pleading, and hot colour suffused her face. She put a hand to her hair, aware it was dangling. 'Oh God, I feel so terrible.'

Rhodri relaxed back in his seat and smiled, one corner of his mouth tilting mockingly. 'Are you saying that Miss Rhianna Morgan, the cocky Miss Rhianna Morgan, is re-questing the pleasure of my company?'

'Yes,' she breathed, and gulped.

The old Rhodri was in his posture, in the animal-like litheness as he moved his legs to a more satisfying comfort.

Rhianna's hand clung to the edge of the door. She suffered a heightened awareness of black-clothed men strolling along the wet pavement, of Mary Johnson giving up waiting at the cottage doorway and turning, disappear-ing, into the gloom of the passage. Mary Johnson was where her mother ought to be, and over the roofs of lower cottages, the wind still threatened from the sea.

Never, in all her life, had Rhianna felt so alien, so severed. She said gently, 'Rhodri. I need your help.'

Something like a chuckle born of bitterness came from deep inside him, and he moved his head as if looking at the chauffeur, seeking a second opinion. 'All right,' he said finally, then slid along the seat towards her and the kerb, the ebony cane held awkwardly. 'But don't think you are getting all your own way again, because you aren't. Maybe it is time Mary and I spoke to each other.'

He got out, onto the pavement. He paused, straightening himself, pulling his wide shoulders back. 'A blind man can't see peoples' faces, Rhianna, but he hears a lot. Do you want me to tell you any spicy bits of gossip I hear?' He was deriding, his mouth quirking.

'No.' She thought she knew these people, knew what they were thinking. She was the upstart who had considered herself too good for them, who had gone to London to find fame and fortune, and look at her now: hair like rope, wearing white as if it were a virgin wedding.

'Right then,' said Rhodri, a mixture of tolerance and irony in his voice. 'Do you guide me or do I bang into things?'

'Take my arm,' Rhianna said. 'Keep close to me,' she remembered how it had been in the old days, when Rhodri Blackmore was always close to her.

His hand linked around her elbow and his body came against her. She felt a great wave of exhausting relief. She was home. Rhodri was with her. She felt her chin tremble and her heart threatened to clog.

The doorway before her remained open. It was the doorway she had continually run through as a child, brought her friends to, and now she was afraid of it. Didn't want to re-enter that part of her past.

Rhodri's grip tightened, a squeezing of his fingers as if to silently give her courage, and she glanced up at him. He seemed bigger than she remembered, and just as adamant. He had decided to enter the cottage, and enter he would.

'Are we going?' he demanded. 'Or are we not?' and she could feel tension emanating from him. This seemed to be a testing time for them both.

She led Rhodri to the door, then into the narrow passage, around the laden hallstand, and sensed he was hating every second. He who had strode everywhere, played cricket for the county, had tennis courts behind his home, and took water ski-ing as casually as other people took a stroll.

He muttered irritably, 'I feel like a poodle on a short lead.'

'You look like Rhodri Blackmore of The Turrets,' she whispered back, and he scowled, his black brows almost meeting across the top of his fine nose.

Then they were in the room she had once called the kitchen, and there were faces all lifted, staring in a curiously awed silence.

'Good God —' someone gasped quietly, and Mary came rushing from the scullery, her hands wiping on the black and purple pinny, her feet bringing her skilfully between sideboard and mourners.

'There now!' she cried. 'There's lovely you came, Mister Blackmore. Welcome to my cottage. Will would be pleased if he knew.' She held out both hands. 'This is an honour. Really it is.'

Rhianna's stomach turned chill. Was Mary making it clear she was permanent hostess here? Mary had been Will's mistress for years, Rhianna knew. Was she now mistress of the cottage too?

'Look, come over here,' Mary hustled. 'Get up, Jim Davies, give Mister Blackmore your seat, there's a good man. Over here, Mister Blackmore. In the armchair by the fire — oh dear, Ree-anna, give me your coat. You're soaked through. Shall I get a towel for your hair? Would you like to go upstairs?'

'No, no.' Rhianna's voice was strong in an urge to protect Rhodri from further unwelcome attention. 'We're fine thank you. Please don't bother.'

She gladly shed the white trench coat, and took the last of the pins from her hair so it fell in all its wet but healthy fullness about her shoulders.

There was movement all around. The room was too small for so many people.

She took Rhodri's hand between her body and arm again and felt him baulk. He didn't want Jim Davies' seat, he had strong second thoughts about being here at all. She smiled as she thanked Mary, then wound her way to the big armchair that used to be Will Pepper's.

59

'There,' Mary exclaimed, helpful but tactless. 'You're by it now, Mister Blackmore. You can sit down.'

Rhodri heaved his shoulders as if a greater degree of tolerance was desperately needed. He felt the chair against his legs, then he sat and jerked his coat securely about him, his square face set; it could be chiselled in granite.

'Cup of tea, Mister Blackmore?' Mary was determined to be hospitable. 'Or something more warming? Brandy?'

Rhodri shook his head. 'Nothing. Thank you, Mrs Pepper. I am quite comfortable.'

Nausea hit Rhianna. Mrs Pepper? Will and Mary had married?

She sat on the wide arm of Rhodri's chair, glad of the closeness of him. She accepted a cup of tea and was glad of the heat. There was a shuddering inside her. Her home had probably gone from her completely.

The tea was sweet, burning her throat, and her brain was ticking away; the cottage had passed from her mother to Will Pepper. Had it now gone from Will to Mary? Was there nothing, as well as no one, belonging to her in the village any more?

Someone at the table said, between mouthfuls of ham, 'I didn't know you were back, Rhianna.'

'All the way from America,' someone else explained.

For a while they stared at her, blatantly curious, not wilfully offensive, but Mary called, 'Eat up, you lot. There's others waiting to come to table,' and the funeral meal went on.

Rhodri sat in silence. No one asked him to remove his coat. He seemed to exude aggression like a guard dog silently listening to the approach of an intruder.

Rhianna bent to him, whispering. 'If I make the tea, will you have a cup?'

His hand moved, found her, and he nodded.

She left him and went to the scullery. It was a scullery no longer. It was now a gleaming blue and white kitchenette.

Mary came bustling after her. 'I'll make it, Ree-anna. You sit down. There's a good girl.'

Rhianna tried not to wince. 'It might be the last time I

come here. I would like to make him a cup of tea.'

'The last time?' There was horror in Mary's voice. 'Not you! This is still your home, Ree-anna. I promised Will and he promised your mother.'

Rhianna nodded and smiled. She felt too sick and tired to do anything else.

'Right then,' Mary said. 'The water in the kettle is hot. Just switch it on and bring it to the boil, then I must take you upstairs. Not because you don't know the way, *cariad*, but because you must be finding everything very strange.'

The older woman stared into Rhianna's face and, for a second, Rhianna expected a quick hug, but someone called from the kitchen.

'I'll be off then, Mary. Thanks for the hospitality.'

Mary hurried to them, her voice calling, 'Thank you for coming. It was good of you. Will would have appreciated it.'

Rhianna made tea, hot and strong with sugar. It was a long time since she had received pleasure from performing such a small task, then she took the two cups to the chair where Rhodri waited.

'There,' Mary called to him, returning from the front door. 'I'm sure that will be just as you like it. Ree-anna remembers things like that,' and Rhianna felt herself blushing again.

She leaned towards Rhodri, glad her thick, yellow hair was almost dry, shielding her face from any curious gazes, but she was still also aware that no one but Mary had made a point of speaking to Rhodri.

She whispered, her cheek close to his, 'The cup's hot. D'you want to try it? Or wait?'

'I'll try it,' he murmured, and lifted both hands, the ebony cane caught between his knees. He took the cup and saucer while Rhianna's fingers hovered, waiting for him to drop or tip them, but he knew what he was doing. He tasted the tea, then nodded, and she saw the slight softening of his mouth. 'Thank you, Rhianna,' and once more her name was a sigh.

Eventually the last guest had gone. Mary sank to a chair beside the table of dirty dishes and left-over salad, while the clock on the high mantleshelf ticked remorselessly.

Rhodri said, 'You had quite a crowd here, Mrs Pepper.'

'Yes,' Mary sighed, then gazed at Rhodri, her slightly full face drooping. 'I'm glad you came in, Mister Blackmore. I've wanted to tell you for a long time. Will never forgave himself. He'd known you such a long time –'

'Sssssh,' Rhodri warned, and moved to the edge of the chair. 'The past has gone, Mrs Pepper. We must forget it.'

'Oh Mister Blackmore, and you, with your eyes –' She clasped a fist to her cheek, pressing, watching him as if she, too, could experience his blindness.

'These things happen,' Rhodri said dryly, and stood up, his ebony cane a waving antenna, ready to feel his way out. 'I must go, Johnnie will be waiting.'

'Johnnie!' Mary cried. 'Oh, your poor chauffeur. And I didn't even take him a cup of tea.'

Rhodri smiled unexpectedly, as if he had done all he needed to do. 'Rhianna. You can manage now. I will say good day.' He was finding his way to the door, and out, to the sloping street.

Rhianna went after him. It was as if she had suddenly been dismissed, discarded.

She tried to take his elbow, but he drew his arm away, 'I am perfectly all right, thank you,' then he held out his right hand. 'Goodbye Rhianna. We will not meet again.' He signalled with the cane and the Daimler came. The chauffeur opened the rear door and Rhodri got in. 'I shall repeat it, Rhianna,' he called. 'We will not meet again.' Then the door closed on him.

Rhianna leaned towards the window. 'Thank you –' she called through the glass, but the car moved away, and she felt snubbed when Rhodri didn't turn his head to acknowledge anyone.

Chapter Five

Rhianna went up to her room alone. Mary stood at the foot of the stairs, undecided.

'You sure you'll be all right?'

'Yes, thank you.'

Now the cottage had emptied it also seemed forlorn. To Rhianna it seemed familiar yet strange.

Mary's hand on the banister knob was strong, a worker's hand, but her face was that of a vulnerable woman in sorrow, pale and puffy-eyed. She said, 'Ree-anna, it's all been a shock to you. I am sorry.'

'Don't worry. You can't be feeling too grand yourself.'

'I should have telephoned you. Told you we got married.'

'Forget about it, Mary.' Rhianna pushed her hair back; it was dry, beginning to bounce again, regain its own glorious colour. 'It was my fault. I should have kept in touch.'

'There were so many things you ought to have been told. P'raps with you it was different. P'raps you had nothing to tell us.'

Rhianna turned, looking down. 'It was I who went charging off. Ready to set the world on fire – and look what happened.'

Mary's hand tightened on the banister knob and her huge, dark eyes became haunted. 'Ree-anna, It was fire that blinded Mister Blackmore.'

Rhianna stared down, her lips parted with a sudden intake of shocked breath. 'Fire! What fire?'

Mary's gaze didn't waver, her face tilted upwards. 'Mr Blackmore went out one night. He left Will in charge to look after the Colonel. He'd had a heart attack – the Colonel. And Fay wasn't capable –'

Rhianna's legs wanted to give way and she moved down

63

a little then sat on the top stair. Waiting. Frightened. As if ghosts would appear and she couldn't escape them.

Mary took her hand from the wooden knob and wrapped it in the pinny still tied about her waist. She put her head on one side, not looking up now. 'You ought to have been told. I ought to have told you. Will didn't stay. He came home. It's why he said he deserved cremation.'

Rhianna leaned forward, loathe to say anything in case Mary stopped telling.

'Fay had candles all about the bed. She liked them. She said they were –' Mary's voice threatened to break – 'romantic. She and Will were –'

'Yes?' Rhianna prompted, yet not wanting to know about Fay and Will, only about Rhodri.

'He came home. He left her. She was drinking. And there was a fire.'

Rhianna crept down the stairs. Mary looked forlorn, a small plump figure struggling for courage.

Mary gazed into Rhianna's grey eyes and murmured. 'When Mr Blackmore got home. There was smoke. And flames. He dragged Fay out. Ree-anna, *cariad*. The heat you see. He was blinded.' Mary rubbed the end of the pinny against her nose, then went on more quickly, 'His hair grew again. And his eyebrows. And his skin came right. But his eyes –'

Rhianna's heart squeezed into a tight torturous lump between her ribs. 'Fay died?' God forgive her. She had felt hope!

'No.' Mary shook her head. 'He saved her. Saved her life. But the old Colonel. He tried to carry water, you see. Throw it. It was too much. That, and the shock of it all.'

Rhianna's fingers were spread, tight to her mouth, suffocating any noisy horror. 'He died?'

'Before the morning.'

Rhianna felt the lower stair hit her thighs as she sat heavily, and Mary sat below her. The cottage seemed full of a silence that caged in the sound of their heart beats.

Rhianna put her arms as if to hold Mary to her, but Mary drew away. '*Cariad*,' she sighed. 'There were many said your mother was unwise. She spoiled you rotten when your father died. Maybe to make up for her loneliness. Then, when Will came along, she forgot you. Maybe that's why you had such airs and graces. Anything to get attention, they said, but no one would wish you a homecoming like this.'

Rhianna smiled wryly. 'I was horrid, wasn't I?'

'Not your fault, *cariad*. You were moulded that way. Life makes us the way we are.' Mary rested a hand on Rhianna's knee. 'But you love Rhodri Blackmore. It was on your face today when you came in. *We* all saw it and more than one heart went out to you. And to him.'

Rhianna stood up, feeling stifled by the thickness of emotion about her. She managed a sound that could be a laugh. 'I hadn't seen him in seven years. He's probably a different person now. Less attractive.'

'He has changed,' Mary agreed, and stood too, a stair and other inches shorter than Rhianna. 'It's a pity. One should never turn one's back on love. There is so little of it about.'

Rhianna climbed the stairs again, gripping the banister rail, her imgination seeing those flames, terrifying, roaring, scarlet, orange, white, all stabbing at Rhodri, and she wanted to rush to him, tell him of her need for him, the insipidity of other men.

'You lie down now, *cariad*,' Mary coaxed from the kitchen doorway. 'They do say this jet lag is a dreadful thing.'

Rhianna glanced down at herself. In New York the cream suit had been chic, fashionable, its loose flouncy lines emphasising she was an actress. Here, in what used to be her domain, it looked ridiculous. She had to get it off, have a bath, sit in heated water and think.

Think? For months she had hoped, planned, even schemed a little, in an effort to further her career, but she hadn't risked taking time to think; that might have resurrected the past.

But now, as the bath water ran, she had to face the fact, the past affected the future. She couldn't ignore it any longer.

She went to the dressing-table, seeking a temporary

home for her undies, and pulled out a drawer. The only thing in it was a shiny black, piano-shaped box, a red rose stencilled on the lid. Memories crowded in on Rhianna; Rhodri and Carl grinning as she helped pull the speed boat ashore, Rodri and Carl handing her this musical box because summer had ended and Rhodri was going up to Oxford.

Slowly she raised the lid and the fairy-like notes tinkled out, 'Twinkle twinkle little star . . .'

'Poor little Rhianna,' her mother had sighed when she first saw the box. 'The world owes you such a lot,' and Rhianna had been young enough to believe it.

Now her brain scolded. Fool, Rhianna, the world owes you nothing. You can demand nothing. You can only earn.

She got into the steaming, scented water and felt the suds begin to soothe. She leaned her head back against the yellow plastic cushion and realised how weary she was.

She dressed in a deep pink jersey dress with a chunky, black necklace and wide black patent belt. Then she lay on the bed.

The rain had stopped completely, a small patch of blue was probing the deep grey of lowering clouds, and Rhianna thought how the Welsh sky varied continually, always moving, presenting different shapes and colours. She thought of how aware she had been of Rhodri, and told herself it couldn't possibly still be love.

She dozed then went down to the kitchen. There were four women with Mary, all relaxed, sitting as if used to being there.

'Would you like a cup of tea, Ree-anna?' Mary said, and introduced her all around.

Rhianna nodded and smiled, wondering if it would be wiser to book into a small hotel in Swansea, get away from the village for a day or two, but Mary seemed to read her thoughts because she said, as she set another cup. 'I have just been saying, Ree-anna, how lovely it is you are here. I shall miss Will. It's going to be lonely without him.'

The other women made noises of agreement, and Mary went on, almost pathetically, 'So you'll stay a week or two, won't you?' and Rhianna smiled because anything else would seem unkind.

'As I was saying,' Mary turned to her visitors. 'Ree-anna is an actress. In New York. In America,' and when no one commented, she added, 'aren't you, Ree-anna?'

Rhianna nodded, faintly amused.

'She's famous. Aren't you, Ree-anna?'

'Oh no!'

'Go on,' Mary laughed, and any awkwardness had passed.

No one mentioned Rhodri Blackmore.

Next day Rhianna offered to do the shopping. It would give her a chance, she said, to see what changes had been made since she went away.

The sun shone and, as she strolled along the promenade towards the shopping centre, the Bristol Channel twinkled and swelled with good humour. The hills encasing the bay were swathed in purple against a sky that was at its deepest, clearest blue.

This was spring, the beginning of the season. Soon, yachts of every size would float *en masse* on the tide, and holiday makers would make the different types of eating houses and pubs along the front full of a clamouring night life.

It wasn't only what Rhianna saw; it was what she felt. A dawning of anticipation, a seaside village preparing to awaken from hibernation. The chrome and glass on parked cars sparkled less coldly, strangers looked at each other, ready to smile, even to chat, and summer colours were beginning to appear in the windows of enticing little dress shops.

Rhianna took time to stare out to sea, a tug bustled to a great tanker, anxious to get it in to dock, and the lighthouse stood, white, aloof, and stark on its outcrop of Vandyke rocks.

Rhianna met people she had once known, but it was as if the reputation Mary had given her was deep seated. The butcher didn't exactly bow, but he smiled wider than was necessary for a pound of shin and two lamb chops. He flicked his boater at a cheekier angle and whispered to others on his side of the counter, drawing their gazes to the mirror that stretched across the back wall, their attention focusing on Rhianna.

She was flattered. It would be nice to be a star, to be famous, and what harm was there in letting everyone have what they regarded as reflected glory? She would be gone from here soon.

She regretted that.

She stood in the centre of the pavement, unaware of people trying to dodge around her, and she tried to renew her feeling of belonging, of absorbing the atmosphere that had once been part of her. The tang in the air made her remember she had lungs, that she was breathing, living, not merely existing hoping Lynsey Webb would break a leg.

She acknowledged people, amused by the way those who recognised her smiled and those who only wondered if they recognised her stared.

She felt young. In New York she had been old, her face a mask of artificial colouring, her hair sprayed into place. Today she had only pale lipstick on her generous mouth, and a lick of brown mascara on her large almond shaped eyes. Her hair blew freely. Her heart was ready to recapture the magic of love. She wanted to run on the beach, lick ice-cream and laugh with Rhodri.

The only problem was that Rhodri did not want to meet her again. He was a married man and, no matter what type of wife Fay was, Rhodri would be forever faithful to her.

Rhianna shopped, paid at the till, and didn't know she was conniving, arranging the next few days. If anyone had accused her of doing so she would have hotly denied it, yet still the plan evolved.

She and Mary lunched together in companionable silence, until Rhianna gestured to the potted plants that made a leafy green bower. 'They weren't here yesterday,' she said, and removed the dirty plates while Mary made a pot of tea.

'I took them out. Better than worrying about people bumping into them. You remember that white geranium? It came from The Turrets.' Mary stood the teapot on the stand on the table. 'They say the garden up there has all gone now. He can't see anything so doesn't care if anything grows. You can understand. Can't you?'

'Yes,' said Rhianna, but couldn't. It didn't sound like Rhodri.

It was two o'clock before she voiced her next move. 'I think I'll go for a walk, Mary.' And Mary didn't seem at all surprised.

Rhianna brushed her hair into a mass of shivering golden tones, then put on a dress of deep mauve in fine wool. It had a cowl collar and she wrapped the wide black patent belt about her waist. She thought ruefully of how few clothes she had brought with her, and it was then that the full implications of Rhodri Blackmore's blindness hit her. She might as well be in rags. He couldn't see.

She lay her black patent leather handbag to one side, not sure she intended visiting him, but disappointed her usual manner of impressing people was now useless.

She thought of returning to New York. Laurence Paget would be waiting, elderly kindness at the ready, promising her stardom if she remained his satellite. She would never be able to visit this part of the world again. Yes to Laurence meant no to Whesley. She had no idea why; it was just some unspoken code inside her that she knew she would have to obey.

Never see Rhodri again, she thought, and was horrified at the affect this thought had on her.

She tried to think of Fay calmly. Had the fire disfigured her terribly? Had the tragedy been a cure for her drinking? Was she a good wife? Why didn't she have someone to look after the gardens? Did Rhodri – the invisible knives twisted in Rhianna's gut – did Rhodri make love to her often?

Rhianna called cheerio to Mary, successfully convincing herself her walk was not an intention to visit Rhodri. She wished to go to the top of Emrys Hill and gaze at The Turrets in the valley below. Just look. Then come back to the

69

cottage and book a Transatlantic flight for the soonest possible moment.

The sun still shone as she went to the street, but the wind was chill, and her trench coat was belted tightly about her. It was a long but pleasant walk, leaving the road early, taking the path that wound behind the cottages then clung to the cliff top.

Gulls screamed warnings of her approach, small birds fluttered, and the gorse was popping from buds to yellow clusters all about her.

Rhianna breathed deeply, glorying in it. She turned inland, crossing fields and a stile before getting to the summit of Emrys Hill and gazing down at the wonder of The Turrets.

She had never discovered why the building had such a name. Certainly it had turrets, but it was no where near the size of a castle. Rhodri had once told her it was built by a Blackmore suffering delusions of grandeur.

'He was a big man,' the twenty-four-year-old Rhodri had stressed to the enchanted seventeen-year-old Rhianna. 'He wanted a castle built on a hill so he could have soldiers marching around the turrets, and more soldiers at the slits of windows all ready to shout, "Enemy approaching!" but all he could afford was this.'

'He didn't have slits of windows,' Rhianna sympathised, 'Nor even a hill. I suppose no one would carry the stones up there.'

She and Rhodri had stood close together, laughing, his arm about her shoulders, a chain of buttercups about her neck, and dry grass stuck to her back, a picture for all to read; she and Rhodri were in love. Their happiness a tangible thing; it was in the way they looked at each other, the way their hands met, the glow on their faces.

'We are not wealthy,' Rhodri had said pathetically, and Rhianna laughed loudly.

'You don't know what want is!'

'Not wealthy!' he insisted indignantly, his face flushing. 'I didn't say we are paupers. But it's all on paper. Father works that way. But I'll be in sole charge one day. I'll make

70

changes. You won't marry a poor man, Rhianna.' She had flung herself at him, laughing and gasping, her arms rising about his neck, the buttercups crushed between them.

'Are you proposing, Rhodri Blackmore?'

'I'm saying I will do. When you are older. Are you saying you will accept, Rhianna Morgan?'

'Oh yes, please.'

His kiss had been one of possession then; she had promised to belong to him, and they sank to the ground together, aware of the scent of the earth beneath them, of sheep calling their lambs.

The Turrets had been beautiful that day. The Colonel insisted on the Union Jack and the Welsh Dragon flying from the south tower. Those flags had been brave, bold, patriotic flashes of colour as they flapped and leapt.

Collared doves had called from the woods where rabbits and pheasants prospered, and where wild deer came in winter from the forest higher up the valley.

Now Rhianna surveyed it all and, at this time of day, the sun glorified The Turrets. The building looked mysterious, old stone in an aura of golden light, a figment of a fairy story, but there was an atmosphere of utter loneliness, even desolation. Rhianna told herself she had known moments like this before, moments that fled and gave way to happiness.

She ran down the hill, into the valley, part of her feeling foolish; she wasn't seventeen any more. She was twenty-six, an age when you didn't run down hillsides with your arms outspread, your mouth open with delight, your hair flying behind you. But she was convinced no one could see her. She was free to resurrect this feeling of fleeting happiness. This was where she had loved, and this was where she had to be, at least once before she left Wales for always.

She went towards the house from the back entrance. The cabbages someone had planted had come to nothing; they were masses of discoloured, caterpillar-nibbled nets.

Rhianna hesitated by the back door, but no creature came to greet her, no big, black cat arching its tail as it purred against her legs, no dogs bounding, barking, sniffing suspiciously.

Rhianna went in, not overly confident but sensing instinctively that she was doing the right thing. She was glad she had come. She was needed here.

'Rhodri?' she called tentatively. 'Fay?' but there was no reply.

She went through the large flagstoned kitchen that looked far from clean, her gaze taking in everything; the pans waiting to be washed, the dirty dishes piling on the draining board. She shuddered at the coldness of the place. It was all so different from what she remembered. In the old days there had been a fat woman, who bossed everyone around and made marvellous Welsh-cakes, while bread was always proving by the great wood-burning stove.

There had invariably been music. Either radio or Colonel Blackmore playing the piano. Rhodri had never played, so the Colonel said – the boy vamped, too lazy to learn the job properly.

Vamped, Rhianna mused now. A woman was a vamp when she tried to lure a man into bed with her.

She walked a little faster. Going to bed had only happened the once with Rhodri; and not at all with any other.

She peeped into the sitting room. The loose covers on the big suite looked as if they hadn't been removed since the year dot.

'Rhodri?' she called, more loudly. 'Fay?'

She came to the spacious front hall and stopped, shaken by the sight of a woman, on her knees, scrubbing the mosaic floor.

Rhianna exclaimed without thought, 'You don't scrub this. You'll ruin it. It was brought, piece by piece, from the West Indies years ago.'

The woman ignored her until that patch of floor was finished, then she sat back on her heels and said, 'It needs scouring. I don't think it's been done in six months.'

'Does Mr Blackmore know you're doing it?'

'Not unless someone else told him. I haven't.' The woman gazed up at Rhianna, her grey curls held back with a yellow band. 'You're Rhianna Morgan, aren't you? I heard you were back.'

Rhianna nodded, still bewildered by what she saw.

The woman held up a rubber gloved hand. 'I can't shake. I want to get another patch done. I'm Mrs Foster.'

Rhianna stared down at her, trying to understand. There was no other sound in the building. Rhianna said, 'The place seems empty.'

'Mr Rhodri's upstairs. In his room.'

'Isn't there any other staff? Where is everybody?'

'There's only me.' Mrs Foster concentrated on moving her kneeling pad, then drawing the bucket of dirty water nearer.

Rhianna stood, undecided. Whatever she had expected, it wasn't this. She said tentatively, 'Is Fay around?'

Mrs Foster shook her head, moving with her equipment. 'She's in a clinic. Down in Devon somewhere. I thought Mary Johnson would have told you that.'

Rhianna looked helplessly about her. The floor was certainly dirty. She said, 'Don't you have any help at all?' and her voice was verging on the incredulous.

'Nope,' said Mrs Foster. 'That's why I've only been here two weeks. A month is usual for anyone that comes here. I don't think I'll last that long. Did you notice the kitchen?'

Rhianna nodded, a tinge of panic in her. She looked towards the stairs and thought of Rhodri in a room above. She supposed Mrs Foster meant his bedroom and asked, 'What time is he likely to come down?'

'Who?' said Mrs Foster as she prepared her wet cloth for another splurge. 'Mister Rhodri? He doesn't come down. Unless it's something unusual, like your step-father's funeral.'

Rhianna brightened. 'He has a chauffeur.'

'My son,' Mrs Foster nodded at the floor. 'I get him to help out now and again.'

Rhianna went through the front doorway and stood on the steps, the portico putting her in shadow. The garden was neglected. The magnolia was in wonderful blossom but

73

needed pruning, the large delicate cups of pale pinky white held out to the sunshine.

Didn't Rhodri know it needed attention? And at the back of her mind was the snippet of news. Fay is in a clinic. Fay isn't here. But Rhodri is. Alone.

She wondered whether to keep walking, go back to Mary, say thank you, then pack her bags and fly away as planned. He didn't want her here. He was no weakling. He obviously chose to live alone. To stay would be to court trouble.

She strolled along the path that was already blocked by clumps of weeds and straying flowers. A row of fat sparrows sat on a broken wooden fence and watched her. She watched them back, then turned to look at the house. Its turrets were reaching as proudly as ever towards the sky, even though the flag poles were bare, and Rhianna knew that if she never loved anything else, she loved this place. And the man in it.

In the same way as her feet had brought her here, so they now took her back indoors. The woman was still on her knees, her arm stretched as it moved in an effort to perform the miraculous and uncover the beautiful pattern of the flooring.

Rhianna said, 'You can leave that. Is there a mop you can wipe it over with?'

'As you say,' the woman said, and got to her feet. She grinned and nodded. 'See if you can get some sense into him. You'll be doing us all a favour.'

Rhianna climbed the stairs then went along the gallery, opening doors as she went, convinced now that she was the only person likely to be interested in what was, or was not, going on within The Turrets. She pushed open the door of the biggest bedroom and gasped. The most atrocious stink hit her.

This had been Mrs Blackmore's room. A shrine held to her memory by an ailing, stubborn, darling of a Colonel. It was black, the walls still showing signs of wet, the satin paper mildewed, peeling from the plaster. Stinking. Stinking.

Photographs of Mrs Blackmore still hung by wires, smoked, splintered, grotesque. The remains of once deep blue velvet curtains dangled about the cracked, blackened windows. The bed was little more than discoloured springs supporting rotting burned covers.

On the charred dressing table cobwebs had begun to form, entangling themselves about the stained jars, the remains of a silver hair brush, a comb.

The stench of fire and neglect was nauseating, and Rhianna thrust her hand to her mouth, not only in horror, but also to stem the feeling of a stomach heaving against all her eyes could see and her nostrils tried to repel.

Against her will Rhianna found herself going further into the room; it had the same terrible fascination as Madam Tussaud's wax works, and Rhianna's fingers couldn't resist touching things. It was as if her brain refused to believe what it was being asked to register.

Black grime moved and the wardrobe door swung further open. Clothes still hung there, mostly ruined, blackened, the mildew creeping insiduously. Rhianna's gaze travelled down, to shoes made like brown tissue paper by heat, and she saw the bottles; rows and rows of bottles. She lifted one and turned it up. There were only dregs to slide.

So this was where the fire had been. This was where Fay had hidden her loot of booze. This room, this erstwhile shrine, had been where Fay had drank. Where the tragedy had occurred.

Rhianna wiped her hands on her handkerchief, feeling guilty that she had seen anything at all; that she had even entered the place. Then she backed, seeing fresh things: wine glasses splintered into small glittering pieces dug into the debris of the carpet, a bottle almost lost in what must once have been a pillow.

In the corridor she leaned against the wall. Closing the door had not taken away the smell. It was as if she had freed a ghost, and that ghost was beside her. She wanted to retch. The stillness, the silence, was unearthly.

And Rhodri lived here. Alone. Thank God he could no longer see that room. It should be cleaned out. Got rid of.

Renewed thought made her move more quickly. She got to his room and tapped on the door.

'Rhodri?'

There was no answer.

'Rhodri?'

'Who is it?' The question was without interest.

'Me.' The relief was in her voice. She had found him. 'Rhianna.'

'Go away.'

'I want to speak to you.'

There was a long silence while she waited, then she knocked again. 'Rhodri!' She was more demanding. 'I said I want to speak to you.'

'Get out of my house!' It was a roar, and she recoiled as if the door itself had struck her.

She backed to where the banister rail supported her, then turned. To the devil with him, let him stew in his own juice. But as she walked past the burned-out room the smell of the dead fire was strong, and she couldn't go on, couldn't leave Rhodri like this. He belonged in the world of commerce, dominating the board room, exciting confidence and brilliance.

Doggedly she went back to his door. She felt near to rebellion, prepared to fight him, even hit him if needs be. No man had the right to wallow in self-pity as he was doing. Had his pride gone completely? Where was his back-bone? In his shoes?

She didn't tap on the door this time, she opened it, quietly.

He sat in an upright, wooden armchair, his ebony stick between his knees, his head lifted, listening.

She closed the door behind her, then leaned against it. All her determination to get him moving disappeared. He looked so independent, so proud, so egotistical, yet so alone.

Silently she warned herself not to go soft. There was nothing pliable about Rhodri Blackmore, and he sat now like a granite statue. She determined not to be the first to speak. She saw the grate had ashes in it, bits of cobwebs clung there, and dust was thick everywhere.

She crossed to the furthest end of the room where two

large screens stood, one was beautifully embroidered with birds and flowers, the other, even more lovely, had come from China and was a tapestry picture of lovers beside a fountain.

Rhianna peered behind them and, as she guessed, there was a single bed that had been ill made, as if a blind person had made it, with the sheets and pillow cases in need of changing.

Rhodri said sarcastically, 'Enjoying your squint around?'

'Not at all,' she retorted.

'I should think not. A man's room is not the place for the famous.'

She didn't answer. So Mary's silly bragging had got to him since yesterday.

'I told you to go,' he said.

'You told me nothing of the kind. You bawled. Like a street kid.'

'Then why stay?' He slid down a little in the chair, crossing his outstretched legs, insolent and, she decided, deliberately goading.

She wondered quickly what would happen if she replied, 'Because I am stupid enough to love you,' but the camaraderie that had built up between them seemed to have gone. In its place was distrust and animosity. He had married another, and she, Rhianna, had taught herself to live without the sensual closeness of a man.

She said, 'No responsible woman could go away and leave a place looking like this. It's a pigsty.'

'And I'm the pig in it,' he accused coldly.

'If the cap fits,' she replied in equal tones, 'you wear it.'

She prowled. There was nothing in the room she wanted to see. She was listening, sensing, needed to know more about Rhodri.

She shuddered, blaming the chill of the room, and hugged her arms about her.

Rhodri said, 'You shiver.'

'How do you know?'

'I heard your intake of breath and your arms moving against the cloth of your coat.'

77

'I'm told you're a hero. You lost your sight in the fire.'

He held the cane between both hands, waving it slowly over his legs. 'Does it repel you?'

'Your blindness? Not at all, but your lack of welcome does.'

He lapsed into further silence and she went to the window, looking out over what used to be well-kept farm lands, lands that supplied The Turrets' family and staff with food, and left plenty over for any charity in the village.

'I gave you a lift in my car,' he said. 'That was sufficient welcome.'

'Is that what you did?' Unwittingly her tone became teasing. 'I could have sworn you accused me of thumbing a lift.'

He became tense, the stick held motionless before him. 'You deride me, Rhianna.' Again her name was a sigh on his lips.

'Was there ever a time when I didn't? You're such a serious old fuddy-duddy when you feel like it.'

'I feel like it now. Only more so. Please go. I don't want you here.'

Rhianna went to the basket chair, dusted it with her handkerchief, then sat. It creaked as if no one had used it in a long time.

Rhodri straightened his wide shoulders. He said, with restraint, 'You also take advantage of my disability. If I could see, you wouldn't behave like this. You would have the good manners to go.'

'It wouldn't be good manners. It would be neglect.'

'There is no welcome for you here.'

'Nor for anyone as far as I can see. The house is rotten.'

'I have a capable housekeeper.'

'You have an overworked slave. This place needs a master. Not a martyr.'

The stick began waving again and his legs drew up, his knees apart. 'So now we come to the reason you are here. To contrive another row. You thrive on them.' His mouth was tightening, and he turned his head away from her.

She said, 'What do you do all day? Sit here?'

'You know where the door is.'

'Do you talk to yourself? Ask yourself if the birds are keeping the estate clean?'

He left his chair, walking from her, carrying the cane but not using it, and he was lithe, even graceful, as a tiger marking its territory.

Rhianna nodded, watching him. Blindness had not crippled him, only stopped him in his tracks. One day he would come back to himself. One day . . .

She said, 'Have you been in the garden lately?'

'I deserve no interrogation, Rhianna. I have asked you, told you, to go – to leave me alone. I need my privacy.'

'You should be in the garden now. The magnolia is a mass of flowers.'

He swung towards her with such vigour she feared he would lose his balance. 'Mind your own damned business!' he rasped. 'Get back to the glitter of New York and your damn fool acting with your Laurence Influence man. You're not wanted here. Understand? And have a bath. Get that damned muck you've sprayed yourself with off your skin.'

'Muck?' she replied quickly, then eased. 'You mean my perfume.' She was pleased he had noticed enough to comment, even in fury. 'I hoped you would like it.'

'There are better smells in the stables.'

'There are no smells in the stables. They are empty.'

He stood facing her, the cane held like a golf club that had just made a faulty swipe, and she went on, 'It's the perfume I used a lot before I went away.'

'You don't say?' he remarked in false surprise. 'I don't remember it.'

'You do!' she cried. 'It's the one I spilled on the cat. She perfumed the whole valley.'

Rhianna saw Rhodri's jaw quiver. A smile, maybe a small laugh, wasn't so far away, but he gripped the back of a chair, frowning, as if he had forgotten to count his steps and now had to concentrate again.

'I will see you off the premises,' he said, and didn't wait for her to move.

Unerringly he went to the door. His hands examined it

and he turned, smiling sardonically, 'You closed it? Well, Rhianna, you have changed. No more leaving yourself a way of escape. How courageous of you.'

She flushed at the irony of his comment. It was true, she used to back out of things, like she backed out of their engagement.

He opened the door and stood relaxed, and she thought of the beautiful masculinity hidden beneath that old tweed jacket and unpressed trousers, how his shoulder muscles moved with gentle rhythm. She walked towards him then said softly, 'Why didn't you come after me, Rhodri? Why did you accept my word the engagement was off?'

He sighed exaggeratedly, one hand holding the cane, the other on the door knob.

She said, 'Was your father right when he said I was too young? Too flighty?'

'Good day, Rhianna. Thank you for calling.'

She went through the doorway and he followed her. She paused and he passed her. She was dismayed at the effect he had on her. Each time his body came close her throat went dry and her heart pounded too fast.

He kept walking as if completely unaware of her, not using the cane, his feet familiar with each step. Even at the top of the stairs he didn't hesitate.

She put out her hands, anxious to help if he tripped, missing his footing, anything, but his confidence was as it had always been. He walked as if he could see, straight, proud, his hips powerful, his legs long. His very independence sensuous.

Rhianna could have wept. His clothes needed attention, his shirt was far from clean, yet he exuded animal attraction with unselfconscious arrogance.

She walked behind him, wanting to touch him, to let her hands feel the strength of him, the warmth and maleness of him, but he was apart from her. He didn't want to be touched.

In the hall the floor was patched with grime and wet, but there was no sign of Mrs Foster.

Rhodri kept walking to the front door, an easy determined

gait, then he was on the outer step. 'Goodbye, Rhianna. Please give Mary my regards.'

Rhianna stopped. Her instinct was saying not to go. She was needed here, but then she was smiling, putting her hand out so it barely touched his, letting him know she was saying goodbye, and he nodded formally.

She stepped further out, down the steps. He went in, and the door closed behind her.

Chapter Six

When Rhianna got out of bed next morning there was just one prime thought in her mind; get back to New York.

So, all right, she argued silently, life awaiting stardom is artificial, and perhaps the stardom will never come, but here in Wales she was on the verge of making a fool of herself, over a married man who made it clear that any contact between them was unwelcome.

In a twist of panic she swung her suitcase to the bed and began to pack feverishly. God, she could end up with nothing; no home, no relations, no career. No Rhodri!

Mary yelled up the stairs, 'Ree-anna! Your breakfast's going cold!' then she came up to find out why there was no reply. She gasped as she took in the scene, 'But you can't. Not just leave. I've told everyone you're staying. They'll think we had a terrible row!'

'Why should we have a terrible row?' Rhianna replied as she made sure nothing was left in the dressing table drawers.

'Because Will left the house to me. Because of what he should have prevented that night up at The Turrets –'

Mary stopped, aghast, her arms plump and bare, hanging limply at her sides. 'I never thought,' she whispered. 'I could accuse him like that.'

Rhianna turned to her slowly, equally aghast at the outburst. She glanced at the almost filled suitcase then back at Mary, her mind shouting, Don't let her stop you. Don't let her!

Mary said, as if all fight had suddenly gone from her, 'It was Dewi Davies brought your luggage up. He saw it down there in the rain and read the label. He guessed then that you'd come back, so he brought it up. Kind, wasn't it, of him to do that.' Rhianna nodded, thinking of how important

Dewi must have felt when he was able to announce to all and sundry that Rhianna was home. She also wondered if Dewi was already marked as the next master of the cottage, but Mary went on, 'He's got a lovely house. On three floors with a lovely garden that he grows beans in.'

Rhianna laughed wryly at the wonder of three floors and a garden with beans, then she pecked a quick kiss on Mary's cheek, and said, 'I really must get back. Maybe I'll come again when the show is finished in New York,' but she could feel the rock of determination inside her. She had no intention of coming back, ever.

She and Mary went down to eat an awkward breakfast then Rhianna was on the way to her own life, the friends who never left her with a feeling of their disapproval.

Back in Manhattan she stood for a while outside her apartment just looking at the place. She reflected that when the company first came she had been so excited she had talked too much to her colleagues, hugged the thought of having made it to America, gaped at the buildings that stretched so high she doubted she would ever have the courage to enter one in case it collapsed. How could mere man make such concrete sentinels safe? Yet she had and the excitement had still not quite worn off.

A cheeky cab driver honked his horn at her as he struggled with the less than walking pace traffic and she laughed at him as he grinned and gave the thumbs up sign. She had never seen him before but this was New York and he was a Yank. A lovely, cheerful Yank who was pleased to see her. She told herself she adored him, adored all that was America. She might even make a permanent home here.

She went up to her apartment and unexpectedly needed to weep. She had been kidding herself. It wasn't New York she wanted for the rest of her life, it was what New York offered; people who would appreciate talent, people who would give her a chance. By God, she was going to be a star or bust and she was going to be a star here before she was a star anywhere else.

She tipped her suitcase contents onto her bed and began to sing. She danced a little telling herself she was now truly home. This, yes this, was where she belonged.

An hour later she telephoned Lynsey and received a glowing exclamation, 'Rhianna! Darling! You're here. I am glad. Can you come over? I have a desire to talk.'

Rhianna immediately shed her Welsh image and, when she descended once more to the street, she wore pink eye-shadow and a pink trouser suit. No one appeared to think it strange. She chuckled a little to herself as she strode along. In Whesley the whole population would have turned to stare or rushed home for a cup of tea. All Rhianna's ambitions were back; there would be no more day-dreaming about an ancient building lost in the depths of a green valley. She was off to the future. Look out world – Rhianna Morgan was on the way.

Lynsey met her at the door, 'Darling, I am so glad to see you.' There were hugs and kisses as if Rhianna had been away years; a greater welcome than she had received in Wales. It re-affirmed Rhianna's sensation of being in the right place.

Lynsey's apartment was opulent; not doorways but arch-ways with eastern type curtains. Shakespeare's plaster head stood on a white pedestal, and a purloined plaque saying Charlie Chaplin lived here was stuck to the white wall over the great fireplace. Rhianna knew the fire was gas fed but it looked real, with coals and flames that Lynsey could make any size she cared.

The settee was bigger than Rhianna's, the cushions huge and softer; there were silks and satins and flowers that were probably also silks and satins. There were also furs. Now, into April, Lynsey still had her furs, left them spread around where ever she had cast them. Lynsey knew how to be a star.

'Drink, old dear?' the star asked, her face a mask of make-up.

'Coffee.'

Lynsey grimaced but swished to the kitchenette and made coffee out of a jar, then she came back to Rhianna, sank into the monster easy chair, kicked off her mules and tucked her feet under her. She smiled brilliantly at Rhianna. 'Darling, I need a holiday terribly.'

'We all do.'

'Well Laurence is going on Sunday for forty-eight hours. He's going to Long Island. Fishing.'

'I didn't know he knew anything about fishing.'

'I don't suppose he does but it will keep him out of the way for a while.' Lynsey's long black artificial lashes fluttered then lowered as if to hide any expression in her eyes. 'I want you to take my place on stage for one night.'

Rhianna's jaw dropped while her brain tried to assimilate.

'I really am feeling very jaded, Rhianna. Please, dear, give me at least one night off.'

'Laurence will go through the roof.'

'I know, I know, but don't tell him. Not yet. Don't tell anyone, not anyone at all.'

'He's bound to know.'

'Not until he comes back.'

Rhianna's heart was banging. Here it was, the chance she had hoped and prayed for.

'Oh Lynsey,' she managed to gasp. 'I couldn't.'

Lynsey re-adjusted the draped neckline of her blouse, took the long steady sort of breath that leads to meditation, and purred, 'Of course you can, darling. You might hit the headlines and be made for ever.' Her smile reminded Rhianna of the wolf in *Red Riding Hood*.

'It would be ghastly, going behind Laurence's back. He's been so good to me.'

'And me.' Lynsey smiled. 'He's a chum to us all.'

Rhianna said, inexplicably nervous, 'You live the part of Miss Fairfax, don't you?'

'Have to,' came the reply. 'There is no other way.'

Rhianna stared at William Shakespeare. He looked blind.

'You will be a darling, won't you?' Lynsey's long polished nails tapped on the arm of her chair. 'Terry's off to Ontario and I do want to be with him. I'll be back in time for Tuesday evening.'

Rhianna tried not to look blank.

'What will you tell Laurence? That you left the show to go with your husband?'

'I shall plead illness.'

'He isn't stupid!'

'I'll supply proof. Eventually.'

Rhianna left Lynsey and wondered why her feet felt as if they wouldn't touch the ground; the sidewalks felt soft, wobbly like balloons.

She went back to her own apartment, got out the script and began to swot. Already she knew the words, now she had to ingrain herself, forget Manhattan, imagine England almost a century ago. Become Miss Fairfax.

It wasn't the finest part of the play. Lady Bracknell had that, but it was the chance that she, Rhianna Morgan, had been given to show New York what she could do, and who knew what then? Would New York learn to love Oscar Wilde and would Rhianna Morgan come back as Lady Windermere in *Lady Windermere's Fan*?

Confidence wrapped around Rhianna and she was cautious when Laurence phoned.

'Hi,' he called. 'I was told you had returned to the fold.'

Rhianna paused, only Lynsey knew she was home so what else had he learned?

'I have heard tales about you, too.' She returned. 'You're going to leave me in preference for fish.'

'No,' he said, 'you got that wrong. On Sunday – all day – I'm taking you with me.'

'You are? Where to?'

'Keep mum about it. Let the others think I'm going alone. Fishing.'

'Is it somewhere nice?' She sounded a child again.

'You'll like it. As long as you keep your mouth shut about it. What about a picnic basket?'

'Huh! We won't be eating there?'

'We probably will, but it's good to pretend we didn't expect to. O.K.?' He sounded bouyant, which wasn't like Laurence at all.

She laughed and snuggled herself deeper into the chair. She told herself he was rather nice; no complications like love, no feeling sorry for him, wanting to take care of him.

That night at the theatre he spoke to her only when it was necessary and then only as a member of the cast, an inferior member at that.

Lynsey did well. At the end of the show there was an extra curtain call. When Lynsey came from back-stage to the front, her head held to the gallery and her arms outspread, there were loud cheers and extra clapping. Lynsey's face was highly coloured, her eyes fever bright.

Rhianna felt ashamed of her jealousy. Lynsey was doing the finest turn she had ever done and loving it, looking healthier than ever before. She couldn't bear to watch any longer so went behind the scenes.

Terry was in the background, listening to the accolades, his red head slightly drooped as if he was tired of being second best.

Rhianna gave him a special smile and for no reason at all whispered, 'How does it feel to be the loved one of a star?'

'Lousy,' said Terry, and walked from her.

Rhianna called softly, 'I hope you enjoy your trip over the border tomorrow.'

'I'm not going down that far,' he returned over his shoulder. 'Pheonix will be the furthest this trip.'

'Oh,' Rhianna said, feeling puzzled.

When Laurence arrived on Sunday morning she was ready in blue jeans and a pale blue shirt that shaped to her waist. He let his gaze weigh her up and down, then he nodded.

'You have what it takes.' She handed him the basket.

Laurence was a good driver, calm and smooth. She lay her head back and gloried in the moments passing fast. She was almost where she wanted to be. She touched Laurence's thigh and he gave her a quick smile. With his shirt neck open and his body relaxed, off duty, he was a very attractive man; the white hair shone, his aquiline nose made him look as distinguished as he really was.

Rhianna decided comfortably that when she was a star

she would make him an even better companion. She said conversationally, 'You know people are talking about us.'

'And what is it people are saying about us?'

'That we're more than friends.'

'How true. We are producer and a company member. Isn't that more than friends?'

Disappointed she turned from him. She didn't know what she had expected in his reply, but it wasn't what he had given.

She sat quietly musing on the fact that men always behaved with this superior attitude, as though they thought themselves above women. Rhodri Blackmore did it; put the stupid little woman in her place and let her be honoured if allowed to sit next to me. Her hands fisted and the rebellion she so often worked to keep submerged began to rise. She said, with an edge to her voice, 'When am I to be given my chance, Laurence? I have been your pupil for so long I'm beginning to wonder if that is all you have in store for me.'

He didn't look at her or show any sign of having heard. Blast the man. Blast all men. She felt so churned up inside and so bewildered by life she couldn't think straight. Why the hell wasn't she a star now? She had been studying and waiting long enough. And where was Lynsey off to this weekend? How confident Lynsey must feel of her star status that she could risk creeping away. Come to think of it, how confident Lynsey must feel of Laurence's trust in her that she could know he'll find out and is capable of sacking her.

The car purred down a narrow hill, swerved and stopped. Rhianna's eyes popped and a gasp was in her voice. 'I haven't been here before!'

The Atlantic Ocean stretched out calmly, so vast it made Rhianna feel infinitestimal. And there were huge yachts; white, gleaming, expensive, barely moving at their moorings.

Laurence turned to her and laughed; a different Laurence, a Laurence who had unexpectedly shed the mask of boss. 'What d'you think of it?'

'Beautiful!'

'Better than Whesley?'

'Well,' she hesitated. 'It's so very different. You can't compare.'

'And this,' he smiled, looking years younger, 'Is where the billionaires come to play.'

That word rang in Rhianna's brain. *Billionaires!* Were there so many that he could refer to them in the plural? What a land this America was; not at all like the America where cowboys looked into saloon girls' eyes, then stood opposite the baddy with gun hand hovering near muscled thigh.

Rhianna burst into hilarious laughter. 'Oh Laurence, what a child I am! How ignorant! I know nothing.'

Laurence slid out of the car. 'I'll keep on teaching. Jeez the breeze is good out here.'

She climbed out quickly, excitedly, and went to his side, gripping his arm. Oh if Mary could see this; if all those people in South Wales could see this. If only Rhodri – oh dear heaven, if only Rhodri could see . . .

She snapped her thoughts back from South Wales and raised her chin, intent on schooling herself for the future. Laurence had not brought her here for nothing; he was not the type to waste time. He had told Lynsey he was going fishing; a cover up – so just what was he after? Her blood began thumping strongly. She had an urge to fling her arms about his neck, persuade him to tell her what he had in store, but already he was striding on ahead, a tall, possibly too slim man who was planning to make money out of her.

The motor boat was at the bottom of the stone steps, a man with a smile of uneven teeth, a smile of respect, a man who was employed and never forgot it.

'Mornin'.' He greeted Laurence first, then acknowledged Rhianna with a nod. Rhianna was reminded of Will Pepper, Will touching his forelock to the Colonel back home, in subservience.

She shivered away the goosepimples and wondered why she couldn't enjoy these moments. Why she had to think of home.

She stepped prettily into the boat, aware of being a starlet, and wondering who was out there on one of those yachts? Who was watching her and Laurence through binoculars?

She caught the hem of her shirt and rolled it up, tying it in a knot just below her breasts. She took the pins from her hair so the breeze caught it and blew it like a fan of golden rays about her head. She had to look carefree. She, Rhianna Morgan, had to be in charge of her life. Use these men when they offered so blatantly to be used.

The boat skimmed across the water and all her hard boiled thoughts crumbled into fragments of regret. Rhodri used to skim like this with Carl. Two boys, that's all they had been – laughing, loving life and the spasmodic Welsh summer time. And she had been in love – really and truly, heartbreakingly in love.

She turned to Laurence, an odd effort at re-assuring herself, that she wasn't the bitch she was trying to be, and he was watching her quizzically, almost, Rhianna thought, as if he knew what she was doing, as if he had seen it all before.

She hung her head and Laurence put his arm about her shoulders. 'You'll like him,' he whispered. 'Just be yourself and he'll like you, maybe more than he should.'

'Who?'

'Thought you'd have guessed. Geoffrey Warren.'

But the motor boat had got where it was going and the long gleaming white metal steps were there waiting for her to climb. This, she thought, is the true ladder to success. She grasped the handrail, smiled at the seaman in smart white uniform and climbed towards her brave ambitions.

The old man sitting under a sunblind on deck looked grizzled, as if he drank too much, and smoked too many of the great stinking cigars like the one jammed between his teeth. He gazed at Rhianna through his thick dark spectacles and clicked his fingers at a young lackey.

Laurence sat opposite him, obviously willing to let the money-maker do the talking.

The money-maker also liked to use both hands at the same time, one to manipulate either the cigar or a drink, the other to touch Rhianna. The grey fingers beckoned her, sat her beside him, patted her shoulder, then found reason to pat her knee. They gently but purposefully squeezed the top of her arm, and the monied grin told her the monied hand received pleasure.

He and Laurence talked about the yacht, Miami and the Bahamas, they dropped names and compliments. Rhianna moved slowly, inch by inch, as if her chair was unsteady and kept wobbling a little further across the deck. She smiled at Laurence and wondered whether the quest for success always came this way, via an unattractive man who owned more wealth than the next.

Money, her common sense told her, brings power in its wake; why blame the monied if they are born and bred that way.

Laurence seemed to understand. He stood up. 'Mind if we dive in for a swim?'

The great smelly cigar waved dismissively. 'If she can swim, take her, but don't let her drown. I can use her.'

Rhianna stood with Laurence, 'I didn't bring a costume.'

'Who needs a costume?' the monied one queried.

'Obviously, my Welsh discovery does,' Laurence replied, smiling.

The cigar stained fingers were clicked again and Rhianna was taken below. There, in a bedroom with silver backed hairbrushes and combs on the dressing table, hung bathing gear.

Rhianna examined the bikinis, high cut holes for legs, straps down from the shoulders and over the breasts. She found an all in one. White. It glittered as if sequined, yet wasn't. She coiled up her hair and wrapped a white scarf about it, then she pattered back up to the deck.

Both men looked at her and Rhianna felt their appreciation cloak her as thickly as if it had been made of heavy velvet. She knew that whatever future plans these men might have, she was in them.

That evening Laurence stopped the car outside her apartment block and he turned to her. His nose was red where the sun had caught it, and he looked more human than in all the three or four years she had known him. He kissed her.

Rhianna responded because she owed him so much, and

because it had been a good day – a day of laughter and a form of freedom, splashing in the sea; a day when, with little effort, she had resurrected her childhood in Whesley – her and two men, salt on her lips and the future calling, enticing in glowing mental golden glory.

'Rhianna?' Laurence never put a sigh in her name and she noticed it. 'If I decided to marry, I would marry you.'

'How nice,' she returned, and knew this was the epic of Laurence Paget's approval. His human Ming vase was about to rise in value and he was about to want to own it.

He smiled into her eyes, the smile of a kind man on the verge of seeing his kindness repaying him well. 'Warren is talking of putting you into a new film he is thinking of speculating on. It's one of those made for television. World rights.'

'Oh?'

'He wanted a long-legged blonde who had experience but wasn't so well known she was already pigeon holed. She had to have talent as well as charisma.'

'Do I have charisma?'

'Warren thinks so.'

Rhianna smiled back at him, inwardly hugging herself, but also warning herself to keep optimism in check until contracts were signed and sealed. She was ready to eat Lynsey; how could she blame anyone for wanting to eat her – and succeeding?

'Has he auditioned many girls?'

'Dozens.'

'How did he find out about me?'

'I told him.' Laurence preened, the expression on his face saying plainly, I am the brilliant one. I found you and I am making you.

Rhianna waited for him to utter the words on the invisible price tag; how much she owed him and how much she would need to pay back.

For a moment she was scared; would the price be one she couldn't bring herself to pay? Like the stories of couches with men like the monied man with the white sparkling yacht.

'Ugh!' she groaned, and Laurence cocked his head.

'Is that an opinion of me?'

'Oh no,' warmth returned to her voice. 'I was thinking of Mr Warren.'

'Then you had better rethink your thinks. He is Mr Make-it and you say yes sir, no sir, three bags full sir. Get it?'

Rhianna got it and knew Laurence was right; nothing was for nothing in this world. She knew what she wanted, Laurence was leading her along the path to get it. She laughed ruefully. 'And what of you now? Do you want to come in for a drink?' But he shook his head and her shoulders relaxed, surprising her as though she hadn't realised they had stiffened.

Laurence gave her a little tap on the top of her arm, a tap that said, off you go, out of my car, and so she slid away, onto the sidewalk.

'As far as you're concerned I've gone fishing. O.K.?' he called.

'O.K.' she returned obediently.

'I am really going back to the yacht. There's a lot to discuss.' He rubbed a finger and thumb together, an ancient sign for bargaining, and Rhianna nodded, understanding; the auction was to begin and end without her being anywhere near it, yet it was her future that was to be sold. 'I'll be back late tomorrow night,' Laurence went on. 'See you Tuesday morning.'

'All right.'

'Be good,' he said, and there was a gap in the traffic. He saw it and slid his car away.

Rhianna found her way into the apartment. She changed then took pen and paper from the small bureau on the corner and began writing a letter to Mary Johnson.

Somehow it seemed terribly important to keep her feet on the ground. Being in touch with Whesley was the only way she knew how to do it.

At the theatre next afternoon there seemed to be an air of conspiracy. The producer and the all important Miss Fairfax could not be found.

'Well,' Rhianna said, 'Laurence told me to tell you all he was taking the day off.'

'Taking the day off!' came the explosive echo of numerous voices. 'Laurence Paget?'

'Afraid so.' Rhianna acted blasé. 'I think he's gone fishing.'

There were roars of laughter mixed with chuckles, 'The old devil!' someone said. 'Wonder what he's up to. And at his time of life too!' But the show went on.

Rhianna suspected Lynsey had confided in the whole company except Laurence because no one made particular enquiries about her. No one telephoned her apartment. To all intents and purposes Lynsey had also got the day off.

It crossed Rhianna's mind that Laurence and Lynsey could be more friendly than people realised, and they had gone off together; after all, it was Laurence who had discovered Lynsey long before he had discovered Rhianna. She shrugged the idea away. Did it matter? She was not in love with Laurence, nor he with her.

When the show opened the auditorium was only half full.

'It's Monday night,' the Director said. 'Never get many in on a Monday night.'

Rianna felt sick. She sat in her dressing room and sipped whisky and lemonade, telling herself this was a big chance, but she knew it wasn't. No matter how hard she tried she could not eclipse Lynsey tonight. She wanted to know where Lynsey was, where Laurence was, and why on earth she had been dragged into this.

Later she wept as she climbed into bed. She knew her performance had been dreadful. She had not forgotten her lines, her actions had been correct, but Laurence had not been there, and it was as if he had taken her will to perform with him.

On Tuesday it was as if Monday had never been; she awakened and the sun was still shining. The telephone rang. It was Laurence.

'Everything's O.K., baby? Keep yourself in trim. You're on the high road.'

'Thank you, Laurence.'

'Don't thank me now. We'll get to that later.'

Lynsey telephoned, 'Rhianna! Does Laurence know?'

'He said nothing to me.'

'Thank God for that. Can you come over? Something terrible has happened. I'm ruined, Rhianna. Ruined. I need a miracle. D'you know any messiahs?'

'What is it? Have you fallen? Hurt yourself?' How she kept harping on that daft idea; Lynsey with a broken leg.

'Get over here. No, meet me in the park. I'll tell you there.'

'Why the park?' Rhianna felt like Mata Hari.

'No one will call me there. We can talk. Oh God, Rhianna how I need a pal.'

The trees were bursting with new green leaves, the sound of traffic was dulled, daisies pried through the grass and Rhianna and Lynsey walked. Lynsey as tall and elegant looking as on stage, a scarlet cloak flung casually about her shoulders, a black hat with a huge floppy brim. Rhianna decided that, however secret the things Lynsey was about to tell, she could never be secret; she automatically announced to the world she was Lynsey Webb, the star, bestowing her appearance upon them. And, going by the smiles and nods that came their way, Rhianna saw the people of New York didn't mind at all.

They had walked almost the length of the park when Lynsey said thickly, 'I'm pregnant. That's where I've been, to a clinic to check up and it had to be a hell of a long way away, where I wasn't likely to be recognised going into the damn place.'

Rhianna kept walking, shock dulling her brain.

'Did you hear me?' Lynsey was cross. 'I said I'm pregnant. With child. Got a sodding bun in the oven!'

Rhianna paused to pick up a twig. She was experiencing triumph, the downfall of a rival. Then she snapped the twig in pieces and flung it away. She felt horrible, and guilty. She said, 'You ought to be happy.'

'Good God no! I'll be finished. Can you see Laurence ever forgiving me? He'll want to kill me. I'm ruining his show, his chance of getting a stronger footing on Broadway.'

Lynsey jerked her body away from Rhianna, a scathing action.

Rhianna said, 'Why are you telling me?'

'You're the one who'll benefit.' For the first time ever there was true malice in Lynsey's voice.

'But I thought you liked me! Were my friend!'

'Why the hell should I like you? You're a sneaky bitch, making up to the man who was mine until you came along.'

'Lynsey! Shut up! I like you. I've liked you all the time!'

'Yea, yea? Now prepare yourself. You were a flop last night. The whole cast told me so. You'll never make it. You lack presence. That thing you need on stage more than you need pretty hair and a fancy accent. To hell with you, Rhianna Morgan. One day you'll be like me – worn out, in the club and bloody finished!'

Lynsey turned on her heel, her face ashen white, her blusher standing out, deep pink with the deep pink lipstick and black painted eyes.

Rhianna stared after her. 'Lynsey! I'm sorry! Terribly sorry!' but Lynsey was past caring. She kept striding towards Fifth Avenue, not looking back, her head high, the cloak swishing about her.

Rhianna thrust her hands into her coat pockets, despondent, not knowing what to do, and her fingers closed over the letter she had written to Mary, a joyful, even boastful letter.

She drew it out and stared at it. The envelope was stamped. All she had to do was find a post box and shove the letter in. Home sickness came, a great wave that made her totter then struggle to correct her steps.

She needed Whesley. Only once more before she entered this intense world for keeps. She needed to sit on Whesley's beach, even if the drizzle was falling, stare at the whiteness of the lighthouse on its rocky outcrop, see the little yachts that she had once thought so wonderful. She felt in need of the little people, the ordinary undramatic people – just for a while, before she plunged into the world of fame, fortune and heartbreak.

Chapter Seven

Laurence was not pleased. He marched through the auditorium and came up on stage calling out, 'Rhianna! My office if you don't mind.'

The rehearsal stopped. Rhianna glanced at Lynsey, but Lynsey was fiddling with her shoe, taking it off and shaking it as if there was sand in it.

Rhianna scowled and followed Laurence. He went to the cluttered table that served him as a desk and began moving things that, Rhianna felt sure, he didn't want moved at all.

She said, 'So Lynsey told you.'

'Told me what?' His scowl equalled hers.

'That I took her place last night and I was a flop. One hell of a flop.'

'You deserve to be a flop. After all I have done for you. Jeez, you Welsh fool, can't you see what you were risking? What if the newsboys had been in, what would they have written about you?'

He came from around the desk and stood almost bending over her, domineering. 'So O.K. Lynsey told me. She had the blasted guts to confess she had put the whole show in jeopardy. Yet you, the one I've nursed, cherished, you have the damned audacity to go on stage and are too pig-headed to see you could land the lot of us in the cart!'

'Lynsey asked me to go on.'

He nodded briskly and began striding around the table, 'So if Lynsey asks you to stick your head in a fire you'd do it!'

'If I thought it would help.'

'Help?' Laurence sat on the table and laughed.

Rhianna stood and stared at him. She had never heard such a weird sound. She said with all the dignity she could muster, 'You laugh more when you're cross than when you're happy.'

'Me? Happy? When the hell do I get any chance to be happy with women like you and Lynsey Webb hanging on to me? You tell me that.' His long, white finger was wagging perilously near her nose.

'In that case,' Rhianna retorted. 'You can stop laughing because I shan't hang around you any longer. I have decided to go home again anyway.'

He took off his spectacles to stare at her and his face looked oddly bereft.

'When Lynsey asked me to take her place I realised I want to visit my home once more. Then,' she added with more courage than she felt, 'I could come back and face all the hard work that goes into becoming successful with a more tranquil heart.'

'Tranquil heart?' Rhianna thought he was going to rock with more laughter, all of it with that caustic edge, and she waited, her inside wondering if this really was the end, if he would say you can go and do not come back.

He didn't. He strode to the door and opened it, then jerked his white maned head at her. 'Come on. We can talk about it over a drink.'

In the corridor he put an arm about her, not about her shoulders as previously but about her waist, and his hold was firm and deliberate. In the street he walked fast, drawing her along with him, her feet taking three steps to his two.

'Now get this straight,' he said, 'I would not have wasted a single second on you if I hadn't fallen for you hook, line and sinker. Get it? You come into my office and have the flaming cheek to yap about a tranquil heart. What in hell d'you imagine has been happening to mine these last years? You look at me with those damned innocent eyes of yours and tell me how lovely and safe you always feel when close to me. You're too damn dumb to see how the man next to you acts, never mind guess at how he feels.'

He ran her across the road, his free arm held up to tell the traffic what it could do with its horn blowing. 'When you went home to your papa's funeral I damn near died. I went around talking to myself. Jeez. You ever been that way about someone who thinks you're safe?'

Rhianna skipped up the opposite curb and kept half running beside him. She felt thoroughly bewildered and the noise about her wasn't helping. She tried to look up as if that would lift her from the mêlée, but she couldn't see the top of the buildings; there were just windows, millions of windows and she thought of Tom Thumb. She wanted to giggle, but there wasn't time.

Laurence swerved her into a bar and held her tightly to him as he ordered, told the barman to bring the drinks to him and, still holding her to him, went to a table.

He sat her down and placed himself opposite her. 'Get this into that dim nut of yours. I intend to make you a star, and then I'll marry you.'

Rhianna tried to wet her mouth with the tip of her tongue, but there was no dampness there. She looked at the barman as he hurried over with the drinks. She watched the payment being handed over.

'Drink up,' Laurence ordered, and she lifted her glass.

She said quietly, 'It is odd how you can be with a person so much and not know them.'

'You mean not even see them,' Laurence returned. 'You took every damn thing I threw your way, but you couldn't look at me, think about me.'

'Oh I thought about you!' she exclaimed.

'You did? What did you think?'

She couldn't tell him. He would have been deeply offended. She looked at him now and saw a man in his early fifties, handsome in his own way, well cared for and immaculately clean, but with slight bags forming under the angry eyes, his jacket shoulders seemingly too wide for him.

'I am sorry.' She seemed to be going all through her life saying sorry – sorry to Will Pepper, sorry to Mary, sorry to Rhodri and feeling sorry for those she wasn't apologising to – sorry for Lynsey, sorry for Terry. Sorry for Rhodri.

She said, 'Am I sacked?'

Laurence sighed, a man who was tired and who couldn't understand. 'Do you want to be sacked?'

'I don't know.'

'So what upset you?'

He waited for her reply, an explanation, and she couldn't give it.

'Rhianna, you've got the wind up, haven't you? I've let life scare the wits out of you.' He raised his brows and replaced his spectacles. 'Maybe it's a pity I never made life scare the pants off you too. You might have thought more of me as a man.'

Rhianna moved her head so she could see the bar with its rows of bottles, its uptipped clean glasses waiting for use. She said, 'I'm sorry, Laurence, I didn't think . . .'

'Drink up. Want another?'

She shook her head, disillusioned. For so long she had thought him safe, possibly with only paternal feelings, but without yearnings, had even suspected him of being gay, and all the time he had been loving her.

She said, 'In my present state I'm not much good to anyone, so it would be as well if I got back to Wales.'

He stared into her face, the expression in his eyes limp and she wanted to soothe him, keep telling him how sorry she was, how selfish and thoughtless.

She said, 'What about Lynsey? Have you been cross with her?'

'Why be cross with Lynsey? She's no chicken and she knows it. If she eats something that upsets her she can't help it. It's more a case of thank God you were here to take her place, even though you failed to do your best.'

'I missed you badly.'

He studied her face, willing to be mollified.

She said, 'Can I nip home?' then added quickly, 'It won't do to let old moneybags see me looking washed-out too often.'

He finished his drink. 'You're certainly going to need all the stamina you can muster. Lynsey reckons she'll be O.K. now, so if you trot off as soon as possible you can be back the same way. As soon as possible. O.K.?'

She reached over the table and took his hand, 'Laurence, you are a nice person, and you are right, I do need improving.'

He put his other hand over hers and squeezed, then

waited for her to rise. Together they left the bar and Rhianna was on a plane to Heathrow before the rest of the cast had time to know what had happened.

Spring had remained in South Wales and the early morning sunshine was as warm, as glorious as Rhianna's memories loved; the breeze was balmy coming over the gorse smothered cliff tops, and Rhianna arrived at the little white terraced cottage with happiness tilting the corners of her mouth.

Already small boats were trying the waters and cars sped along the main road with surf boards fixed to their roofs.

Rhianna called from the open doorway along the passage, 'Anyone in?' and Mary came from the kitchen, the inevitable pinny tied about her waist.

'Ree-anna!' There was no doubting her pleasure. 'You don't have to stand there waiting. Come in. Come in. Oh dear, dear, why didn't you tell me you were coming. Look at the place. Such a mess!'

Rhianna gestured to the sewing machine on the kitchen table and the cotton skirt halted in its run beneath the needle, 'Making something nice?'

'I am going – that is I was going – with Doreen, that's my friend from down the road. She's going on a trip.'

'When?'

'Oh, don't you worry about that now. I can always go another time. Only to Bath to see the monkeys.'

'Bath?' Rhianna put her suitcase at the foot of the stairs. 'Why go all that way to see monkeys?'

'Not just monkeys,' Mary bustled to the kitchenette, filling the kettle, reaching into a cupboard and bringing out a glass stand loaded with fairy cakes. 'Lions and elephants. The lot.'

'You can still go. I'll be quite happy here unpacking and having a rest.'

'Oh no!'

'Oh yes.'

'Well, we'll see then. It's early yet.' Mary turned quickly

and saw the washing still waiting in a plastic bowl on the draining board, 'Oh, now look at that. So involved in my sewing I forgot to put it out. Watch the kettle, Ree-anna, will you, while I go and peg these out. Won't be long.'

Then she was gone, bowl under her arm, bag of pegs swinging from her fingers, her face a little flushed with trying to keep pace with the unexpectedness of life.

Rhianna watched her through the window for a few moments, pensive, thinking that Mary was still less than forty years of age, yet she had married Will Pepper who, in spite of rough hewn good looks, was sixty. Had Mary married for love? Or out of loneliness?

Once the tea was made Rhianna called in her best happy voice, 'Mary! Tea up.'

She poured then took the cups to the table and Mary came, bringing the stand of cakes with her. 'It smells lovely out there, but there's a bit of blackspot already.'

Rhianna nodded trying not to wonder about her own life, about the way she had always taken it for granted she could be a great star, yet Laurence had been right when he said she was scared.

She tried to shrug away her sense of disquiet and was glad of the smallness of the room, the cosiness of Mary's litter; threads of cotton on the floor, discarded fragments of material on a chair, photographs of her mother and Will Pepper on the high wooden mantelpiece.

Mary heaved the sewing machine to the narrow end of the table then sat at the long side opposite Rhianna, both stirring their tea. She said, 'You'll have a cake, Ree-anna, I made these with butter, not old margarine. Must have known you were coming.'

They smiled at each other, the sunshine pouring in through the sash window, the thick leaves of the rubber plant glossy with attention.

Mary peeled the paper cup from a cake and said, as if to encourage confidences, 'You don't like it in America. You don't belong there. Nor in London. As Welsh as the rest of us, you are.'

Rhianna didn't answer. She knew she was Welsh; it was a

feeling that sometimes swept through her like some reverential wonder, especially when familiar mountains loomed on the skyline as she travelled back to South Wales. She thought of those mountains the day of Will's funeral. They had been almost black, like shadows of great gods waiting to enfold her. She chuckled at her nonsensical thought and Mary said, 'Now what?'

'Hwyl,' Rhianna replied. 'I haven't thought about it for a long time.'

'Pity it isn't in every other country,' Mary said flatly. 'Quarrel them. Quarrel with everybody.'

'They certainly quarrel in New York and in London, but it's not like quarrelling with your own tribe.'

'Tribe? What d'you mean, tribe? Nation, mind you. Nation.' Mary munched her cake, one elbow on the table. 'Of course, if you do stay a while this time you can't be ignoring Rhodri Blackmore.'

'He needn't know I'm here.'

'Ah now,' said Mary, *sotto voce*. 'There's a man needing help. What with Fay not being there and only trouble when she is.'

Rhianna gave a sigh of exasperation, but a call came from the ever-open front door sparing her the need for reply.

'It's Doreen.' Mary said in undertones, and took off her pinny, folding it and pushing it in a sideboard drawer, then calling. 'Come on in. There's only Rhee-anna and me.'

Doreen came, broad cheeked, nodding an acknowledgement to Rhianna, 'Mary! I thought I ought to remind you. The coach leaves in half an hour –'

Rhianna excused herself and escaped to her room. She didn't know if she was happy at having told herself she must stay a while, or furious with herself for being so pliable.

A short while later Mary and Doreen were waved away in a coach leaving the square, and Rhianna went back up the hill into the cottage. She realised she was completely alone with her memories. She wandered from room to room, thinking of her mother, her father, her grandparents, all of whom had sat beside that grate, died and been laid out in that parlour.

Basically all was the same, the shape of the stairs, the cupboard under them. Mary had even kept the old mangle out at the back; dented and rusty now, but there.

It was still the cottage of Rhianna's childhood and unconsciously she reverted to her teen days, reclining on the old sofa with cake and another cup of tea, not surprised that all Mary's reading matter seemed to consist of romance.

When the telephone on the sideboard rang its loud jangling startled her.

'Yes? Hello.'

'Rhianna!' A sighed name. An exclamation.

'Rhodri!' Surprise.

The line was perfectly clear, as if he was in the room beside her.

'Is Mary there?' The startled tone left him fast; he became crisp, to the point.

'No. Shall I give her a message?'

He exuded a long breath.

'She's gone to Longleat.'

'She's in mourning!'

'You're old-fashioned. She's gone with a friend.'

There was silence as he considered, then, 'She called here yesterday. Brought me one of her apple tarts.'

'Did she?' Another surprise.

'She did not give the impression you were returning.'

'She didn't know.'

'Well, all right –' He was preparing to end the call.

'I can give her a message!' Blast her traitorous tongue.

'No,' he said, half heartedly. 'It was merely that I would have appreciated her views on a certain matter.'

'Mary's views?'

'She and Mrs Foster – er – suggested I get in touch with the Job Centre. Get extra staff.'

There was no end to the surprises.

'So I did,' he said. 'This morning. And they have people already. They're coming up this afternoon. Women.'

Rhianna felt sympathy and amusement. He sounded as if the idea petrified him. She said, 'Mrs Foster will show them in, I'm sure.'

'It isn't the showing them in, Rhianna,' he retorted. 'It's looking at them, gauging them. Are they clean? Honest?'

'Ask Mrs Foster. She'll probably know them anyway.' Rhianna's hand was lowering the receiver. She was not going to offer. She was not.

'Rhianna!' It was a command.

'Yes?' The receiver didn't come right back to her ear, only half way.

'What about you?'

'Me?' She gazed at the mouthpiece with excitement and despair. She was drowning, drowning. 'Tell them to come another time,' she cried. 'Tell Mrs Foster –'

'Mrs Foster gave her notice in last night.'

It should not have been another surprise, but it was.

'She said there is too much to do for one pair of hands. Although she did say she – er – would stay on if I obtain extra help.'

'Fine,' Rhianna managed heartlessly. 'It's time someone brought you to heel.'

'I did you a favour. Now you may return the kindness. These women will begin to arrive about half-past-two. Thank you, Rhianna,' and his receiver was replaced.

Rhianna consoled herself with the thought that sometimes it did no harm to be the scrapings at the bottom of the barrel, and looked at the clock.

She wore the dark pink jersey dress with the black belt and black chunky necklace, decided the day was warm enough to leave her coat at home, and set off.

Mrs Foster was washing a bed sheet in an old zinc bath in the yard, and Rhianna gazed at her in horror. 'Why don't you use the washing machine?'

'It doesn't work.'

'Have you told him?'

'I've told him enough. Mary Johnson and I joined forces yesterday afternoon and he did nothing about it, so last night I got him to myself and told him a thing or two. And more.'

'He says you're leaving.'

'Well, he's wrong there. As long as he behaves himself I'll

stay. I like the man, in spite of his high and mighty ways.'

'Couldn't you get someone to repair the washing machine?'

'On what authority? He could refuse to pay the bill.'

'That's not likely.'

'Huh!' scoffed Mrs Foster, and went back to bashing the sheet.

Rhianna watched for a while longer, then said lightly, 'I suspect you are a masochist.'

'A which?'

'A masochist. You enjoy being in pain.' Rhianna grinned.

Mrs Foster scowled, 'Just try me. You phone the washing machine bloke up, then you can pay him if Mr Rhodri doesn't.'

Rhianna nodded, 'You're on.'

She went to the hall. It did need scrubbing. Inch by inch. There were Corinthian pillars, supposedly holding up the ceiling, but all Blackmores knew they were doing nothing of the kind. An ancestor had seen them coming from a demolished building and bought them; no one knew where to put them, so they had been fitted into the hall. Now they looked as they must have done when they first arrived, straight from dust and debris. They, too, needed attention.

Rhianna wandered around, examining the downstairs rooms, then returned to Mrs Foster. 'Wouldn't it be possible to close some of these rooms off?'

'Supposed to be,' Mrs Foster panted over the sheet. 'No one goes into them, so that's that. They're closed off.'

Rhianna went back to the hall. Not only extra help but also extra equipment was needed. Slowly she climbed the stairs. She went past the burned out room trying to pretend it wasn't there, and made for Rhodri's. To her surprise there was music, muted but unmistakable. Rhodri had the radio on.

She tapped the door and, to her further surprise, Rhodri opened it. He looked breath-taking in beige cords and tan shirt, the collar open so she could see some of the hairs spreading from his chest.

'Rhianna?' There was no sign of the ebony cane.

106

'I've been looking around downstairs,' she said, to cover a momentary awkwardness. 'What staff d'you intend taking on?'

'A cleaning lady,' he said, stepping back, opening the door further.

'And?'

He twitched his head to one side, then raised an arm in derision. 'Shall we say a butler or two, a first maid, a second maid. Anything to stop these busybody women trying to take over my life.'

Rhianna wanted to laugh. Here was Rhodri. The Rhodri she adored, and had been determined to possess.

He strolled from her, agile, as if his full weight never touched the ground, his hands expertly finding signposts on the way, and she wondered at the stupidity she had practised, trying to cage him, keep him, as he often said, on a short lead.

He moved to a table then lifted a pair of sun glasses and put them on, turning, he said, 'How do I look?'

'Wonderful!'

'Not blind.' He was unimpressed with her enthusiasm. 'Not blind.'

His head lifted in that unconscious posture of arrogance. 'I have an idea.'

'Yes?' It was an old familiar beginning to a next move.

'We'll interview them on the lawn.'

'Rhodri! What a lovely idea!'

'Mary Johnson's,' he said drily.

'It sounds as if she gave you a hard time.'

'I suspect she is fighting not to hate me. It's psychological. By asking her husband to stay here that night, I made him responsible for the fire.'

He stood, as if surveying her. 'Do you understand?'

Rhianna nodded, then remembered he could not see. 'We're all a mess of hang-ups I suppose.'

'You,' he said curtly. 'Has this Laurence man asked you to marry him?

'Well –' The sudden apparent change of subject made her frown. 'Yes. He did.'

'And you will keep him dangling. Enjoying the attention he is pouring on you, enjoying the power you have over him.'

'I neither accepted nor refused.' Her head high now, the blonde hair loose, shimmering.

'Good girl,' he mockingly approved. 'Stick to your career. It's what you have always wanted. Public self-expression. But do have him as well.'

'And you?' she snapped. 'Your psychological hang-up?'

'I have none,' he returned confidently. 'I always make my own decisions. Like now. I have decided to end my period of mourning.'

Rhianna sighed. It didn't matter what name he gave the last months, or whose decision it was to snap out of it, as long as he did so. She clasped her handbag against her body, an unconscious buffer between him and her.

He said unevenly, 'What are you thinking?' and she had to jerk her brain to find a suitable answer.

'That interviewing in the sunshine will be lovely.' She wished she wasn't breathing so rapidly. He was bound to hear. She said quickly, 'I've told Mrs Foster to get the washing machine repaired –' but Rhodri didn't seem interested in any washing machine.

He cut in, 'Your hair is free today.'

'Yes.' Instinctively she put up her hand, pushing a stray golden band back behind her ear.

'You change with your hair style, Rhianna. You always did. When it's piled up you have a touch-me-not front. When it's loose you clasp your handbag close and glow with admiration. Are you admiring me now?'

She took a while to answer. She felt stupidly shy. 'Yes.'

'Because you can't see my blindness.'

The comment took her off guard, and she stopped to think.

'So it is,' he said flatly.

'Not really.' She tried to make amends. 'It was just so unexpected seeing the old Rhodri return.'

'The old Rhodri. Then I have changed?'

The interrogation was un-nerving. 'Not in appearance.'

He sauntered around the room, one hand feeling for the furniture and finding it, pressing, as if to assure himself he was doing fine.

He said, 'Move about. Keep talking,' and she did, knowing what he was doing. He was following the direction of her voice; Rhodri was practising for an examination he had set himself.

Her heart thudded a little more erratically with each step he took, and when the exercise was over and he stopped moving, her hand was out to welcome him.

He stood before her and said prosaically, 'The sun is still shining,' and she nodded.

He smiled crookedly, feeling the movement of her head through the touch of her hand. He preened, 'I can feel it. Coming from the window.'

She gazed up at him and he was truly a blind man, not gazing down at her. She put up her hands and caught his face, 'This way,' she laughed. 'I'm just a little to this side,' and touching him brought all the old fire scorching through her, as if he and she were caught up in some erotic magnetism that made her shiver.

Hot colour flooded his skin. 'Are you flirting, Rhianna? Or trying out the latest stage technique?'

She snatched her hands away, her voice icy. 'I simply thought that if your head was properly directed, you might catch a change in the light. Some blind people do.'

'Kind of you,' he derided. 'So it isn't just my home that is to be managed. It is also the direction of my head.'

Rhianna scowled, 'Shall we go?' and walked from the room, not waiting for him.

In the hall Mrs Foster stood gazing with wide inquisitive eyes. 'Going out?' and the pink band around her head slipped, giving a rackish look.

Rhianna smiled, compelled to like her. 'To the garden,' she said, and Mrs Foster screwed up her mouth as if she was sharing in a conspiracy.

'When we come back,' Rhianna explained. 'We'd like a meal served in the dining room. Could you manage it?' She gestured with a movement of her head to the door at the end of the hall, in case Mrs Foster wasn't sure where the dining room was. 'Salad would be nice.'

'Salad?' echoed Mrs Foster. 'I haven't any salad. I was going to do chips.'

'There are carrots still available in the vegetable plot, and I'm sure I saw a swede there. If you grate a few slices of those they'll go nicely with the lettuce I brought, and a couple of hard boiled eggs.'

Mrs Foster was open-mouthed, her brows up, and Rhianna wondered if the poor woman had ever tasted the coconut-like flavour of raw carrot or the mustardy tang of raw swede.

Mrs Foster said with an air of high dudgeon, 'As you like,' and marched away, while Rhianna waited at the front door for Rhodri to come abreast of her, then she took his arm.

As they strolled along the path, skirting the shrubs, to the lawn, Rhodri said, 'She'll be getting the impression you're in charge here.'

'Yes,' Rhianna said, without looking at him. 'She will, won't she.'

'I wish I could have seen her. Was she pop-eyed?'

'A little,' Rhianna said, 'and open-mouthed. I suspect she hasn't been given an instruction since she came here.'

'She shouldn't need instruction,' Rhodri replied. 'She can see what has to be done. I trust her to do it.'

Rhianna took him on to the grass and felt the pleasure of achievement run through him before he released his hold on her. 'I know where I am now. Thank you.'

He went cautiously to the centre of the lawn, the clutching and unclutching of his hands showing his tension, and Rhianna wondered what his deepest thoughts were. It must have seemed as if in one night the whole of his world collapsed, yet now someone had set the ball rolling. Her? Mary? Mrs Foster? Or Rhodri himself by going to the funeral? But it was Rhodri's game and now there was no doubt he was set to win.

He scuffed the grass with his sandalled feet, then crouched to feel it with strong slim fingers. 'This needs

110

mowing,' he said, as if the idea had not previously occurred to him.

'It looks beautiful. All daisies, dandelions and periwinkles.'

'Dandelions!' He was affronted.

'Oh, come on,' she cried, and her voice shook. 'Who minds dandelions in this valley? They look gorgeous.'

She stood gazing down at him, enjoying his pleasure, rivers of admiration running through her. He wasn't just an attractive man. He was an exciting man.

He left his crouching position and turned his back to her. She let her tongue moisten her lower lip. She had been silly to let so much emotion into her words. They were a cry, a cry that said, 'Why do you have to be blind? Why can't you see the gold of the dandelions?'

She clapped her hands, 'I suppose the table and that are in the summer house?'

'Probably,' he answered, subdued, and she ran from him.

It was all easy for her to carry, the white chairs that were more supple backed and comfortable than they looked, the large scarlet and green umbrella that Rhodri was able to help her fix in the hole in the centre of the round white table. Then the pad and pen ready for making notes, plus the list of applicants.

Rhodri sat in his chair and stretched his legs, the ankles crossed, a picture of casual elegance. 'Aaah,' he breathed, the sun glasses firmly in place on his straight nose. 'Howz that?'

'Fine,' Rhianna beamed, and felt smug as well as deplorably miserable. It was terrible. She loved him. She hated him. How dare he marry someone else, and Fay Hanson, of all people. She wondered how often he visited the clinic, if Fay ever came here?

He said, 'All we need now is something to drink.'

'Coffee? Tea?'

He shook his head so the black curls that really were too long, quivered in the shade of the fringed umbrella. He got to his feet. 'I'll look in the fridge –' then he sat abruptly, his lips jammed tightly, his brows coming together in anguished frustration. 'I couldn't see a can of coke if it hit me on the nose.'

'Why not just enjoy the sunshine,' Rhianna said quietly. 'Start getting a bit of a tan.'

'Why? Do I look pasty?'

'Yes,' she said honestly, 'And as ill-tempered as hell.' Then she stood up. The situation was almost unbearable. She needed to help him, console him, love him, yet all she could do was direct him.

She went from him with an easy walk she knew he would listen to, but all the time she longed for a miracle. People did regain their sight. Sometimes after years and years. Didn't they.

But another thought was creeping in: if she hadn't gone away, if she hadn't flung his ring, if she had been a kinder person, he would not have married Fay. There would have been no fire. He would have seen today.

She took her time finding the coke. She needed time to calm her heart, quell her guilty conscience, try to be insular, but the cans were there. And Rhodri waited.

He flung his head back as he drank and she said conversationally, 'What did happen to your staff, Rhodri?'

He took a long time before answering, then he said drily, 'I sacked them on the spot.'

'All of them? Just like that?'

It was as if he was looking at her, his mouth faintly quivering. 'I knew the whole thing was my fault, Rhianna. I should not have passed my responsibilities onto an employee. There is no way I can describe the atmosphere of those first weeks. I couldn't even go to Father's funeral. You went to Will's. You came from the States. I couldn't come from the blasted hospital. Fay was a wreck – I wouldn't have cared after that if the whole damned place had gone up in flames. I wouldn't have cared.'

Rhianna clasped her hands on her lap in case they moved towards him. 'It's all right,' she said softly. 'You survived.'

She needed to touch him, let him know in some way other than words how she felt for him. 'I just had the silly idea that if you talked about it, it might help.'

112

'You think I need a psychiatrist,' he scathed, 'and you will be his stand-in.'

She didn't answer. It was as if everyone was blaming themselves for his father's death, his wife's injuries and his loss of sight.

The applicants came one by one, completely unaware of the stress inside the man or The Turrets. They got out of the car in the drive and approached the languid looking Mr Blackmore with the can of coke in his hand.

If their eyes noticed Rhianna, their brains didn't register the fact. Rhodri dominated every scene, and Rhianna told him so.

'This one looks intelligent,' she breathed, as yet another woman advanced. 'Smoothly clean, straight backed, tidily dressed. Probably dependable and honest.'

Rhodri gave a nod of acknowledgement, then took over. He heard the woman approach, heard her say, 'Mister Blackmore?' and the afternoon wore on.

Rhianna witnessed that Rhodri could not only interview with all his old style from behind the screen of sun glasses, but that he was also enjoying it.

It was later, when he and she sat in the silence broken only by bird calls, content with their afternoon, their minds not yet made up as to who to employ and who not to, when a taxi sped up the drive, unloaded a very fat lady with a floppy. white hat, plonked three large suitcases about her, took her money and sped away, that Rhianna let exuberant laughter escape her.

'Rosie Jones!' she called. Then, 'Rhodri! It's Rosie.'

Rhodri stood up. He took a step, then decided to wait, his face wreathed in creases of welcome, and the fat woman stomped her way towards him.

'Well,' she bellowed. 'I hear you come back to your senses, young man. Discovered you need me.'

Rhianna shook her head in wonderment. Rhodri opened his arms. Rosie Jones opened hers, and the two met in a gasping, crushing hug.

Rhianna sat, tapping her teeth with the end of the pen. 'Who would think you two are employer and employed?'

'That means I'm re-instated,' Rosie grinned, all dimples and quivering chins. 'The moment I heard you were re-staffing I thought, right, that's my bugle call, and here I am.'

'Where have you been?' Rhianna glowed.

'In the Regency Hotel. Cooking for people I never set eyes on.' Rosie drew up a chair and placed her treble sized hips on it. 'So what's the news?'

'Here, Rhianna,' Rhodri instructed as he found his way back to his seat. 'Give Rosie the list of names. She'll know who to choose. She'll have to work with them,' and the stab of jealousy that shot through Rhianna flashed to her face.

Rosie said, more diplomatically than was usual for her, 'Oh, I don't know. Miss Rhianna could run this place as easily as falling off a bike.'

Rhianna said quickly, 'I'm returning to America in a few days. I'm doing quite well there.'

'That's nice,' said Rosie, and had a hard shrewd look into Rhianna's face. She took the list then turned her head, 'I heard you lost your sight, Mister Rhodri?'

'Yes,' he said curtly.

'Ah well, never mind. Worse things than that have been put right in this world,' Rosie said, and did not sound callous.

A short while later she stood in the hall with Rhianna and said, 'He's a good boy. Gave me excellent references.'

'That's something,' Rhianna replied, ashamed of the jealousy still twisting inside her. 'My step-father got none.'

'I should think not!' huffed Rosie. 'Not after the way he'd been carrying on. Her and him on Mrs Blackmore's bed!' She puffed hard and patted her stomach. 'No wonder the old Colonel died. Enough to kill any self-respecting mortal.'

Nausea rose in Rhianna. Her imagination flicking pictures through her mind.

'But it's all over now,' Rosie beamed. 'Rhodri'll get over it. He's got spunk, that boy.' She caught sight of Johnnie coming from the kitchen area. 'Come on, young man. Give me a hand with these bags, then I'll get and make some Welsh cakes. We can have them for supper with a nice cup of cocoa.'

Chapter Eight

It was clear that Rosie Jones was in her element; her demeanour said The Turrets had fallen apart without her. Rhianna watched with a mixture of chagrin and relief as the fat one puffed up the stairs carrying a suitcase, with Johnnie in the rear carrying the other two. Mrs Foster, who appeared to feel her nose had been pushed out of place, followed with an anxious expression all over her.

Rhianna leaned against a Corinthian pillar and sighed. It was comforting to know Rhodri was again in good hands, but she was experiencing a sense of desolation; she could walk out now and probably not be missed.

Not only did Rhodri have Rosie, Mrs Foster, Johnnie and, possibly, Mary, but also a list of others, all bright eyed and ready to serve him.

Those who called applying for jobs today had made it clear they found Mr Rhodri Blackmore an exceedingly attractive man; blind, married, he might be, but he needed a woman to care for him, and no woman was likely to miss the opportunity.

Mrs Foster returned from upstairs first, her shoulders very straight, as if battle had commenced. She glowered darkly at Rhianna, 'Just because she used to put napkins on him she thinks she owns the place.'

Mrs Foster disappeared towards the kitchen, then re-appeared lumbered with the vacuum-cleaner and dusters. As the woman trod her vexed way across the hall Rhianna said, 'Will you tell Mr Rhodri I shan't stay –' and Mrs Foster swung around.

'Miss Morgan,' she intoned. 'I have not only grated carrots and swede, arranged lettuce and hard boiled eggs, but I have also made a fresh fruit salad. If, after all that, combined with this –' and she nodded to the pieces of vacuum-cleaner and cloths, '– you make no effort to sit at table. I definitely will not stay, in spite of my promise to do so if he got more staff. I will walk out with you. Now.'

Rhianna smiled and inclined her head in sympathy. 'You've been a gem, Mrs Foster.'

'Right then,' said Mrs Foster. 'Help me carry this lot,' and Rhianna hadn't the heart to refuse.

She uncoiled the flex from around Mrs Foster's shoulders. 'This is supposed to be drawn from the machine,' she said.

'It doesn't work,' said Mrs Foster predictably, but looked less thunderous as she and Rhianna climbed the stairs together.

When they got to the room Rosie had ordained was hers, Rhianna was delighted and dismayed to see Rhodri lounging in one of the deep leather armchairs, his legs stretched out, his feet wide apart, the sun glasses still on his nose. He was grinning, preening, like a supercilious sixteen-year-old, and Rhianna couldn't refrain from shaking her head. The difference forty-eight hours had made!

'Rhianna?' He didn't turn to her.

'Yes. And Mrs Foster.'

'Ah, but I smelled you.'

'Smelled me?' Rhianna's chagrin infiltrated her voice. 'I haven't a dab of perfume near me.'

'Soap,' he said. 'Shampoo.'

'Huh,' said Mrs Foster. 'I know what I smell of. Dirt. I've been struggling alone through masses of it for days,' and her tone said, there, Rosie Jones, stick that in your pipe and smoke it.

Rosie snapped an empty suitcase shut and swung it to the top of the wardrobe, then began to unpack another with white podgy hands that fluttered now and again as if a cobweb had caught them. 'All that will soon be changed,' she said confidently. 'As first in, Mrs Foster, you can choose your position in this household.'

Rhodri's fingers gestured gently and Rhianna knew he was calling her. She crossed to him, leaving the two ladies to plan their future. He tapped the arm of his chair, inviting her to sit there. She did so, obediently, but couldn't curtail the shudder of familiarity, a wave of deep, scared trepidation as his arm slid about her hips, his hand coming around to rest on her thigh. He gave a hug, 'Comfy?'

'Yes,' she answered dutifully, but was wary. Had he got over his love for her so completely that he could not envisage what his touch did to her? That he could believe she was totally immune to him?

He said softly, 'I just want to say thank you for your help today. You did your duty well.'

'Thank you,' Rhianna returned and her body involuntarily stiffened.

His fingers against her jerked, the happy smugness fading from his face. 'Now what have I done wrong?' he murmured.

'Nothing.'

'There was something.'

'No.' But he had. He had put a lovely afternoon down to duty, not friendship. Or love.

When they went downstairs Rosie was with them, leaving Mrs Foster with the vacuum-cleaner and racing spiders.

Rosie said, as if she had prepared it. 'If you will go into the dining room I will bring in your meal. It is ready on the trolley.'

Rhodri put an arm about Rhianna's waist, directing her as if she didn't know where the room was, and Rosie's face creased into dimples, 'Ah,' she groaned, 'There's nice, seeing you two together again.'

'You mustn't get the wrong impression,' Rhianna told her. 'I have my career to consider these days.'

'Fancy that then,' Rosie said archly, and stomped towards the kitchen.

Rhianna tried to draw from Rhodri but his hold tightened. 'You can't tolerate me being blind, can you?' he hissed. 'I felt you shudder upstairs when I touched you.'

'You imagined it –'

'Stop underestimating my intelligence, Rhianna. D'you think I don't feel it, sense it?'

'It's only a few days ago you told me to get away from

here. What do you want? Me to go to hell, or me on the arm of your chair?'

She waited for his reply and saw his face harden. 'You're at it again,' he whispered. 'Trying to create a scene.'

'I'm doing nothing of the kind.'

'Rhianna, be careful. I am not the fool you keep mistaking me for. Today I tasted pleasure for the first time in months. Now I wish to make it sweeter.'

Sharply he turned her to him and, with one arm about her and the other holding her jaw, he kissed her, forcing her lips against his, hungry and vengeful.

She writhed, rasping his name against his mouth, but his closeness, his warmth was as wine to her. She became enfolded to him, the response of them both moulding and welding, her fingers traipsing up the nape of his neck, combing through the thickness of black, curling hair.

His hand left her jaw and pressed the small of her back closer to him. She heard a soft moan and realised it was herself.

Shocked into sensibility she forced herself from him, 'Don't Rhodri! Don't!'

She stumbled backwards, against the edge of the dining room door, then struggled to save herself from falling. She was bitterly shaken, disgusted with herself.

'That,' he said, 'was nice, wasn't it, Rhianna? It's what you threw away.'

Her legs barely supporting her, she fled from the room. She was aware of the table neatly laid for two, of the pink-tipped yellow tulips Mrs Foster must have placed in the tall, narrow silver vase, but Rhianna couldn't stop. She kept hurrying away, from Rhodri, and temptation.

He was being vile. Out to prove he could master her, repay her for belittling him with the sapphire ring.

The french doors were open to the garden and she went through them, along the path, her scorching face held in hands that had no cooling power. She came to the bench and sat, her heart pounding so hard that her ear drums thumped and she couldn't stop panting.

Horrified she watched Rhodri become framed in the wide

doorway, and realised he didn't have his cane. Slowly he came along the path, pointing each toe before he took a step, feeling his safety inch by inch.

Rhianna felt mean, desperately mean, but she couldn't go to help him, not then. His kiss had been so unexpected, so violent, so perilously, frighteningly needed. At this moment she stared at him and was glad he was blind, glad his eyes couldn't see the turmoil that must be in hers.

He came closer, and his nose wriggled. 'Rhianna! I can smell you. Say something.' His hands were held out, the fingers spread.

'I'm here,' she said soulessly. 'On the bench.'

He waited, and she went to him, his fingers plucking at hers, then he was seated. 'How you despise me,' he said as a bee flew past, intent on a clump of dandelions among the blackcurrant bushes.

'You say I despise you,' she prevaricated. 'Then you make a question of it.'

His right hand felt along the edge of the bench as if he missed his cane, and he said caustically, 'You came that first day out of pity. And, of course, you came today because I left you no option.'

Rhianna couldn't answer, couldn't explain her desire to see The Turrets again, to see him, be near him.

'Didn't you?'

'Yes,' she replied lamely. 'If you say so.'

His wide shoulders humped forward like those of a rugby player preparing for defence. His voice was controlled but the sinews on his neck were drawn tight, betraying the swamping emotions he was suppressing.

'Rhianna,' he said. 'Every person to enter these gates during the last months has been filled with pity. Every one of them waiting for the chance to tell the world how much they did for me, boosting their stupid egos on my back, expecting me to grovel my thanks. Have you ever been taken across the road by a school boy, heard the pity in his voice as you mutter, yet again, those immortal words, thank you for helping me?' He stood up restlessly. 'I'm sick of do-gooders, Rhianna. Sick of being in need of them, of being led around. Thank God, Rosie will never condescend –'

'Sit down!' Rhianna snapped, unable to suppress her reaction. 'For a while it will do us no harm to openly despise each other. In the meantime there is nothing wrong with being helped.'

'You refuse to understand!'

'All right, then,' she retorted. 'Go and hide in your little hole. Pretend Rosie Jones is God and your responsibilities are over. Is Rosie attending to your investments too?'

She stopped abruptly. She had gone too far. He towered over her, thoroughly masculine, proud, egotistical, yet vulnerable.

She hated him. She loved him. She longed for his arms. How dare he kiss her like that!

She could vaguely imagine his ancestors; builders of commercial empires, probably whipping blacks because they didn't harvest enough sugar cane.

'The only person suffering pity is yourself,' she said quickly. 'Millions of people go blind. Some are born blind. They *never* see the dandelions and the grass.'

'You are tactless, thoughtless, incapable of loyalty, and completely lacking in any type of understanding,' he accused.

Rhianna was spurred to standing up, glaring at him as if he could see, as if the fire in her eyes could burn through those dark glasses. 'Me?' she almost squealed. 'Not loyal? You were on the terrace – the terrace of this house – just one week after we were engaged. Another woman in your arms. And you have the blasted cheek to tell me I lack loyalty?'

She wanted to hit him, punch him, vent all the misery and fury of those first awful, lonely, heartbroken months.

'She was drunk!' The words tore from him, his lips twisted in a snarl, his head bent towards her. 'Paralytic!'

'You had both arms about her!'

'How was I supposed to hold her? With my little finger?'

'You were engaged to her in no time!'

'I'd have got engaged to the devil to be free of you!'

Rhianna sat again. 'My God! And you had the damned

cheek to accuse me of despising you.'

There was a long, anguished silence while floods of anger made her body go hot and cold.

Rhodri sat too, but well away from her, his hands still unconsciously seeking the ebony cane as if he needed something to hold on to.

She waited a little longer, watching two blue tits hopping fussily along the fence, their heads cocked as they watched a blackbird gorge a worm, then they turned their backs as if in disgust at such gluttony, and Rhianna managed a wan smile. Well, she thought, you pay your money and you take your pick. She had picked Rhodri to fall in love with, and got nothing. Thank God she hadn't married him.

Manhattan was there, promising, beckoning; Laurence Paget loved her and old moneybags was willing to invest in her. Fate was showing clearly where her future lay and she was glad. She need feel no more guilt over Mr Blackmore.

She stood and smoothed the skirt of the dark pink dress around her hips and thighs. She took a quiet, deep breath, but Rhodri heard and turned his head towards her, his face calm. She reflected that she had been, as he said, self-centred and thoughtless. It would have been better to have obeyed him in the beginning, and stayed away.

She said evenly, 'I am going now, Rhodri. You can find your own way back to the house the same as you found your own way out of it.' He stood, his right hand held out, but she ignored it and walked away.

She was on the path against the wall of the house, still trying to regain her composure, when Rosie filled the french doorway and beamed out. 'The salad is all ready.' Her glance took in Rhianna's tormented scarlet face, then shot to where Rhodri should have been on the path.

'Master Rhodri!' she bellowed, and glared at Rhianna as if to say, this is your doing, m'girl. 'Master Rhodri? Come along. Your food is ready.' Then her fat arm was about Rhianna's shoulders. 'In you go,' she said sternly. 'If you still want to cry after you've eaten I won't stop you, but at the moment you are not spoiling my first evening back.'

Mrs Foster came, squeezing between the french door

121

jamb and Rosie, determined Rosie would not usurp her for attention. 'The lettuce will be going all soft,' she grumbled, 'and it did look so nice when I laid it out.'

Rhianna gaped at her, thinking how apt were the words; laid out. The whole of her homecoming had been one long funeral, so why shouldn't even the lettuce be laid out?

She began to giggle. It was uncontrollable. No amount of gripping her mouth or squeezing her lips could stem it, and Mrs Foster stared at her in alarm.

Rosie said purposefully, 'Pull yourself together, Miss Rhianna. D'you want to upset him more?'

Rhianna couldn't answer. The giggles were severe.

'Mister Rhodri!' Mrs Foster called, the pink band supposedly supporting her grey curls even more awry. 'You'd better come and help!'

Rhodri came comparatively quickly, as if instinct was guiding his steps. 'Rhianna!' His voice was crisp. 'You on the verge of hysterics?'

'Yes,' Rosie said. 'She is.' And Rhianna sniggered while the great, refusing-to-be-hidden tears emerged from her shocked, dismayed eyes.

As if radar had directed him Rhodri came to her and his arm took the place of Rosie's. He said quietly, 'Did someone mention tea or coffee earlier on? I suggest we also find the sherry bottle. We'll have it with the meal. All right, Rosie? Mrs Foster?'

'Certainly, sir.' Mrs Foster flew in to a tizzy, her hands pressed together.

Rosie nodded, approving that the master was in charge again.

Rhianna could feel what she sensed was irritation, cold fury, emanating from him, his fingers hard against her shoulder, gripping as if he would like to choke her.

She gulped, 'I'm sorry –' and her mind struggled for something different to say and found it. 'I've left my handbag somewhere.'

His voice was non-committal. 'There's no rush for it. We can eat first,' he said as Rosie and Mrs Foster wandered reluctantly away, their heads swerving as if seeking an errant handbag.

'There are private things in it,' Rhianna murmured, hysterics still dangerously close.

'Letters from this Laurence fellow?' How casual Rhodri sounded.

'I don't think so.' Rhianna tried to remember, just to oblige him, but couldn't.

Rhodri persuaded her forward, towards the french doors, 'Cheer up,' he said. 'He'll probably give you a bigger ring than I did.'

She tried to draw from him, but he gripped hard, smiling, as if enjoying imprisoning her.

She said unevenly, 'I didn't want Laurence's ring.'

'Of course not,' he soothed deviously. 'You didn't want mine either.'

Bewildered she let him propel her forward. Mrs Foster had certainly made the salad look delicious. There was the deep pink and gold of the grated carrots and swede blending with the scarlet of the tomatoes and yellow and white of the eggs. All were presented on a bed of cool green crisp lettuce.

Rhianna instinctively led Rhodri to his chair, then prized his fingers from her. 'You sit there,' she said waveringly, then went to the other side of the table and took her own seat.

Rhodri sat quietly, waiting to hear her settled, then his fingers felt for the glass Rosie presented. 'The bottle, Rosie.'

'Yes, Master Rhodri. Here it is.'

Rhianna watched, aghast. When she ordered the food she hadn't stopped to consider Rhodri's blindness. Now she wondered how he was going to manage.

She watched him place the neck of the bottle against the rim of the glass and watched him pour. Rosie said quietly, 'Half full, Master Rhodri,' and he nodded and carefully put the glass down. He did the same with the second glass.

'Rosie, will you see that Miss Rhianna receives one, please? And, if you like, pour one for yourself and another for Mrs Foster.'

'Thank you,' Rosie beamed fatly, but didn't move, and Rhianna wondered what instruction the woman awaited. It wasn't long in coming.

'Now that Miss Morgan is more herself, Master Rhodri. I think it might be time to wash your hands.'

Rhodri laughed a little derisively, 'No bowl brought to the table, Rosie?'

'Not at all, sir,' Rosie said firmly. 'Mrs Foster tells me you wash your hands regularly before food, and I took it for granted you did so properly.'

'Of course,' he smiled, and Rosie handed him his cane.

'You know the way,' she said, and Rhianna bit her lower lip. She should have thought of that; not led Rhodri straight to his chair.

He paused and made a little half bowing gesture in her direction. 'You will excuse me for a moment. A blind man depends a lot on his fingers while eating. Especially when the food is grated.'

He walked away, deliberation in every lithe step, in the wide shoulders, as if his words had been a satisfactory thrust at her.

Rosie followed him, her fat arms wide spread, as if behind a child learning to walk.

Feeling humiliated Rhianna heard them go to the hall cloakroom, then she rushed upstairs to a bathroom and swilled her face. It made her feel calmer, and she swooped on her handbag when she saw it on the hall table. When she returned to the dining room, Rhodri was already sitting there.

A few moments later he said quietly, 'Rhianna. Close your eyes. Tightly.' He paused while she did so, then he continued, 'Now, without opening them, pick up your knife and fork and eat your salad.'

She found her knife and fork easily because she had seen where they were placed. She even scooped up grated carrot and got it into her mouth, but small shreds missed her lips and slid down her chin. She opened her eyes quickly. 'I'm sorry. I didn't think.'

He smiled, gratified. 'No need to apologise,' he said gently. 'I made my point. So now you won't mind if I use my fingers.'

'Please do,' she agreed quietly, then watched Rhodri

124

Blackmore, over six feet tall, with a square strong face topped with thick, black, curling hair, use a spoon to scoop up food. Sensitively he felt it with his fingers, making sure it wasn't over laden, then putting it in his mouth, and she realised, not for the first time, how expert tuition could help him.

He said, 'Now, maybe, you understand why I prefer to eat alone.'

'No,' she said, 'You manage extremely well.'

They ate in silence and Rhianna tried not to think of Rhodri and Fay, Fay and Will Pepper. What was Rhodri thinking as he ate? No wonder he despised her. She and her step-father had caused such havoc in his life.

Eventually she said tentatively, 'Rhodri?' and he lifted his head, listening. 'What do the specialists say about your eyes?'

'Nothing.'

'How many have you seen?'

'I haven't seen any of them. They saw me.' There was a wry twist to his mouth and she guessed his words were meant as humour.

She pushed the point. 'Did they *all* say they can do nothing?'

He rolled a leaf of lettuce expertly and bit off the end. 'That is precisely it.'

'Someone must be able to do something. Don't they realise the rest of your life is at stake?'

His voice became edgy, their quarrel still under the surface. 'All blind people have the rest of their life at stake, Rhianna.'

'How circumspect of you,' she snapped. 'I was trying to help.'

'And I have warned you to do nothing of the kind.'

In the hall the telephone was ringing, and a moment later Mrs Foster popped her head around the door. 'That was your accountant again.'

Rhodri nodded. 'All right, Mrs Foster. Thank you.'

'Just a minute!' Rhianna called, as the woman prepared to back out. 'What did you tell him?'

'I told him what I always tell him. Mr Blackmore does not wish to be disturbed.' Then Mrs Foster had gone.

Rhianna glared at Rhodri. 'That's a stupid way to run a business!' She wished her hands would stop shaking. It was as if every sensation was catching up with her at once.

'Rhianna.' He pointed a long forefinger in her direction. 'Keep calm and mind your own business. My affairs have nothing at all to do with you.'

'They have everything to do with you, yet you are too damned sorry for yourself to get off your backside and talk to your own accountant!'

'Shut up, Rhianna, or we'll quarrel again.'

'If it gets you moving it won't matter. You've wasted months as it is.'

His head thrust forward, accusing, 'Anything for a scene!' and she had the nonsensical urge to either kiss him or hit him. She felt the giggles coming on again.

He frowned, his hands resting on the table, 'Rhianna! What has life been doing to you? Your nerves are as taut as violin strings. Is stardom worth the cost?'

No, her heart cried, but her mouth retaliated, 'And your nerves? Haven't they been injured? Isn't hiding away a nerve complaint? A phobia?'

'Certainly not. I am keeping out of people's way. I do not seek to impose my troubles on others.'

'Stop kidding yourself,' she said. 'You're afraid you'll have to cope with life again. Make decisions. And you're using your blindness as an excuse.'

There was a long, terrible silence and, in the end, Rhianna sighed loudly. 'I can't go back to America and leave you like this. All right. I agree. We are not suited to each other, and it is as well the engagement ended, but we have known each other a long time and I would not be your friend if I did not care what happens to you.'

He poured himself half a glass of wine, then held the bottle in her direction. 'I suggest you help yourself. I shall surely poor the stuff on the wrong side of the glass.'

'Now you're being facetious.'

'It's probably the only weapon you haven't torn from me.'

126

She took the bottle, but put it on the table. She didn't want more wine. Sitting opposite Rhodri was having an odd affect on her. His fingers feeling for the food made her remember the sensuous way he could touch her skin; his mouth accepting food made her remember his kisses on her body, the light touch of his lips caressing her throat, her breasts.

She tried blinking rapidly, as if that would wash away her thoughts. She tried shaking her head briskly, as if that would vanquish all memories. It wasn't logical to be furious with the man, ready to row, to wound him viciously and, at the same time, want to love and caress.

They each finished their salad in silence and she tried not to look at him. She gazed about the room. It was aesthetic. The windows draped as Rhodri's father had liked them, with deep green velvet. The mantleshelf still held the big, black marble clock flanked by two rearing horses, their riders trying to restrain them. There was an atmosphere of ease and contentment in here, and she had known some wonderful moments on that deep, soft settee at the side of the room.

She said, in the calm way that was characteristic of the aftermath of quarrels with Rhodri, 'This room is still lovely.'

'I'm glad something is equable to you.'

'Maybe because it faces south.'

Mrs Foster brought the bowl of multi-coloured fresh fruit salad topped with meringue, then beamed at Rhianna. 'Didn't know I could do things like that, did you?' and Rhianna nodded, amused and appreciative.

Mrs Foster went on, more happy than Rhianna had as yet seen her. 'I hate cleaning, but let me cook, prepare food. Chips and curry. Cordon bleu. I don't mind.' She grinned at Rhianna's startled face, then set a finger bowl beside Rhodri's hand. 'Never mind what Rosie says,' she explained. 'I know you like to dip your fingers, Mr Rhodri,' then she sailed out.

Mrs Foster had made a point and Rhianna put it to Rhodri. 'Why don't you,' she said between mouthfuls of truly delicious meringue. 'Let Mrs Foster be your cook?'

'She is,' Rhodri said. 'It was one of the first things Rosie ordained.'

Rhianna didn't sigh, but she did wish she had kept her mouth shut. Of course Rosie had ordained it. Rosie was in charge.

Rhodri seemed to sense her displeasure and he turned, looking towards the french doors, and Rhianna's heart missed a beat. Had he looked that way because the light attracted him? Was it possible his loss of sight was partly psychological?

She wondered whether to ask him if the possibility had been considered, but stopped herself. He would be deeply offended at such a suggestion.

She sat back in her chair and stared at him. She would have to watch him more closely. See how he did react to light and dark. See if there was a tiny hope that no one else had noticed.

He said unexpectedly, 'Rhianna. Stop staring. It is ill-mannered and uncomfortable.' He directed his attention towards her and removed the sun glasses as if to prove his eyes were still as tightly closed as ever.

She said quietly, 'How d'you know I'm staring?'

'I can feel it. Sense it. You send out rays.'

She laughed softly. Was it possible the closeness was still there? Quarrel as they might, the bond between them could prove unbreakable.

She said, 'I was thinking how incredibly attractive you are.'

He laughed, his lips turning up in derisive pleasure. 'That is a gambit that other people try. Flatter the fool and he might let me run his life for him.'

Rhianna made a loud 'Huh!' of exasperation, then asked, 'Are you still chairman of the Board of Blackmore Incorporated?'

His laughter fled, and he leaned forward, making sure his cuffs were not in the fruit salad or touching his glass of wine. 'In case you haven't noticed,' he said caustically. 'I am blind, Rhianna. *Blind!*' His voice cracked. 'Now will you try to understand?'

'That shouldn't stop you being anything you want to be.' Her voice softened. 'Sooner or later you'll need to talk about it, get it out of your system. And it might as well be to me.'

He straightened himself and lifted his head proudly, his lips twisted. 'Shall we retire to the settee? And I will make light conversation.'

'I want to know, Rhodri. I want your side of the full story.'

She was surprised at the firmness in her voice. Somewhere at the back of her mind a lost voice was still warning her that she should not be here at all; the man despised her, didn't want her, and he was married.

Mrs Foster returned, bright faced and cheerful. 'Coffee?'

'Yes please,' Rhianna smiled back. The sun had moved from the direction of the french doors now and the loss of its golden glow made the room seem drab, the paintwork unclean, the oil paintings on the walls dusty. 'And do you think we could have a fire in here?'

'No!' Rhodri snapped, and Rhianna turned to him so quickly she cricked her neck.

'Why not?'

'I'm sorry.' Dull colour flooded his face. 'You are right. I am a fool. Though – er – wouldn't it be more simple to turn on the central heating?'

'No,' said Mrs Foster, with a tightening of her lips. 'It wouldn't.'

'No?' Rhodri asked.

Rhianna said, with Mrs Foster, 'It doesn't work,' then she laughed, and Mrs Foster's face filled with shared mischief.

'How did you know?' she asked.

'Elementary, my dear Watson,' Rhianna quipped back. 'Nothing works here except you.'

'Quite right too,' Mrs Foster agreed, and Rhodri asked, 'Why doesn't it work?'

'No oil,' Mrs Foster said. 'You have just survived another winter and not had a refill.'

Rhodri tugged the lobe of his ear with embarrassment. 'Yes, of course, I should have realised.'

'Logs in the grate, then,' Mrs Foster said.

'Will it be an awful lot of trouble?' Rhianna asked.

'Only to the spiders,' said Mrs Foster comfortably. 'They'll have to shift themselves. Johnnie is in the kitchen listening to Rosie. He can come and do it.'

Rhodri and Rhianna remained at the table to drink the coffee; it was smooth, creamy, and Rhianna let it roll around her tongue, sip by sip.

Rhodri said quietly, 'You feel better Rhianna,' and there was the sigh in her name again.

She moved her head, acquiescing, forgetting for a moment he couldn't see, but it was as if he sensed that too, because he nodded and smiled in return.

Johnnie lit the fire so it crackled with logs that had been drying a long time in the stables. He stacked more beside the grate, looking more bull-like with his striped shirt sleeves rolled above his biceps, his blunt face with its pug nose alert, as if hoping to hear any conversation Rhianna and Rhodri might have. Then he winked at Rhianna. It was an unspoken message that said, 'You're doing fine, old girl.'

Rhianna blushed and averted her gaze. She hadn't thought she was doing fine, but now, as Johnnie went, she stopped to consider. Rhodri did look better, far less drawn, his lips no longer pulled down at the corners. He had laughed and he had interviewed strangers.

'What are you thinking?' he asked, as Johnnie left.

'You.'

'Something wrong with me again?'

'No. About how well you know me.'

'Ah,' he said, comprehendingly. 'That might help you understand why I asked you, yet once more, to stay away from here.'

'You did ask me to come today.'

'That was because of an unusual circumstance. Rosie is here now. I shan't have to encroach on Mary's kindness if another such occasion arises.'

'If you know me as well as you think you do, you already know the answer to that. Until I go back to New York I shall continue telling myself to keep away – while I continue to enter your doorway.'

130

'We'll fight incessantly.'

'It will prevent us getting bored.'

In the hall the telephone became insistent again and Rhianna listened. Was this the accountant trying once more? If so why was he so determined? Ted Knox was not a worrier; there must be something in the air.

She waited until she heard Mrs Foster's quick steps pass the door, then Rhianna hurried out to her. 'Mrs Foster. Who was that on the phone?'

'Mr Knox again.'

'What did you tell him?'

'Same as I always do. That Mr Rhodri —'

'Did he say what he wanted?'

Mrs Foster shrugged disparagingly. 'He wouldn't, would he? Not to me.'

'Is his number easily available?'

'It's on the pad beside the phone.' Mrs Foster waved a hand towards the other side of the hall. 'He keeps asking us to phone back.'

Rhianna went to look, hearing Rhodri call, 'Rhianna?', his voice a threat. She ignored him and dialled Ted Knox. The man answered instantly.

'Ted? Rhianna Morgan here. I'm at The Turrets.'

'Good God! I didn't know you were back in town!'

'I'm visiting Rhodri. He has trouble getting to the phone. Can I give him a message?'

'Rhianna! Bless your cotton socks. Tell him the Board is preparing to sell out three of the Manchester shops. I know they're not doing too well just now, but who the hell is? They ought to hang on.'

'Rhianna!' Rhodri was in the hall. Stiff, emanating thick fury. 'I told you to mind your own damned business!'

His voice was so strong and vibrant that Ted Knox heard it over the wires and called back, 'Rhodri! That you?'

Rhianna said calmly, 'Hold on, Ted. He'll be with you in a moment.' Then, with her hand covering the mouthpiece she said to Rhodri through tight lips. 'Come and listen to one of the few loyal friends you seem to have left.'

131

She turned back to the receiver. 'Hold on, Ted. The great man is on his way right now.'

Rhodri's tread was purposeful, his whole attitude promising her with things dire when this episode was finished, and when she put the phone in his hands he took it ungraciously. 'Ted!' he barked. 'I have made it clear –' but he got no further. Ted's voice was stronger, more urgent than Rhodri's. It was evident the man was not just worried, he was prepared to go beserk with concern.

Rhianna heard him shout, 'What the hell is wrong with you, Rhodri? Is your head affected as well as your eyes? I've been over to your place twice and couldn't get in.'

Rhodri listened, his face white, his mouth pulled into a thin straight line, his jaw jutting more and more.

Rhianna retreated, and the men went on talking, planning. 'What time is the meeting?' Rhodri asked. 'In Cardiff. Yes, yes, kind of you.'

Rhianna came back to his side. She could hear Ted's voice clearly, almost as if he was in the hall. 'I'd better come and get you or you'll back out –'

'Never!' Rhianna called. 'A Blackmore never backs out. He keeps his word.'

Rhodri turned towards her, the frustration and exasperation coming from him like steam. 'Blast everything!' he stormed. 'If only I could *see*!'

Rhianna smiled indulgently and the smile shaped her words. 'I'll drive you to the meeting. Where is it? Cardiff? What time?'

'Tomorrow. Two o'clock,' Rhodri muttered, then he turned back to the phone. 'Yes. All right. Yes. I've said so. I'll be there. Miss Morgan has just kindly offered to –' he hesitated as if on the verge of saying 'hound me there', but he said, 'accompany me.'

Rhianna went back to the room where they had eaten. She felt emotionally exhausted and hoped she had done the right thing.

The fire was promising great warmth, and she drew the settee so it slid on castors towards the blaze, then she waited.

When he came she ignored the cloud of animosity that

poured from him. She said sweely, 'Over here, dear. I've drawn the settee around. You promised to tell me how your blindness happened,' and her hands were ready to lead him.

But the idea was not a success. He sat at the very end of the settee and, when she tried to come closer, he found reason to stand up, to stretch; his foot had gone to sleep and needed exercise.

'Rhodri. Please. Let's talk.'

'Rhianna. Please. I do not wish to discuss the fire.'

'About us then?'

'No!'

'You loved me –'

'Any love I had for you died. Died.'

She gripped her hands between her knees, seeing the dent made in her skirt. 'When you kissed me today –' She moved back to her own corner and his foot became miraculously better. He sat, the settee's full width away from her.

She rebuked, 'You wanted me.'

'I wanted a woman. I get hungry.'

'You had Fay often?' The peeved question almost suffocated her.

His foot went to sleep again and he had to get up and wiggle it about with an agonised grimace on his face.

'We're friends though, aren't we?' Rhianna asked, and hoped there was no hint of tremor in her voice.

'We're friends.' He hesitated, then sat and grudgingly let his hand reach for hers. 'We should have stayed that way seven years ago. Some people do make better friends than lovers.'

'Yes,' Rhianna agreed dolefully. 'They do. Don't they?'

She watched the logs die down, settling into embers and knew she ought to get up and throw an extra log on, but not now, not while Rhodri held her hand.

She whispered, 'Did you love Fay more than you loved me?'

'Why?' he demanded. 'Why can't you leave the past alone? Forget it,' and he moved restlessly, stretching a leg out then drawing it in again. 'I told you. I brought Fay in from

133

the terrace that night. Someone needed to get her home. To bed. To sleep it off. She was slobbering over me. Then I realised no one was dancing.' He licked his lower lip as if in vexation. 'The party had come to an end. Carl held out the ring and said you'd dropped it –'

The embers collapsed to glowing ash, but Rhianna didn't move, and he went on. 'She took it. She was laughing, crying. She announced we were engaged –'

He broke off, as if his breath had become chokingly tight, and put his hand through his mass of thick, black hair. 'My God,' he groaned softly. 'When you said I should talk it all out you didn't know what you could be in for.'

He turned his head then, as if trying to see her, and his arm went across her shoulders. 'Rhianna.' A different tone entered his voice. 'Never once did you consider me as a human being, with deep feelings. I said, yes Carl, we are engaged.'

Rhianna moved from him, not aware of thinking or feeling anything. She went to the logs and lifted one, deliberately and gently she laid it on the almost dead glow in the grate, then she remained crouching, watching it. She said quietly, 'She wore my ring.'

'No.' He sat with his hands loose on his thighs. 'I told her she could have another. A better. When she kicked the drink habit.' He leaned forward, putting his elbows on his knees. 'She handed the ring to me. Like a naughty child trying to be good. Then she went home. To bed, they say.'

In the garden a magpie gave a high pitched croak before flying away, and the room was dark, except for the faint spread of orange and scarlet growing beneath the new log.

There were no tears from Rhianna, more an odd feeling of relief. Now she did know where she was.

She let him kiss her goodnight; no passion, no emotion, just a kiss, and she decided that, to give her just one feeling of achievement, she was going to see Rhodri through his trip to Cardiff, then she would leave for always.

Chapter Nine

The following morning Mary decided the trip to Cardiff warranted a special business-like outfit, so Rhianna rushed into the village, thanked providence she was what manufacturers regard as normal size, and bought herself a suit. Its blueness accentuated the yellow gold of her hair, and the drawn out collar of the crisp white blouse gave her a glow of freshness that went well with the sunshine that continued to bless South Wales.

She dressed carefully, then waited for Johnnie to bring the Daimler for her. Today she felt less bewildered. She thought she knew exactly who she was. Rhianna Morgan – the girl who was pleased to see Rhodri Blackmore getting back on his feet, metaphorically speaking. All dreams of love had gone. Her future belonged to Laurence Paget.

Johnnie came for her right on time and drove her to The Turrets, then she waited like an ordinary visitor, in the newly cleaned library for Rhodri to appear.

He wore an immaculate, silver grey suit, and a cream shirt with a blue and grey striped tie. Rosie had replaced his cane with a hooked walking stick so he could, Rosie said, slip it over his arm when he didn't feel in need of it.

'Rather elegant, what what!' he teased the fat woman, and he and Rosie laughed together.

Once in the car again Rhianna gazed at him sitting beside her. Her heart ached with her knowledge of the future, yet was filled with an admiration for him. This was Rhodri going to work. Heaven help the fools attempting to sell off part of the Blackmore kingdom.

He drew a sheaf of papers from his brief-case as the Daimler sped smoothly on. 'Rhianna. Will you read these aloud for me, please? I need facts and figures.' He switched

135

on a pocket sized tape recorder. 'There's a letter from the Lemington Trust. Let me hear that first.'

She found the letter still in its long envelope. 'Did anyone read it to you at the time?'

'No.' He smiled then. 'I could feel the insignia on the letter head. It's surprising how deeply indented some of them are. It's the actual typing I can't make out.'

'You've been practising,' she laughed encouragingly.

'While others thought I was brooding,' he replied dryly.

She twitched her head, acknowledging the rebuke, then read the letter aloud. He frowned and she read another, then another. When she finished he drew his hand tightly across the lower half of his face, deep in thought. 'Blasted idiots!' he said succinctly, and Rhianna made no comment.

'It seems to me,' Rhodri went on, 'The Board now consider Rhodri Blackmore to be a non-executive chairman. All decisions having been taken over by them.' He clenched his hands on the closed brief-case, and still Rhianna said nothing.

As they entered Cardiff he drew a deep breath, his hands pulling his jacket less casually about him, tapping the knot in the blue and grey tie, checking the handkerchief Rosie had tucked into his breast pocket, then he hooked the walking stick over his arm.

'In winter,' he said. 'I could replace this with a hooked umbrella.'

'Of course.' It was evident to her that he was no longer thinking of yesterday. He was very much in the present and the future. He was planning next winter.

The Daimler stopped outside the large, grey stone building with the arched doorway and curving steps, and Rhodri made a visible effort to lift his chin and prepare for what could be a battle.

Rhianna let him leave the car without her, Johnnie holding open the door, then she too, slid out, while Rhodri waited on the pavement.

As naturally as if he could see, she took Rhodri's arm, and together they went up the steps and into the building. They entered the lift, and Rhodri's shoulders were as straight and firm as they had ever been. Rhianna couldn't quell the little fluttering of excitement; it was as if today was make or break for Rhodri, and she would be here to witness it.

The corridor was lengthy and, at the end of it, were two highly polished doors like sentinals of the future. She let Rhodri set the pace. He was like a coiled spring, waiting to be released and, when her arm tightened about his, he pressed it to him and whispered, 'Stop fretting. I'm all right.'

Rhianna pushed open the double doors and Rhodri stepped into the room. A group of well heeled men stood chatting before a wall sized window. They turned, and their gasps were audible.

A short fat man exclaimed, 'Rhodri! By all that's holy!' and he came, striding on little legs, to take Rhodri's hand and stare up at the sun glasses. 'By God, I'm proud of you. We didn't think to see this happen –' He turned to his colleagues and slowly astonishment and the initial pleasure, drained from their faces. Plainly they were wondering, 'What the hell is Blackmore up to? Why is he here?'

The fat man looked at Rhianna. 'How d'you do?' She let him take her hand for a moment. 'You are?'

'My secretary and confidante,' Rhodri said swiftly. 'All right, Rhianna, take me to my chair at the head of the table, then you can go for a stroll around the shops.' He added in an undertone, 'Buy yourself something particular and chalk it up to me.' His hand found hers in the crook of his arm and his fingers squeezed, quietly saying thank you,

Rhianna was even more aware of his strengthening confidence. Impending combat was soaring through him. He would enjoy whatever lay ahead.

She gave his hand a perfunctory reply as she led him to the only chair with its back to the window. Through the huge pane she could see Cardiff teeming below, but here in the room the men were sober, almost ashen faced, gradually sinking into the high backed seats around the leather topped table.

The fat man found a cigar in the inside pocket of his green suit jacket and stuck it, unlit, between his imperfect teeth.

137

'You don't have to send the girl away, Rhodri. You'll need her to make notes.'

'I have a tape recorder,' Rhodri said, with a mocking little smile, 'and my memory is almost perfect. I have had months in which to train it.' He looked splendid, calm, truly a man born to inherit authority.

Rhianna smiled at everyone and stalked from the room. There was nothing more she could do now. She must let them get on with it.

But such ideas were more easily thought than done. She didn't want to go around the shops, and she certainly didn't want to buy herself anything on Rhodri's account.

For a while she sat outside the Board Room. It was like sitting in the gallery of a stately home just before the public poured in. She tried to eavesdrop at the double doors. She could hear the men's voices, but the wood was thick and any sound was muted.

In the end she left the building. She stopped where Johnnie stood on the corner. 'Hi!' she said, which, she knew, was not the accepted way to speak to the chauffeur, but Johnnie was not merely a chauffeur; he was, like Rosie and Mrs Foster, a confederate in the effort to get Rhodri Blackmore to assume his rightful place in the world.

'Hello, Miss Morgan,' Johnnie said. 'Is he in?'

'He's in.'

Johnnie sucked his teeth, his hands clasped behind him. 'Did you hear on television that Woolworths is selling off some of its stores?'

'No.' She laughed. 'Don't tell me you're a business tycoon.'

His uniform cap was pushed to the back of his head, emphasising his protruding ears. 'I read the *Financial Times*, if I get the chance, but my money goes into the little blue book with the post office.'

'Very wise too.' Rhianna smiled. 'Where's the car?'

'Up near the castle. I can soon collect it when the meeting's over. Will he want to go somewhere to eat before we go back home?'

It was something she hadn't considered. Her aim had

been concentrated on getting Rhodri to the Board meeting and, that done, she had been tense, awaiting the result.

'That's a darn good idea,' she enthused. 'Where d'you suggest?'

Johnnie shrugged. 'Any number of good restaurants about, but I don't think they serve a full meal until tonight.'

'It might be tonight before Mr Rhodri appears,' Rhianna said thoughtfully. 'On the other hand he might appear at any moment.'

She looked back at the grey arched doorway. Her desire was to return there as fast as possible, get up to that Board Room, go in, find out what was happening, but she knew that was out of the question.

She caught sight of a deep blue trouser suit in the window of the shop behind Johnnie and peered closer to look at it. Johnnie moved to one side, grinning cockily. 'Be my guest. Get right up to the glass there. I don't mind.'

She laughed with him. He did seem a nice person, and together they window shopped, their glances jerking from time to time to that great grey doorway with its three wide stone steps.

The meeting began just after half-past-two and it was gone four when Rhianna recognised one of the directors coming from the building.

'This is it, Johnnie. They're on their way out.' She ran, and entered the building, up in the lift and to the corridor that had been so empty. Now a small group of men stood there, still talking, the thick aroma of tobacco smoke oozing from the open doors of the room beyond them and, unless one queried the sun glasses, no one would know Rhodri was blind. There was no sign of the hooked stick. He was gesticulating freely, talking, trying to convince, and the little fat man took his arm, drawing him along.

Rhianna walked up fast. 'Was the meeting a success, gentlemen?' she smiled, and her heart was thudding with a weird type of trepidation. This meeting had nothing to do with her; it was Blackmore business and she was not a

Blackmore, but Rhodri had introduced her as his secretary and confidante so, she decided, she could enquire about how things went.

'Well, now,' chuckled the fat man through a lit cigar. 'That depends on the way you look at it, and whose side you are on. For us, seeing your Rhodri here was a success in itself, and I hope he won't leave us without his company for so long again . . .'

'Rhianna,' Rhodri said. 'This is Mr George Gubb. He joined the company recently and has been acting as my stand-in.' Rhianna held out her right hand, hearing the inflection in Rhodri's voice that this fussy little man was nothing more than his 'stand-in'.

As the soft plump hand took hers for the second time that afternoon, a younger man came sauntering from the open doors of the Board Room, a file of papers under his arm, his brown eyes bright as they centred on the group. Then he saw Rhianna, and unadulterated admiration filled his fine chiselled, continental looking face.

'Carl!' she gasped. 'How nice to see you,' and she heard Rhodri's great intake of breath.

Rhodri said, 'He almost got his own way, but for the first time in a long time, he failed.'

'Ah,' smiled Carl Jurgan. 'I would have tended my new investments with care. You would have been proud of them, Rhodri.'

He turned again to Rhianna, and his voice became most unbusiness-like, low, husky, tantalising and brazenly flattering. 'How long is it? One hundred years, heh?'

'Seven,' Rhianna laughed, and knew she was blushing.

'Ah, Miss Morgan,' said George Gubb. 'You know Carl Jurgan, I see.' He, too, laughed, deeply, so his big belly quivered. 'I don't suppose there is a beautiful woman in the world who doesn't, heh Rhodri?'

Rhodri gave a smile that held no humour. 'He was late for the meeting, Rhianna. Said his car had broken down.'

Carl Jurgan bent over Rhianna's hand, his lips barely touching her white skin, his dark eyes turned up to watch the expression on her face.

Rhodri said sharply, 'Rhianna. Will you bring the brief-case, please? I left it on the table.'

Carl let her hand go reluctantly. 'Not my car,' he corrected smoothly. 'The firm's car. My car is like a woman. Dependable when correctly treated.'

Rhianna hurried for the brief-case and found the walking stick resting on it. With both she went back to Rhodri and tried not to look at Carl, but there was something about his charming audacity that was most attractive. She reflected that he ought to have taken to show business; he had the looks, the personality, and the need to show off.

As they all began to stroll towards the lift Carl Jurgan came to Rhianna's side. He said, pleasantly, 'And what brought you back to the fascinating Rhodri? Is it the *amour*?'

'I came home from America for my step-father's funeral,' Rhianna said, and Carl's face drooped in exaggerated sympathy. 'I am sorry. So sorry. It is terrible to lose one you love; and you, Rhianna, know how to love.'

He offered his arm, but smilingly Rhianna refused it, though she had to admit to herself, that here was a man many women would give more than an arm to be seen with.

'We must all take refreshment together,' Carl addressed everyone. 'I have gained nothing from today –' he gazed meaningly at Rhianna, and added, 'yet, but we can, at least, enjoy each others' company for the next hour or so. The bill, it can be for me.'

'How magnanimous,' the fat man beamed, but Rhianna had the feeling he was not being sincere.

Carl took her elbow, guiding her from Rhodri to the lift. It gave her the feeling she was being treated like a piece of Dresden china. It was a nice feeling. She could not imagine this man ever saying the nasty things that Rhodri threw at her, or her ever flinging them back.

She saw Johnnie waiting at the corner and, leaving Carl's side, she went to Rhodri who strolled with the fat man, the walking stick in full use as an antenna.

'Rhodri,' she said quietly. 'What instruction shall I give Johnnie?'

Rhodri touched the braille watch on his wrist. 'An hour

and a half?' He turned his head towards the little fat man beside him. 'Will that be all right?'

'Yes, yes, of course.' The words came jovially through the end of the cigar. 'Your man you're talking about? Yes. Tell him there's a car park behind the hotel.'

Rhianna hurried to Johnnie and gave him the message. Johnnie grinned, 'What happened? Do I transfer my stocks to Blackmore and Co, or leave them with ICI and FWW?'

Rhianna laughed aloud. She felt foolishly happy. The sun was shining, falling maybe, but still shining, and Rhodri had not only survived the meeting, but looked well, revitalised on it.

'Put them with Blackmores. I think we're on to a winner.'

He winked and straightened his cap, then he was striding away, the blue-grey uniform suiting his cocky swagger.

She hurried back to the men and tried to walk beside Rhodri but the pavement wasn't wide enough. Mr George Gubb was not only fat but he liked room. As he talked he swung his arms, gesticulating a lot, and his feet continually pointed to ten to two.

Rhianna found herself walking alone behind, until Carl Jurgan joined her. 'Hello,' he teased, as if they were just meeting after a long parting. 'You are feeling lonesome, heh?'

'No,' she said, but didn't realise how her unusually almond shaped eyes widened with pleasure.

In the restaurant George Gubb led Rhodri to a table and remained immersed in talk. Carl held a chair for Rhianna, and it was Carl who handed her the menu. It was Carl who suggested the wine she might, and did, prefer, and it was Carl who followed her to the foyer and bade her adieu when she and Rhodri left.

'We must meet again, Rhianna. Before you return to the States. And again after,' he said throatily. 'Many times a year I fly to America.' Then he was brushing her knuckles with his lips, shaking hands with Rhodri, and saluting courteously as Johnnie drove Rhianna and Rhodri into the stream of traffic.

They were on the motorway before Rhodri said casually, 'I assume Carl is still remarkably attractive.'

142

'He always was,' she returned enthusiastically, and Rhodri jerked his shoulders in disdain.

He said scathingly, 'I would not trust the man any further than I could throw him. Now that I am blind I realise he has a voice like crushed velvet.'

'He has been your friend for years, in spite of being a business rival,' Rhianna reminded. Then she remembered it was Carl who picked up the deep blue sapphire ring; Carl who had handed it to – whom? Rhodri or Fay?

Rhodri said a trifle stiffly. 'You appeared to be enjoying his attentions.'

'Why not?' she countered. 'I'm single, and he made me feel good.'

'Huh,' said Rhodri, and lapsed into silence.

Rhianna gazed at him. He was sulking. She was sure of it. She wanted to laugh, tease him, make his mouth turn up at the corners again, but something warned her to say little. Rhodri had gone to a business meeting. He had survived it and triumphed in his intentions. Now must come any reaction.

They were half way to Swansea before she said tentatively, 'How did the meeting go?'

Rhodri took his time before replying, then said grudgingly, 'They listened to me.'

'And you won your argument.'

'Naturally. I would not have gone if I had not been certain of the outcome.'

'So they are not going ahead to sell the Manchester shops?'

He turned quickly, his whole body coming to affront her. 'They told me that Woolworths are selling off some of their stores!'

Rhianna nodded, then remembered he couldn't see, 'Yes,' she said. 'Johnnie told me.'

'Johnnie?' He was askance. 'You mean Johnnie? Him?' He nodded in Johnnie's direction. 'He knew Woolworths were selling out?'

She saw Johnnie's shoulders move as he overheard. 'On television!' he called.

143

'Good God!' Rhodri gave a forceful and shocked expletive, then sat back. 'I *have* been letting life slip by. I deserve to lose *every* damn thing the family worked for.'

Rhianna didn't comment. She felt it was enough for Rhodri to sit and work things out for himself. The process had truly begun. The rest was up to him.

She gazed through her side window and, now that she felt her job at The Turrets had been done, an aching sadness was taking over. Thoughts of New York, of fame and fortune, lacked their former strong attraction. In retrospect the rat race seemed as nerve tautening for her as Rhodri had suggested yesterday. While here, in Whesley, there was the Welsh *hwyl* – and Rhodri's blindness.

No matter how well he coped, it could not be the same as if he could see. A businessman needed to look upon people's faces, to gauge their foxiness, see their gestures. Rosie could never do that for him.

Chapter Ten

Rhianna didn't rush back to America next day; nor the next. If anyone had asked her why she could not have told them. She only knew she lacked the inclination to pack her suitcase. She leaned on the high thick window sill of her bedroom and looked out over the tiled roof tops to the sea, wondering why she had ever dreamed of a greater world. Had it been a way of saying, I don't care if Will Pepper is in my father's chair, if he does take all my mother's time and love. I am going to be famous.

Now she shook her head derisively; how little she had known of the world beyond Whesley. Her bank book, containing every penny her mother had left her through endowment policies, had seemed a fortune.

She thought of Laurence, how he had 'popped in' to the little theatre that evening because it had been pelting with rain and he had been at a loose end, bored. She giggled a little at the memory of her playing Abigail in Rae Shirley's version of Lady Godiva; *Not Even A Wimple*, unaware the influential American producer was watching as she enjoyed letting rip with her, 'Woe is me, oh woe is me!' Tall, thin, bespectacled, so apparently safe she had turned to him like a puppy to a warm neck.

She moved her position against the window sill, seeing a pigeon settle on the guttering of the cottage across the narrow climbing road, and she wondered whether to telephone Laurence, tell him yes, she wanted to marry him. He produced successes. He had no time for anything else – his plays, his companions, all had to be on the road to fulfilment. And she needed success; her self-esteem was low.

She and Laurence got on well together and, by being

together, they kept less welcome relationships at bay. Laurence, Rhianna told herself, was all right.

The pigeon flew off cooing loudly and Rhianna lowered her head, shame sweeping through her. What a selfish, unfeeling creature she had been. All her love, all her romantic dreams had been wrapped in Rhodri, and when they were sacrificed nothing else seemed worth keeping, except that promise to become famous. Be a star.

She left the window as if the light was showing up too much of her soul, and she lay on the bed, a fore-arm across her eyes. She told herself she should not be feeling depressed like this. Her choice had been made for her. Stardom.

When she got off the bed she had the feeling it might be Laurence who would telephone her, not her telephone him. He was bound to be getting concerned about not hearing from her, not knowing when she would be back.

When he did call her he asked simply, 'You coming home tomorrow, baby?'

'Afraid not.'

'You got things to do?'

'Yes,' she said, and was glad she had never told him Will Pepper was not her father.

'Yea,' he said slowly. 'I guess it is awkward. You got solicitors to see. A will to get sorted out.' And she didn't put him right.

'Another few days, then,' he said. 'But we'll be in a mess if we need you and you're the other side of the ocean.'

If they need her. Rhianna tried not to think of the if. There was no *if* about Rhodri. He *did* need her – even though he might not know it.

And so ten days later she was still in Whesley, though Laurence phoned again, his voice barely hiding his growing lack of patience. 'We've no one in your place, chick. If Lynsey falls sick we're finished!'

'I'll be back.' Rhianna called. 'I know I will.'

She visited Rhodri regularly, usually on the pretext of seeing how Johnnie and his hefty farming friends were working on the garden. Carl Jurgan also found a reason to visit Rhodri, and Rhianna found a reason for refusing his invitation out. The sun continued to shine, and Rhianna gave in to a happiness she had not known in years.

One afternoon at The Turrets she hissed, 'Sssh,' and Rhodri breathed back, 'Why? What is it?'

They stood on the narrow path together, transfixed, and Rhianna whispered, 'A jay. On the lawn. It's lovely. Glorious deep blue flashes on its wings. Oh Rhodri! If only you could see it!'

'Through you I can.' His hand tightened on her arm. 'I know it's only a crow, but you make it sound like a thing of paradise.'

'Paradise?' Rhianna was surprised. 'What a lovely word.' She turned to Rhodri as if to gaze up into his eyes, remembering the sky blue they used to be. 'Today, I too feel as if I'm in paradise.' She lifted her finger tips to his cheek, infinitely tender, and as she touched his skin a gentle wave of emotion rolled through her. 'Rhodri,' she said softly. 'I would like you to kiss me. Now. Here.'

His head bent, directed by her guiding hands, and he kissed her like a man savouring wine after years of abstinence, not demanding, but tasting and wanting more.

'Rhianna,' and there was that deep sigh in her name that she loved to hear, a breath of wonder. 'Don't you mind being held, kissed, by a blind man?'

She shook her head and he felt her body quiver. 'You say no.'

'And you have the nerve to say you are blind. You can see as much as anyone, but in a different manner.'

His hands travelled up from her waist, to her arm pits. He said cautiously, 'You sure you don't mind?'

'Did I ever?'

'The crippled can be regarded as obscene.'

'But you wanted to kiss me.'

'I wanted to.'

'Isn't that odd?' she laughed, 'I've been wanting to kiss you too. Like this.'

The black bird called 'pop-pop' from the middle of the flowering cherry tree, and Rhodri murmured against her mouth, 'Sounds as if I have a jealous rival,' then their lips were tantalising, meeting, clinging, and her body was curved tightly to him.

Rhianna had known she wanted him, but never dreamed the want was as terrible as this. She wanted to drink of him, fill to overflowing, and her lips were parted, hungry, sensual.

The tip of his pointed tongue caressed her mouth and she was replying, swept into acceptance by the unexpected fierceness of her need.

'Darling!' her mind called. 'My love. My love.'

Rhodri drew back, holding her away. All softness gone from his features. 'Rhianna! Witch! Get to hell out of here. Before we both do something we'll always regret.'

'Like what?' she teased, still trying to hold him.

'Is your ego so inflated you can't understand? A prostitute would do.'

Her arms fell from his shoulders, her fingers no longer touching the skin of his neck.

'You're a tease!' he accused. 'Asking for trouble. Now get back to America. Fast! Practise your technique on some other fool.'

She gazed up at him. He meant it. The conviction was in his voice.

She went to the bench and sat, hoping her footsteps sounded calm, unperturbed, then she gazed back at him. He was standing resolute, wearing a gleaming white shirt tucked into a pair of light weight trousers. She peered into the cherry blossom to see if the black bird was still there. Anything in an attempt to regain her equilibrium. Blue tits acrobated about the container of nuts she had hung out for them, and she managed to almost ease a smile into her mind.

Rhodri turned his back on her, making for the house, using the toe of each foot to find his way, the hooked stick still somewhere in the room.

He was entering the french doors when she heard the car roar into the drive at the front of the house, and she recognised the sound of the engine. Carl Jurgan had found another reason to visit South Wales.

Deliberately she ran and laughed as if her excitement was intense. The car door slammed with echoing vibrations, and she shouted. 'Carl! I'm here. In the garden around the back!'

To her disappointment Rhodri didn't pause. He went on, into the house, and closed the glass doors behind him, then his outline was absorbed by the inner gloom. Rhianna went back to the bench and tried to pretend she was glad to see Carl Jurgan.

There was no doubt the man was a charmer. He strode towards her with his dark eyes dancing, his lips quirking with merriment, and both hands held out in greeting.

He bent over her hand as if she were the first lady in the land. 'Rhianna!' he exclaimed, so huskily it gave the impression they already had deep secrets together. 'I have tried for so long to get you alone, but always that Rhodri Blackmore is before me.'

He was laughing and she laughed with him. If Carl Jurgan wanted to pretend that today was a wonderful day, let him.

The kisses with Rhodri had unsettled her, her senses were stirred with hunger. His thrusting her away had been an agony she had not expected, though, she tried telling herself, only her pride had been hurt; she had anticipated too much.

Carl Jurgan was still laughing, bright eyed, settling himself beside her on the bench, reaching for her fingers which had become entwined in her lap, but as his hand settled warmly about hers she extricated herself and stood up. His touch was something she couldn't tolerate. Not then.

She smiled, 'You have come just in time for a cup of tea. Shall we go indoors?'

He frowned, thinking hard, and she knew he sensed a quarrel or, at least a disturbance, but he just gave a huge continental shrug. 'You run from me all the time, Rhianna. Why is this so?'

'You imagine things,' she returned, using all her acting ability to look pleasant, but he shook his head.

'I am too old a hand to imagine it when a beautiful young lady gives me the shove-off.'

She really laughed at that. Carl looked so much a man of the world, doubtlessly wealthy, yet his phraseology must be unique.

He gazed up at her, squinting against the sun's rays, his sun glasses swinging from his fingers. 'Is it that you are –' he hesitated, obviously seeking the right word, then he shrugged again, giving up, and said bluntly, 'still in love with the man?'

Rhianna turned from him in embarrassment, colour making her cheeks as pink as the sunset would be that evening.

'Ah ha!' Carl laughed, his hand reaching out and catching hers. 'So that is the truth. The lady suffers the unrequited love.' He pouted and slowly shook his head as if in the depths of deep sorrow. 'It is sad. So very sad. I hold passion in my heart for you, and you hold passion in your heart for the man who has been my friend for many years.'

Rhianna pulled from him and walked quickly up the path. 'I suggested tea, but maybe you would prefer coffee. When you are ready please join us.'

She knew she was doing what she had promised herself she would never do again. She was pressing her company on Rhodri, straight after he had repulsed her.

Carl called softly, 'Does it not matter to you that he is blind?'

'Not at all!' She turned as if to accuse him. How dare he suggest such a thing. 'I knew him for years before he lost his sight.'

Carl wagged a hooked forefinger at her, calling her back to him, and she surprised herself by obeying. 'Sit here one little moment.' He patted the bench beside him. 'If I cannot be your lover, then I must be your friend, yes?'

He was so serious, so intent, that she did as he said and sat facing him.

'Now you must listen to me, *chère amie*. Have you not thought what happens to a man when his life breaks into

150

splinters? Have you not thought he is not the same man any more?'

She opened her mouth to retort, but he shushed her. 'If you please. This man, who takes responsibilities so hard, goes to the theatre, an assignation perhaps, leaving his ailing father with only the farm manager and a silly woman to care for him. He feels bad at leaving them at all when the nurse is away. Everyone is away . . .'

Rhianna drew herself up indignantly. She knew all this.

Carl smiled as if guessing her thoughts. 'Quite so. He had most likely told you so much but not of what has happened in here. So –?' and his forefinger tapped his chest where his heart was hidden. 'I have asked only that you listen, not that we judge. That is not so.'

Rhianna subsided. Carl was too sincere for her to ignore.

'So –' Carl went on, his hands moving in wide gestures of explanation. 'On his return he runs up those stairs because he is frightened. What had he left these people he loved to? Isn't that what he is calling to himself? Isn't he in the panic? Isn't his stomach, as you say, fighting with this – er – this terrible thing, the guilt?' Carl watched Rhianna's face, and she bowed her head. She had accepted the fire story as she had heard it. It had sounded like another terrible accident. There had been nothing of Rhodri's thoughts.

Slowly Rhianna nodded, and Carl took it as a sign she was beginning to understand. 'He opens that bedroom door, chère amie. What does he see? Heh? Can you tell me?'

There was a lengthy silence and Rhianna felt the slight chill of evening whisp across her shoulders. The blue tits swung about the peanuts and a chaffinch came. She was aware of life going on all around her, but here, on this bench, it had temporarily stopped.

'Well?' Carl whispered, his hand on her arm, his head bent in an effort to see her expression. 'You tell me. Lift your lovely face and look at me, and tell me, Rhianna. What did the man your heart cries out for see when he burst open that door?'

'Flames.' The tragedy was no longer something that happened to someone else; it was happening to her.

151

'Flames?' Carl echoed. 'Is that all? And in those terrible, monstrous flames?'

'Fay,' Rhianna breathed. 'Fay . . .' She snapped her eyes shut, ramming them tightly, blinding herself against the heat, the horror.

'So now you understand the better, my dear, dear Rhianna.'

Rhianna's whisper wavered. She felt so sick it was like a slithering serpent deep in her gut. 'A human torch. Screaming –'

'And he thinks, his fault for leaving them so.' Carl pressed her arm lightly. 'His father trying to bring water. Collapsing. And now you ask him to forget?'

'Not to forget!' she cried rebelliously. 'I wouldn't expect him to forget. I want to help him live. To start again.'

'With you? Not the woman he holds guilt for?'

The sympathy was defined in Carl's cultured voice, and when she didn't reply he said, 'You will need much patience, Rhianna. He might never turn to you again. The sight in that room blinded him. As it did you. Yes?'

Carl leaned forward so she could smell his aftershave, see each individual hair of his strong eyebrows. 'If it could blind his eyes to the beauties of the world, what do you think it did to his heart?'

'He wanted me!' Rhianna burst out. 'A moment ago. Not her. Me!'

Again there came that big expressive shrug from the man on the bench beside her. 'Of course,' his hand lifted and his fingers found their way to her hair, beginning to twist a strand. 'Many men have wanted you –'

'No!' she said forcefully. 'No.'

He laughed at the startled expression on her face. 'Have you forgotten that men also gossip? Do you not think that even a Board of directors do not talk of these things over a glass of wine and a cigar?' He gave a little laugh. 'Come *chérie*, men are human, like women, but where women gossip, men say they show the interest. Is that not right?'

She moved her head away from his caressing fingers, and didn't correct his words. Rhodri had wanted her, a matter of twenty minutes or so ago. Rhodri's tongue had questioned, probed, awakened forces that had lain dormant.

She stood up, hoping her face had become as expressionless as she wanted it to be. 'Shall we go in for that coffee?'

Carl shook his head quickly, admitting a lack of comprehension. 'You British women. You take things so –' He moved his hands again, palms up, as if gesturing to the world, the sun glasses precarious between his finger and thumb. 'Is none of what I have said of importance to you? Do you not understand what I have been trying to show you, Rhianna?'

'I understand. You have shown me, but that doesn't mean I have changed my mind. You have only helped to clarify it.' Her tone was business-like, and she felt a pang of regret that she could speak so to a man who was apparently trying to help.

He took a deep breath and stood beside her. 'As you wish,' he consented. 'We will have coffee, and while you wait for Rhodri Blackmore's heart, I will wait for yours. *Compris?*'

She nodded, but couldn't smile. She let Carl slide open the french doors and precede her. The place was empty, chill. She looked instinctively to the grate. Logs were there, but no fire had been attempted. She excused herself temporarily to Carl, then went in search of Mrs Foster or Rosie.

'You haven't,' she said to the former, 'put a match to the fire in the main room.'

'Mr Rhodri just gave special orders,' Mrs Foster said importantly. 'There are to be no more fires in this house. He doesn't like them and he doesn't want them.'

'In that case maybe you won't mind supplying Mr Rhodri's guest with coffee,' Rhianna said calmly.

Mrs Foster smiled as if a nasty interview was at an end. 'I'll fetch it myself,' she said. 'You just sit yourself down in there and wait.'

Rhianna went back to where Carl had made himself comfortable in the corner of the settee, but she didn't like

what she saw in the huge mirror behind the clock and rearing horses on the mantelshelf. She looked pallid with a veiled expression about her eyes, as if the Rhianna in the mirror didn't want anyone seeing what was in her mind – or her heart.

Carl smiled as she neared him, 'The man has returned to his cell?' he asked, as if slightly amused.

'If you mean has Rhodri returned to his room, then the answer is yes,' she returned sharply, and he grimaced in self disparagement.

'I forgot. You do not like me to be less than kind to him.' He snapped his fingers in the air as if to dismiss such a minor matter. 'So that is good. We no longer talk of him. We talk of you. And me. Now,' and he moved more comfortably. 'When are you coming to London, heh? You used to like the ballet. You would like to see *Coppelia*? The lightness, the fun of it will do you good. I like to see the laughter on your face, Rhianna, and not the heavy heart you carry with you at this moment.'

She wished he would go away as easily as he came but, if she were rude, might not Rhodri, at some future date, scold her for being so to his colleague?

Mrs Foster came with the coffee, the cups sending up steam from their placing on the silver tray, while small, obviously homemade, cakes with glazed cherry toppings, accompanied them.

Mrs Foster was smiling, wearing a brilliantly white apron. 'I made the cakes just an hour ago. I put coconut in them.'

The telephone rang and she excused herself, then crossed the hall. She came back anxiously, 'It's for you, Miss Rhianna. Your step-mother. Says it's urgent.'

Rhianna felt a surge of panic, while noticing that Mary was now regarded as her step-mother. That was something else she had not properly considered, and why should Mary phone her here? Had there been an accident? Another fire? God, she had fire on the brain.

She said to Carl, 'Help yourself to coffee. I won't be a moment.'

He smiled. 'I have upset you, Rhianna, when you were so

upset already. I wanted to help.'

She tried to smile, but the confusion inside her only brought a moue, and she was aware of Carl's gaze following her through the doorway.

Across the hall she lifted the receiver. 'Hello Mary!'

'Oh, Rhee-anna, love. I am glad I caught you.' Mary's words were quick, excited. 'There's been a call from America. Your boss, that Mr Paget. He sounded awfully worried. Said to tell you Miss Fairfax is pregnant and you must do something about it.'

Rhianna said nothing. She couldn't. Her mind was agog. So Lynsey had told, or had been ill and others had guessed. Poor Lynsey. Poor Laurence. The whole company could suffer.

Me? Rhianna thought. I am the understudy.

She became aware of being deeply involved in the phone call, of Mary's voice – and of another sensation; like the one she always had when Rhodri came silently into a room. She knew his presence. She glanced about, looking for him, then realised he was upstairs, listening in.

Mentally she scolded herself. She was becoming hypersensitive, not thinking properly, becoming Rhodri-obsessed. She heard her voice as if it were an echo in an empty cathedral.

'Thank you, Mary. I won't be much longer. Rhodri has gone to rest and I am entertaining one of his business friends. I will come –' and she had to pause, the word still sounded so alien, '– home, as soon as I can.'

She heard Mary go off the line, then there was another click, and she knew her instinct had been right. Rhodri, upstairs, had been on the extension.

She replaced the receiver thoughtfully; everything pointed to her leaving here and returning to her career. It was as if Fate was saying, you have done your bit, now get on with your life. The problem was that at this moment she felt that her life was the least of her problems. She wanted Rhodri's life; she wanted it interlinked with hers.

His voice jerked her from her reverie. 'Rhianna!' There was no sigh in the name, it was a command, and he stood at the top of the wide staircase. 'There is an opportunity for you in Manhattan?'

'Yes.' She gazed up at him, and a hint of awe entered her soul. Blind, he might be, but he was Rhodri, and he was taking it for granted that here, in his domain, he was king.

'Of course, you will go at once.' It was a statement.

'Of course,' she echoed, but already her mind was questioning the idea, not because she didn't believe the 'of course', but because she felt it had to be her decision, not his.

She turned as Carl came from somewhere behind her. He went to the foot of the stairs, laughing up. 'Hullo Rhodri. Did you hear the shares of Amalgamated are already on the way up?'

'So it is you, Carl.'

'I thought it was possible you heard my car. She is so noisy.'

'I heard a car.'

Rhianna watched the two men and considered them, then a guilty thought swept through her. Was it possible Rhodri's attitude was irreversible, that the flames had warped his nature for ever? She dismissed the idea as fast as it came. No, her common sense cried; he is too great a man to let that happen.

Abruptly she needed to escape from both men. She forced her smile from Carl to Rhodri, as if Rhodri could see her.

'Well, I'll be off,' she cried. 'Mary is expecting me.'

She waited for Rhodri to answer, but he stood, quite still, at the top of the stairs. It was like a tableau, two men and her, waiting for something to happen.

Carl said expansively, 'Well, naturally, you must allow me to drive you.'

'No! Really.' She tried to laugh, but Rhodri's disapproval was enveloping her like a thick grey fog. 'I will enjoy the walk.'

'Walk?' Carl exclaimed in exaggerated teasing. 'How can we let you walk? It would not be gentlemanly.' He laughed up at the immobile Rhodri. 'You agree, heh, my friend?'

'I agree,' Rhodri returned, guessing the words were addressed to him, but he didn't smile.

Rhianna wanted to run up to him, ask him to tell her not to go, but Rhodri was in no mood for giving solace.

She ran back to the room and got her white cardigan, then flung it about her shoulders. She tucked her handbag under her arm then smiled again. 'Bye, then. Bye.'

Carl came with her. 'Cheerio Rhodri. I will call again. Then we can talk. It will be good, yes?'

'Yes,' Rhodri returned, but still made no move, not even of a face muscle.

Rhianna knew she could stand it no longer. Here was an atmosphere she couldn't tolerate. She ran for the door, out to the sunshine where the blackbird was singing. She hurried down the path, and the thin heel of her black sandal caught in the crack of a paving stone. Rhianna yelped, then laughed to cover her confusion. She ran a few feet to regain her balance and the sandal was left behind.

Carl picked it up, his laughter loud. 'One day, I will drink the champagne from your slipper, Rhianna, *chère amie!*' and he held the sandal above his head, the toe pointing to his mouth.

Rhianna took it from him, her face flaming. It had been undignified and silly of her to try making such a hurried exit, but all the time her mind was asking, when will Rhodri say goodbye?

She bent, putting the sandal on and, as she half turned to look down at the heel, the corner of her eye caught sight of Rhodri. He had come downstairs, to the doorway. He stood in the shadow of the portico, looking like a model in a gents' outfitters window: tall, wide shouldered, slim hipped, curly haired, attractive, but so stiff and straight, his arms hanging at his sides, his hands tied into fists.

Chapter Eleven

Carl's car was low and red with the hood down and riding in it caused a false sense of exultation. He drove fast, his tanned hands on the steering wheel resting so lightly he gave the impression of not steering at all, yet the way in which he took the winding corners on the narrow parts of the road proved to Rhianna he knew what he was doing, and she sat back to enjoy the rush of wind lifting her hair from the back of her neck as if to blow all her misgivings away.

Carl's joy in living became infectious and, for a short while, Rhodri became a blur in her mind, a tormenting anguished blur, but not as painful as if she had been walking alone.

The car had to cover more miles by road than Rhianna would have done by foot across the fields and, as it came to the coast road, the Channel was set, a panorama before them, unbelievably blue, the sand a thin golden crescent framing its edge on this side and the Devonshire hills marking its limit on the other.

Carl stopped the car where the view was framed by two sycamore trees. For a few moments he gazed down at the swell and twinkle of the tide, then he turned to Rhianna, his dark eyes bright, his head nodding just a little. 'You inherited a very beautiful country, Rhianna.'

She agreed. 'Have you seen much of it?'

'London, a little. Cardiff, a little more. The castle there has a fine history, but I am told the one at Caenarfon has better.'

'It has,' Rhianna enthused. 'Caenarfon is where the Princes of Wales are crowned.'

Carl raised a finger as if listening while he thought. 'Ah yes, I do remember a charming story. About the first Prince

158

of Wales. Is that so?'

Rhianna clasped her arms about herself. Soon she would be leaving here for ever, so now was the time to relish every scrap that was available. 'What a fox the first King Edward must have been,' she exclaimed. 'The Welsh had been harassed on all sides from the Isle of Anglesey right down the borders. The King announced we could have our very own prince; one who had done no harm to any man and had never spoken a word of English. And do you know what he did?'

Obligingly Carl shook his head.

'He arranged for his first son to be born there, at the castle, and the place hadn't even been finished, then he carried the new baby out to the waiting crowds and yelled, "Here is your prince who has never harmed another, nor yet spoken one word of English." '

Carl's lips twitched at her seriousness, and his thick eyebrows rose as high as they could go. 'He yelled like that! Tut tut, that was indeed a dreadful thing for a King to do.'

Rhianna collapsed back in her seat, laughing with him. 'Well, anyway,' she said, a little shamefaced at having been so intense about something that happened hundreds of years ago, 'since then, every first born son of the English ruler has become Prince of Wales.'

'Yes now you all speak English, yes?'

'No,' Rhianna corrected less merrily. 'You should go down to Carmarthen. It's only twenty-seven miles away. Go on market day when the farmers are in town and listen to them gabbling to each other – all in Welsh. And they talk so fast. I tried to learn the language once. It seemed the right thing to do when you're born and bred in a country, but I couldn't. An odd word or two, but nothing more.'

Carl nodded, as if he understood. He moved his shoulders. 'I too, am not so good with languages. French, yes, because my mother was French. And Danish, because my father was Danish.'

Rhianna was staring at him, thinking, what a mixture he was. He obviously saw it because he laughed. 'You are thinking I am one hell of a mongrel, yes?'

Aghast her thoughts were so apparent Rhianna shook her head, but his laughing went on. 'So, yes, I am a mongrel. Who is not these days? And are we all not better for it? We are a bit of everybody, which is good.'

Rhianna didn't know whether to nod or argue. She said, 'The Welsh-Welsh would never agree with you.'

'Welsh-Welsh?'

Rhianna prepared to explain. The wind was a warm breeze, carrying the scent of gorse from the cliff tops, while yachts with red sails set out from the Mumbles Head, lining up as if for a race.

She said, 'Here in Wales, you have different grades of Welsh; the Anglo-Welsh, the Welsh – that is me; I am Welsh born, but I don't speak the language – then there are the Welsh-Welsh.'

Carl enjoyed her company, the balmyness of the air. 'I know. I know. The Welsh-Welsh are the people born here, who stay here, pass the language on to their children, and are patriotically possessive of their inheritance. So?'

'Yes,' Rhianna agreed. 'Now tell me about you. Your mother was French, so you are a French Dane.' She laughed teasingly, and he started up the engine of the car, apparently not so pleased to talk about himself.

'She was a concert pianist,' he called, as he drove. 'So we lived wherever she played. I thought I had been everywhere in the world – even Moscow – but always I like to come to Wales.'

'What brings you here these days? Rhodri?'

'Business,' he said curtly, and Rhianna knew that that particular subject was closed.

Even so, her mind was working. Rhodri must really be back in the swing of things. She reflected that it was possible Carl had investments in Switzerland. It would not surprise her if Blackmore interests were worldwide. She had no reason to be concerned for Rhodri now. His confidence was back and his money would take care of everything else – his home, his staff, his general health – but she did long for a miracle to bring back his sight.

Had his eyes actually been burned? Was the trouble

partly psychological as Carl had hinted? Rhodri certainly had a will that could cure or kill him. Could it blind him also?

Abruptly she brought her thoughts back to the present. She wasn't being fair to Rhodri. If he said he was blind, then he was blind.

Carl obeyed her instructions and stopped the car outside the whitewashed cottage. Mary appeared as if she had been watching from the window, and Carl gazed at Rhianna, then at the open doorway with an expectant look. He was waiting for an invitation, but Rhianna didn't give it.

She held out her hand. 'Thank you, Carl. It has been a pleasure.'

'More of the shove-off, heh?'

'Afraid so.' She smiled, and left her seat. On the pavement she closed the car door and turned to Mary whose eyes were wide with curiosity. Rhianna called to her pointedly. 'I won't be a moment.'

Carl gave a perfunctory nod. 'If that is the way it is to be.' He smiled and held out his hand. Rhianna extended hers and he took it, his lips lightly brushed her knuckles. 'Only you can make your happiness, Rhianna.'

His gaze held hers, questioning. 'You sure you want to leave this beautiful country of yours? These mountains and valleys? All this lovely so green-ness?' But Rhianna knew the question really was, do you want to leave Rhodri?

'Yes,' she said, dishonestly. 'I shall be away on the first available plane.'

Still he gazed at her, even though she could no longer look at him. She said, 'It's only once in a life time that a girl gets a chance like I have been offered.' She wondered, though, why she was trying to justify herself and turned quickly from him. 'Good bye, Carl. And thank you – for everything.'

He shrugged. 'Just one friend trying to help another.' Then he drove away, the car making more noise than ever, as if Carl was furious and was taking it out on the pedals at his feet.

Indoors, Mary could hardly contain her curiosity, 'Are you going to phone America now? I was telling my friend, it isn't really New York you are in, it's Manhattan. That is right, isn't it?' At Rhianna's nod she went on, 'Oh, you'd never believe the ignorance of some people. I had to explain that Broadway is in Manhattan . . .'

Rhianna let her natter on. Mary was doing no harm and, while she talked, it meant that Rhianna needn't.

It was half an hour later when she telephoned Transatlantic and heard the familiar American accent on the line.

'Hya Chick,' Laurence called.

'Hya,' she replied easily. 'I hear Miss Fairfax is pregnant.'

'Not just pregnant,' Laurence Paget said agreeably. 'We could take that a little longer. It's the fainting all over the place that upsets the routine. Like we all go running around with cold wet pads to stick on her head, then hope everything will be all right on the night.'

Rhianna laughed in a faintly highly-strung way. There was that certain type of excitement growing inside her; it made her hands damp and her knees weak.

'So when'll you be here?'

'As soon as possible,' Rhianna retorted. She was relieved. She was getting away at last; away from The Turrets and the man who was blind in more ways than one. She was relieved. Of course she was.

She put the receiver down and waited for the operator to call her back, to let her know the cost of the call so she could reimburse Mary. She wanted to cry. She told herself it was because here came her big chance, presented on a plate as Laurence always promised. She was not crying because of the man who looked so proudly alone in the shadow of a portico.

Before the day was over she had got a flight time.

She was up early next morning, then rushed to the shops to buy a gift for Mary. She didn't think the unlined cape in Welsh wool was worth the price asked, but she did know Mary would never buy one for herself, and it would help keep out the cold when winter set in once more.

She also had a strange feeling of guilt as she handed the cape over, as if she was saying, 'Mary, I forgive you for taking all I thought was mine – my home and all the bits and pieces in it,' when she couldn't forgive anything of the sort. She actually only said, 'There's a little musical box upstairs that used to be mine. May I take it with me?' and her voice quavered, shy of asking.

Mary beamed, 'Oh Ree-anna, how I wish you would. I told Will I'd feel awful, but he said you'd understand, and you have. I'll look after your home, love. It'll always be here for you. and when I die I promise it will all pass back to you.'

'Oh no!'

'Oh yes, love,' Mary insisted. 'The will is already in the solicitor's hands. Though, mind you, I'm not promising to die early so you can move in.'

Rhianna hugged her and Mary's arms went about Rhianna. For almost a minute the two women clung together, neither realising how much they needed each other, but each knowing full well how much the cottage meant to them both.

'Thank you,' Rhianna said at last. 'I'm glad Will left it all to you.'

'Only as caretaker, mind you,' Mary quipped. 'I told him that and he didn't argue.'

They were in the kitchenette a short while later when Mary said, 'Oh, by the way, while you were out Mr Rhodri phoned.'

Rhianna's head jerked to look at the older woman, and Mary's eyes clouded over as she hung up the blouse Rhianna had just ironed for herself. 'He asked what your plans were. That's all.'

'Did you tell him?' Rhianna stood against the wall cupboards, the steam iron in her hand.

Mary said, 'I told him you'd be leaving about two.'

Rhianna pressed the pleats in the french-navy skirt she intended wearing on her journey, then emptied the iron, put it on the work surface to cool, and folded the ironing board away.

Rhodri had telephoned. He had thought enough about her to telephone. She felt unable to think clearly, the mixture of happiness and sadness was taking so long to sort

163

itself out. She had to be happy, pleased with herself, and not let this deep-gut anguish spread any further.

Mary said tentatively, 'I thought it was nice of him, phoning.'

'Yes,' Rhianna said, and wished her chest didn't feel so constricted. America was such a long way away.

'He said he would ring again before you go.'

Suddenly Rhianna didn't want to go, didn't want to be a star. She wanted to be with Rhodri before the log fire, with Rhodri in the garden listening to the black bird. She said quickly, 'I'll nip upstairs, time is flying.'

They were having their last meal together when the phone on the sideboard a few feet away rang, and Rhianna found she couldn't leave her chair, couldn't lift her gaze from the cucumber sandwich she had just cut in half on her plate.

Mary looked at her and hesitated. 'That's probably him now.'

'You answer it,' Rhianna said. 'I hate goodbyes.'

The ringing became insistent and Mary bustled to oblige. 'Hello? Yes, she's here.' She held the receiver out and Rhianna left the table. She needed to swallow but her throat wouldn't work.

'Hello, Rhodri.'

'Rhianna —' and there was the sigh as she had never heard it before; it was a verbal caress that floated around and through her. 'You are going this evening?'

'Yes.' She imagined him there. In his room, alone, the receiver held to the side of his head. 'Are you wearing the sun glasses?'

'No.' The words meant nothing. It was the silences in between that meant so much.

Rhodri said, 'Carl came back here. He is going to America shortly.'

'Is he? He didn't say.'

'He told me.'

The clock in the hall at The Turrets chimed and Rhianna said quickly, 'You're in the hall!'

'Yes. Why?'

164

'No reason. I just imagined you in your room, that's all.'

'One o'clock,' he said. 'You'll be off soon.'

'The taxi is coming at quarter past.'

The silence was long. She could hear him breathing.

'Well, have a good journey.'

'Thank you. I'll try.'

'Goodbye then.'

'Bye –'

And it was over. The final goodbye.

She was shaking, a sort of ague. Her lips trembled. She felt awful.

Mary said quietly, 'Come and sit down *cariad*. I've made a fresh pot of tea. You've just got time for it.'

The first hour in New York exhilarated Rhianna. She sniffed the diesel filled air and didn't attempt to compare it with the sea-smell of Whesley. It was one big challenge. The world was waiting and she was ready. On the plane she had re-studied the play, rememorised her lines and as she went through customs she had been murmuring them to herself. She had to be as one with New York again. Fast.

Once in the silence of the apartment her bravado sagged. She had been proud she could manage without sharing, but now she longed for a welcoming voice, to hear someone say they were pleased to see her.

God, she missed Rhodri. She made coffee and lit an old cigarette. All right, it was bad for her, but so was knowing she loved Rhodri Blackmore. She had been wise in the first place to have doubts about going back. She could have guessed what would happen. Her head had said one thing and her heart had said another. Her head had been right.

Subconsciously she must have known a man like Laurence was waiting in the wings. Poor Laurence. For so long he had been understudy to Rhodri. She needed to make it up to him.

She stubbed out the cigarette. It tasted vile and probably did do an awful lot of harm. She didn't want a cigarette. She didn't want anything. She wanted everything.

She wanted Rhodri and The Turrets, the sunlight in the garden, the blue tits swinging upside down. She wanted stardom, the topmost peak, her films translated into every language of the world and, yes, she wanted Laurence to be happy to.

Blast! Blast! Blast!

She had a bath. She put in lots of scented mixtures and lay among them. She told herself no bath at The Turrets could be as enjoyable as this. The system for heating the water probably didn't work.

She knew she was thinking like a spoiled child. Well, she would get over it. At least this time she hadn't flung Rhodri's ring into a welter of dancers, hadn't shamed him unmercifully. But she felt she had walked out on him, hadn't even said a proper goodbye. She should have gone to him, put her arms about him and whispered, 'Rhodri, I love you. I love you and I'm going to miss you.'

She got into her dressing-gown and heaved her suitcase onto the bed. The sooner she got unpacked the sooner she could kid herself she was really where she ought to be.

She opened the case. The deep pink jersey dress lay on the top and sitting on it was a small package. She lifted it, wondering. The handwriting was vaguely familiar. Mary? Rhianna smiled, so Mary had decided to return gift for gift, and slipped it surreptitiously into the suitcase as a surprise. Poor, dear Mary.

The telephone rang and Rhianna went to answer. It was Laurence.

'Ah, so you're back, darling.' His voice was relaxed.

'Yeh.' She slipped into the Americanism easily, and her tone was sarcastic. 'Thanks a lot for meeting me at the airport.'

'I intended to. You know me.'

'I know you. It doesn't matter. Thanks for giving me so much time off, but now I'm back. I have a snorter of a headache, I'm suffering from home sickness. And I want to be left alone.'

There was a pause, as if Laurence was not happy with her attitude. He said, still relaxed, 'I happen to be your mentor and friend, as well as your producer, Rhianna. You are not supposed to talk to me as if you don't give a damn.' The reproach was strong in the clear way the words came. 'I told you. I meant to collect you, but Lynsey Webb went and had an abortion.'

Rhianna's brain clicked. An abortion? The one thing she had never considered. Of course, other people had to make decisions too, and Lynsey had made this one. Dear heaven, what a rotten, stinking world it was.

Rhianna wanted to slam down the receiver, block Laurence Paget and all he stood for out of her life, but a thin line of common sense refused.

'Oh yes,' she commented.

'So she might be back,' he said, as if it made no difference to him.

Rhianna said, as if she didn't care either. 'So what happens now. Am I Miss Fairfax or her understudy?'

'She'll be laid up a coupla weeks. It's hit us all sideways and we cancelled tonight's show. You're on tomorrow. Silly bitch went off this morning to some darned quack. Thought she could be on stage again tonight. She couldn't. She looks ready for her box.'

'Charming,' Rhianna said, and felt sick. 'Was Terry awfully upset about it?'

'He's gone. Left her.'

'Oh! no!'

'So you're on. See you in the morning.'

'I'm not ready yet!' Blind panic.

'I'll make you ready. I'll be there. In the front row every performance. Watching you and I shall will you ready. Will you ready for all Warren has planned, ready for our wedding in Madison Square. Make no mistake, sweetheart, this is it. Get it? You are not going to fail. You've got it and you're going to let them see it. O.K.?'

'O.K.' Rhianna murmured.

'Good girl. Now get plenty of kip and come out sparkling.'

'I need to study –'

'You know it all. It's all there! In you! What you need is

167

that extra stamina to flash over those footlights. Stun them, Rhianna! You're going to stun them! Every damn one of them. Get it?'

'All right.' There was no confidence in her voice and she told herself Laurence probably guessed she could have come back sooner than this. His disapproval had been shown in him not meeting her, now he was the business-man, the man grasping this chance to give her all she had claimed she lived for. 'Thank you,' she said softly.

He blew her a kiss along the wires. 'Good kid, chin up.'

The call ended and she felt shattered. So this was Laurence when things got going. Could she spend the rest of her life with him?

She went slowly back to her suitcase and the intriguing package, turning it in her fingers, having to draw her mind away from the vigour, the overpowering ambition in Laurence's voice.

It had to be from Mary. She was the only person who had access to the suitcase before it was locked.

Inside the crinkled envelope was another, smaller pack-age, but first there was a letter: '*Dear Rhianna, it was lovely having you home with me. You looked thin when you first came but you look better now. Mr Rhodri phoned when you had gone to the village and he said Johnnie was bringing a message. When he came he gave me the enclosed but said you were not to open it until you got to Manhattan, so I hid it in your case. Hope you don't think I nosey-parkered be-cause I didn't.*'

It was signed, 'Mary,' but already Rhianna had put the letter aside, the package from Rhodri in her hand. She held it tenderly, as if trying to transfer every touch he gave it to herself.

She left the bedroom and sat in the deep armchair in the sitting room. The place was basically decorated in green while the cushions were all the shades of autumn.

Rhianna's anticipation grew into a sensation almost as strong as passion, but remained as gentle as the first kiss. He had thought enough about her to send her this package. He had sat in that lonely room and decided to send her a gift.

168

She opened it on her lap as if afraid it contained grains of gold sand that might shiver from its wrappings and fall away. There was tissue paper. Then?

The sapphire ring.

Rhianna stared at it, gasping, twisting it so the light caught the deep blueness of it, flashing reflections of beauty, the small enclosing diamonds glittering like tiny snowflakes dissolving on a window pane.

She shook. She felt she would choke. He must have kept the ring all this time. Carl had picked it up from the dance floor, Fay had snatched it, and Rhodri had taken it back on the promise of giving her another. Then Rhodri had kept it. All this time.

She lay back in the chair, flummoxed. She had kept something too – the box the ring belonged in. It was still in the bottom of the suitcase.

What on earth was wrong with the man? If he could keep her ring so long why couldn't he love her? He had wanted her with his body. Surely, with a little effort he could also want her with his heart and, she whispered, with his soul?

She slipped the ring onto the finger of her left hand, then took it off. Laurence would query it. She put it on the third finger of her right hand. Even when she was Mrs Paget she could use it as a dress ring. She stared at it, at the blue of Rhodri's eyes, remembering. It looked young, every bit of the nineteen years she had been when she chose it.

'Are you sure you like it?' Rhodri had asked dubiously as they stood in the jewellers like any other romantic couple.

'Of course I do. I wouldn't have chosen it otherwise.' Her voice had risen a little in exasperation. Why did he have to be so obtuse? Always treating her like a child.

'There are others. Better –'

'I like this one. I want this one. It's like the sky over The Turrets.'

She had meant it's like the sky when we lay on the grass and you kiss me; she had meant, it's the blue that belongs to you and me, deep and glorious.

With the ring twinkling Rhianna opened the envelope that had been wrapped about it. The handwriting was

Rhodri's, and her inside lurched as if all her need of him had risen in one great sweep.

'*Dear Rhianna, This is probably not in a straight line. Maybe I should learn to type but no one else could write this note for me. I would like you to find a use for the enclosed. Maybe give it to your first daughter. I am sure many men must ask you to be their wife, but choose Carl. The stage will discard you one day. A man like Carl never will.*'

None of it was what Rhianna wanted to read. None of it was what she wanted to be told. It was signed 'Rhodri'. Not love Rhodri. Just Rhodri.

She took the little sapphire ring off and found the box. Placing the two together she put them back in the suitcase. A tight band crawled around her love for Rhodri Blackmore. Her memories and dreams moulded into one then became entangled in the lock that held the band fast. All that had been buried. All she had to do was forget; concentrate instead on tomorrow evening and impending failure on stage.

When tomorrow evening came Laurence quietly instructed the make-up girls to see that Rhianna had extra attention around the eyes, get rid of those dark circles and, for heaven's sake, put some colour into her face.

Rhianna wanted to hold his hand perpetually. She peeped out as the audience began to file into the theatre. 'I can't do it,' she whispered. 'Everyone knows I can't do it.'

Laurence spun her round to face him, his expression relentless. 'I have said you can not only do it, but you can do it better than it has ever been done before!'

'No Laurence. I made such a hash of it last time.'

'Every man jack of those people paid good money to see this show and I worked like hell to get Warren to back it. He believes the Yanks don't want Oscar Wilde. You are going out there to prove that they do!'

She was shaking. 'I can't remember the first words.'

'Those people are expecting Lynsey. They liked Lynsey – Some of them loved Lynsey – and they are not going to be pleased when you first get out there!'

'No Laurence.'

'You want to be a star? The greatest since Garbo?'

'Oh yes, Laurence.'

'Then go and lie down in your dressing room, close your eyes and slowly count ten backwards. The worse you feel now the better you'll be on stage. Get it?'

'Yes, Laurence.'

She lay in her dressing room. She counted ten tens backwards, then went on stage ready for the silence of failure, for the end of everything.

Her first line quavered out, 'I am always smart! Am I not, Mr Worthing?'

Mr Worthing's reply came, 'You're quite perfect, Miss Fairfax.'

And suddenly Rhianna wanted to believe him, knew she had to believe him. She saw Laurence, as he had promised, in the front row, mouthing, 'You are quite perfect,' and she felt his belief in her add strength to the lines. She truly was 'quite perfect'.

Her lips moved and the play began to grow. '. . . I intend to develop in many directions . . .' and she knew it was true. She was going to develop in many directions.

Laurence pursed his lips in a silently thrown kiss, then he smiled and sat back in his seat, his arms crossed. Rhianna knew that, come what may, she owed Laurence this, he deserved all she could give in repayment for all he had tried to give her. She straightened her spine and felt the mantle of Miss Gwendoline Fairfax slip over her. She was Miss Fairfax.

Three weeks later all New York knew of her. The gossip columnists no longer ignored her. New York had a new over-night discovery. Theatre goers were delighted with her English accent; it had a Welsh lilt. Hadn't Richard Burton come from South Wales? Jeez, maybe this Rhianna Morgan had known him.

They invited her to parties. She was the new craze, a new fashion, and she threw herself into it. Even off stage she was Miss Fairfax. She had needed a new identity. Rhianna

171

Morgan had too much to remember. Gwendoline Fairfax had only her lines.

One evening as Rhianna once more became Gwendoline she glanced out at the audience. There, sitting in the front row, was Carl Jurgan.

She averted her gaze back to the suave actor standing, supposedly nonchalantly before her, a moronic smirk on his smooth skinned face. She had forgotten her lines.

Keep calm, her mind screamed. Keep calm!

The prompter whispered. She heard him, her lips moved and the words came. Carl was entranced. Even from up here, from behind the footlights, she could see his eyes, alive, admiring her.

Finally the curtain came down, the applause dying at last, and she hurried to her room and removed her make-up. When the knock came she knew who it was. 'Come in.'

Carl would have kissed her, but she moved back. Space was limited and he was wise enough not to chase her. He shrugged, 'I did not come to gobble you up, *chérie*. Maybe perhaps we could have supper together, yes?'

She had no need to reply. Her face told him she would be ready and willing in no time. He nodded, as if guessing what she was hoping. Did he have news of, or maybe from, Rhodri?

She found Laurence and told him without any sense of guilt that she had other arrangements that night, then they set off for a small place behind Tiffanys, a place that was not crowded, the food simple and the wine good. Carl talked of the flight over, of the weather in England and France, of the snows having gone from Austria, and Rhianna smiled, and nodded, and ate. She made the right comments, and all the time that tight band that imprisoned her love for Rhodri strained to break its lock.

It was after midnight when she could stand the suspense no longer. She said, as if merely interested. 'What are you doing in New York?'

'Talking to a beautiful woman,' Carl returned softly, and she flushed, looking down at her wine glass.

'I meant why are you in New York? You flew over today?'

172

'Yesterday,' he said, and watched her quizzically.

'Because?' If only he knew the anxiety, if only he would tell her what she wanted to hear.

'Business,' he said, and sat back.

Her sigh was audible and she was ashamed of it. Tiredness swept through her, and antagonism, as if Carl had deliberately led her to believe he had come from The Turrets.

She wanted to ask, but she didn't dare. All her longings might become verbal, and she would never live down the indignity of it.

'More wine, Rhianna?'

He watched her closely, and she writhed imperceptably, wanting to escape. She didn't want him, nor any other man, if she couldn't have Rhodri.

She scolded herself, for God's sake, grow up, Rhianna; stop mooning like a fifteen-year-old.

Carl poured her another glass of ruby coloured wine, then lifted it, silently asking her attention. His fingers were deeply tanned, as if the sun shone where ever Carl Jurgan flew, and they seemed to walk around the glass as he gently turned it, making her want Rhodri more; Rhodri's hands touching her, loving her.

Carl said, 'But I have changed my mind.'

Rhianna put her head on one side, trying to remember the last thing he had said, her golden yellow hair loose from its Miss Fairfax plaits.

'About my business,' Carl smiled, and put the wine glass down gently before her. 'I had come to take you home.'

Rhianna's gaze shot to his and held.

'Home?' She didn't dare touch the glass in case the shaking of her hand spilled it.

Carl nodded shortly, watching her a few moments more, then he turned his attention to his own glass. 'But, I made a mistake. You are at home here, just as you were at home in Wales. It is not my place to take you anywhere.'

Dismayed she tried to remain looking pleasant.

'You are like the chameleon, *chérie*. You take on the colours of your surroundings. You give yourself to them so

173

well that you belong. And now you are a succes. Do you know I heard people talking about you at the airport? First class passengers, not peasants.'

He was teasing her, trying to make her laugh, trying to ease the pallor that had come to her face.

The tip of her pink tongue slid along her lower lip. She could taste the tang of lipstick and disliked it. In Whesley very little had been necessary. She said seriously, 'You came because of Rhodri? Something has happened?' She was tense, hoping for, yet dreading, his reply.

Carl nodded and stretched his legs under the table so his feet touched hers. He linked his thumbs into the edges of his trouser pockets, his brow furrowed as if he was wondering how to phrase his next words.

He said without expression, 'He is to have an operation.'

'On his eyes!'

Carl nodded. 'Tomorrow.'

'But when did he arrange it? He didn't tell me.'

'Of course not. It was not known then, though I knew.' Carl tried to look modest. 'There is a surgeon – a Russian. You understand? So procedure was difficult.'

'A Russian!' Rhianna blinked.

'There was such a lot of palava –'

'Has Rhodri gone to Russia?' The idea appalled her.

'No. No.' Carl wagged his head as if placating a small child. 'There are channels through which one can do things –'

'You mean the Russian has come here – gone there – to Britain?' It was incomprehensible.

'He is to arrive –' Carl glanced down at his wrist watch without moving his thumbs from the edges of his trouser pockets '– about now,' and Rhianna sat back in her chair, feeling limp with trepidation and hope.

'Is he a good surgeon?' she asked.

'Very good.'

'Someone must have friends in high places,' she said flatly, wondering who it could be and how much Rhodri's money had influenced things.

'Someone has,' Carl agreed, and his gaze was excep-

174

tionally sober as it settled on her puzzled face. 'You are not happy at the news, Rhianna.'

'Oh but I am!' She spoke sharply, pulling herself together. 'Yes. Of course I am. It's wonderful. It's also scaring. What if it goes wrong? What if –'

'What if it goes well and he is able to see again? You have to be positive thinking, *chérie*, not the negative. Compris?'

'Yes.' She was still gasping. 'Yes. Of course.' She sipped the wine, her shaking becoming less severe. 'Do they know exactly what is wrong with his eyes? Were they burned? What is the Russian going to do to him?'

Carl shrugged, 'I have seen no one but you. They transplant hearts, maybe he is to have transplant *eyes*, heh?'

Long minutes past, minutes in which other diners left their tables, paid their bills, collected their coats, minutes in which new diners appeared, perusing the menu, ordering. Life went on, and the lock about Rhianna's love began to slowly come apart.

She said calmly, 'How long will it be before we know?'

'We will have to find out these things.'

Rhianna had much to think about. 'I suppose his attitude to the operation can mean a lot.'

'That was my thinking also. That is why I have come to you.' Carl sat up to the table again and lifted his glass. He drank greedily as if the time had come to take the next step. 'So, you understand,' he smiled. 'That was my business. To see you and to tell you, but how was I to know you were so successful so quickly? Heh *chérie*? I cannot possibly ask you to throw all that away.'

Rhianna didn't answer. Amid her anxiety was a state of pique; Rhodri could undergo an operation that could make such a difference to his life, yet not tell her, not ask for her support.

Carl took her back to her apartment, but the only kiss he gave her was on the back of her hand. He said nothing more about Rhordri. He talked of impersonal things, like the country's re-armament plans, of inflation, and the litter in the gutters, then his dark eyes gazed into hers before he was going, going. Gone. She felt as if a great chunk of herself had gone with him.

Next day Rhianna did not sleep on. It was foolish of her. She needed rest. How could one become a household name, an *artiste*, if one neglected oneself?

She went to visit Lynsey Webb, and asked her if she felt fit enough to return to her part in *The Importance of Being Earnest*. Lynsey sat and stared. This sort of thing did not happen. Actors did not walk out so others could regain a chance. She touched her dyed yellow hair and said tentatively, 'I feel sort of washed out, you know.'

Rhianna did know. She said, 'I need to go back to Wales, so as soon as you feel up to it, get in touch.' She left her chair and Lynsey followed her, then Rhianna was striding to the door. Her life seemed to be filled with moments of decision. She said, 'You wanted the part badly enough to – to lose your baby. Success doesn't mean all that much to me.'

Lynsey couldn't understand. It was there, in the blankness of her eyes, the nervous movement of her fingers as they twisted together. 'You sure, Rhianna?'

'I'm sure.'

'It's good of you. Does Laurence know?'

'Not yet,' Rhianna pulled on her white cotton gloves. It was funny how she had built up this external picture of the English young lady. All she needed was a parasol. She smiled at Lynsey, then was in the street. 'Here we go again,' she sighed. 'For right or wrong, I've done it.'

Chapter Twelve

On the plane Rhianna tried not to think too much. She had finally put all her eggs in one basket. To put it mildly, Laurence had not been pleased. In fact he had told her not to come back – ever. The backers had not been pleased and the Director had said it was only what he had expected all along. The columnists had a field day, and Rhianna felt sick in an anxious sort of way. She had lived up to Rhodri's image of her. She had walked out, and there was no way of knowing yet how Rhodri would feel about it.

She gazed out of the port-hole shaped window at the blanket of white clouds below her, thinking that this was the end of June; the month old songs said rhymed with moon, which was above and rhymed with love. Morosely she agreed with her thoughts. She was, stupidly, very much in love.

Seeing the desolate face of Lynsey Webb had hardened her resolution. Everyone knew that Lynsey's husband had left her because of the abortion. He was reported as saying, 'I married because I want a wife, not an actress.' So Lynsey could be an actress. Rhianna wanted to be a wife, or – as the wife part might not be possible – the other woman.

She looked at the blue sapphire which was on the third finger of her left hand, and she remembered being taught that if you wanted something badly enough to want it long enough, it would come to you. She wanted Rhodri.

When she left the plane at Heathrow, Carl was there to greet her. He looked splendid in a cream linen jacket and white slacks. He hurried to her, took her suitcase, and she allowed a chaste kiss. It set him laughing, his dark eyes twinkling. 'You trust me so far, heh Rhianna?' Then he was explaining that he knew a quicker way to his car, through here, down here, hey presto; here they were.

'How is Rhodri?' She could wait no longer before asking.
'So-so. The operation went well. Now we wait.'
'Does he know I'm coming?' She glanced at Carl's face.
'Of course.'
'What did he say?'
'Nothing at all.' He helped her into the car before going on. 'I do not think it was necessary for him to be told.' He got in beside her, checked the gear lever and prepared to turn on the ignition.

'Was he pleased?' Rhianna asked, barely hiding her eagerness, and Carl took such a long time to reply that she prompted. 'Was he?'

'It was − er − difficult to say.'

'You mean he was cross.' She sat back disappointed but not surprised. 'I just dropped everything and came. Seventy-two hours − that's all it took me to fix things up − and he has the nerve to be cross.'

'Furious,' Carl confessed. 'Red in the face,'

Rhianna clamped her teeth together as the car sped out onto the open road. Rhodri Blackmore, she seethed beneath the roar of the engine, I am sick to death of you.

Carl stared through the windscreen, his hair flapping in the wind. 'And you?' he called. 'You are furious too? It will be a splendid fight.'

Rhianna sagged, her teeth unjamming. Carl was right to be sarcastic. She had come because she wanted to, and not because Rhodri needed her. She must remember that.

She watched an England basking in a heat wave rush past her − pavements dusty, windows glittering, gardens brilliant with flowers and shrubs − and she prayed that Rhodri would soon be able to see, even if he didn't want to see her.

Carl took her to a small hotel hidden in a side street near the hospital, and his gaze rested on her too long as he prepared to leave her in the foyer. 'Do not expect too much, Rhianna. Rhodri's mind was under stress before this. The time of waiting will be worse. He has been told there is a less than fifty-fifty chance.'

Rhianna wanted to cling to Carl, make him stay with her, let him listen to her talking about Rhodri, but she said, 'You will be coming to the hospital tomorrow?'

He smiled. 'No. I regret that is not possible.'

She didn't ask why. Jet lag had caught up with her, the loss of five hours made her dizzy, but she waited until he got to the street before she went to the lift, then to her room.

She telephoned the hospital. Mr Blackmore was comfortable. Yes, she could visit tomorrow. No, it was too early to make predictions. Sorry, they did not give information over the phone.

Rhianna washed, sighed a lot, then stretched on the bed. There would be no more Miss Fairfax for her. She was out of work. Her name, as far as the company was concerned, was mud. Soon she could be living in a dingy London backstreet, a tiny room at the top of a decrepit old house, with only the Social Security coming in.

She fell asleep fully dressed. Rhodri may not want her, but she was as close to him as she could get, and her body screamed for rest.

Next day she dressed with care in floaty nylon, the same yellow gold as her hair; just in case the miracle had already happened, and Rhodri could see.

She had not expected to find him looking healthy, but neither had she anticipated finding him in a chair with two young, very pretty nurses fussing about him. One was combing his hair, patting and fingering it into position.

'Oh, Mr Blackmore, your hair is gorgeous. All curly and shiny.'

He was enjoying it. Rhianna could see the pleasure on the bit of his face that was showing beneath the eye bandage. He was smug! She had a tremendous urge to flatten his hair immediately with lashings of castor oil, and kick both nurses out.

They smiled at her, making happy sounds, all blue and white in their uniforms. 'A visitor for you, Mr Blackmore. We'll leave you now. See you later.'

As they went Rhianna put her hand across her face in self disgust; so this was what true jealousy felt like. She said unsteadily, 'I'm afraid it's me, Rhodri.'

'Naturally,' he replied. 'Who else would the staff see I was tarted up for?'

She sat on the chair the nurses had placed for her. 'It's a lovely day.'

'Why have you come. Did you think I was incapable of living without you?'

She looked around the room. It was almost bare; his bed, a locker, a washbasin in the corner, a radiator below the high window. She wished he would greet her lovingly, lift a hand, touch her.

She said quietly, 'How d'you feel?'

A little nerve was throbbing in his neck. She could feel his tension, as if Carl had understated his fury.

She said, 'Aren't you pleased I'm here?'

He threw the thin blanket from about his knees. 'It's warm,' he said, and she swallowed quickly, not sure what to say next.

He stood up, as if her presence made him uncomfortable. 'Rhianna! Just why are you here? Did Carl tell you to come?'

'No!' she snapped. Why bring Carl into it? Anyway Carl hadn't *told* her to come.

'You're suffocating me.' Rhodri walked from her, as if already used to finding his way about, and she wondered if those pretty nurses had taken his arms and trained him, their voices gurgling with pleasure. 'I am not,' he rasped, 'on the market for pity.'

'Pity?' He had the nerve to stand there and accuse her of pitying him?

He reached the bedside locker and took a folded newspaper from it. 'You enjoy this sort of thing? Is your career so important you have to sacrifice friendship on its altar?'

He flung the newspaper towards her and she left her chair to pick it up. The front page horrified her; there was Lynsey Webb's photograph, and her own.

'Oh no –' she gasped in dismay.

'Someone else's fault, Rhianna? You didn't give any interviews? You haven't sold your story?'

'No! I haven't!' Her voice rose. 'No one has approached

me. There wasn't a single reporter at the airport!'

'They've tried approaching me. Here, in this hospital. Get the sob story out of the man. Fill the nation with pity. Look at it, Rhianna. Read it! Enjoy it!'

She lowered her head, her eyes unwilling to focus on the heavy black print.

Rhodri was quoting, 'Rhianna Morgan, British Broadway star, rushes to the bedside of ex-lover.' Then, caustically, 'Tell me, Rhianna Morgan, have you made sure your smile will be on the front of every newspaper in the country? Surely you aren't satisfied with only one?'

Her reply was icy with anger. She must not lose her temper. She must not. 'You are deliberately trying to cause another quarrel, goading me. I came to be friends. I would like to be here when your sight returns.'

'It's not going to return! Haven't they told you?' His head was lifted, arrogant and defiant. 'The whole thing is a farce. I should never have demanded it in the first place.'

'Demanded!' she exclaimed. 'Demanded? Who from?'

'Oh, come on,' he jeered, one hand on the cold white radiator. 'Don't say Carl didn't tell you how I demanded, begged for, his help in getting my eyes seen to?'

'He certainly did not.'

'Of course not.' The jarring note was stronger. 'He wouldn't. Fine upstanding man that he is.' Then he bent in her direction, his voice losing some of its venom. 'Carl goes to Moscow on my behalf. He comes back with an eye surgeon. And you weren't told the demeaning details?'

'No,' Rhianna said wonderingly, and things began to click into place. Carl meeting her at the airport, whisking her to a small hotel. He had been outwitting any reporters likely to be interested in her. Carl manipulating. Carl who said he loved her, trying to give her Rhodri.

Her nerves felt so jolted they were ragged. Why hadn't she realised before? And could all this be a great part of Rhodri's fury now; the knowledge that Carl wanted to be part of her life, yet had done so much for Rhodri?

She said calmly, 'The day I pity you the sky will fall in. You're a Blackmore. Why should I give you pity?'

'If I stay blind –'

'You won't stay blind. Another man might. But not you.'

He turned his back to her, both hands clutching the radiator. 'Did Mary give you my ring?'

'Your ring?' Her side of the quarrel hadn't ebbed as fast as she would have liked, and she lifted her hand. The sapphire glittered in the sunlight that poured into the hygienically white room. 'I thought it was *my* ring.'

'It would enhance the story if I obliged you by arguing. It's my ring.'

She stared at him, trying to understand his behaviour, and not sure how to deal with him. She said, 'You don't want me here and, rather than be honest and say so, you create a scene. You hope I'll walk out. Well, I won't. I came. And I'm staying.' Why tell him there was no point in going back? It was too late.

He half turned, and he clapped, the palms of his hands resounding in the small room. 'Encore!' he called softly. 'Encore!'

She watched, momentarily silenced by his animosity, and he waited, as if wondering how she was going to react, awaiting her onslaught, but she drew close to him, gazing up into his square face, at the curling black hair, at the small cleft in the set chin.

She said, 'Haven't I done enough to try and put things right between us? I thought you had sent the ring because –'

'Put things right!' he scorned. 'Do you honestly believe that things can ever be put right? Have you ever thought of what that ring does for me? It nauseates me. Deep down here.' And he thumped his groin with a hard fist.

She looked at the ring on her engagement finger. 'I thought you had sent it to me with –'

'Revenge!' he spat and, when she didn't answer, he went on. 'Let me fill you in, as your American friends would say. And you can begin to think of how I felt that night. "Look what I found!" Carl says, so everyone can hear. "Look what I found". And it was your ring, my ring, our ring. We could still hear you screaming in the hallway: "He's out there now. On the terrace. With another woman!" '

182

'I was not screaming. The band had stopped and so my voice sounded louder.' She put her hands to her ears. He had remembered the exact words.

'And the drunk took the ring,' he said more slowly. 'She yelled as well. Just as you were doing, but she did it from my arms. "Let the silly bitch go! I have just been his!" and I'll swear there were those who believed her.'

'No, Rhodri! Oh, no.'

'You did,' he reminded, and his hand came up, touching her cheek, trailing, the tips of his fingers against the corner of her mouth. 'I wanted to kill you that night, Rhianna. I wanted to take your head in one hand and your body in the other, and twist. Like a farmer takes a chicken. Break your neck and hear you squeal.'

She reached up and brought his face down to hers. Their lips met in a sweetness that comes after bitterness. She whispered as she let their lips part a fraction. 'I waited for you. Waited and waited. Will kept on to me to phone you, but then it was too late.' She kissed him again, and his arms went about her.

'Making a monkey out of me?'

'I was so silly.'

His mouth silenced hers and his hunger was there. She brought her body closer, curving into him, longing to feel his warmth within her, never to be separated.

She whispered, 'You want me, don't you?'

'I can't –' It was almost a groan. 'I can't marry you –'

'I'm wearing your ring.'

'Your ring,' he said huskily. 'It has nothing to do with me any more.'

His hands moved to her waist, caressing her curves, then rising sensually to her breasts, and Rhianna's lips were apart, inviting, 'Rhodri . . . Love me . . .'

The tip of his tongue found hers. She was quivering, her body eager, needing to give. She glanced at the bed and her left hand moved from him; the sapphire ring glinted and his last words hit her. That ring nauseated him; it was nothing more to do with him.

'Rhodri,' she said, and a terrible calmness held her. 'I'm

the stupid one. Not understanding. Fay did wear this ring that night.' She drew from him, her body stiff. 'While she was drunk!' Like a bomb exploding in her head the pictures came to her, all passion roaring away as water roars over a dangerous drop or fall. 'She wore it. Didn't she? Flaunted it! Wouldn't give it back to you.'

Rhodri didn't move. One hand still held her, the other on the swell of her breast, the heat of his fingers searing through the thin nylon of the golden yellow dress.

'I told you what happened, Rhianna. She was like a child, trying to be good. Drunk as she was, she knew she had done wrong. She was contrite –'

Rhianna glowered at him. Naturally, he was defending his wife. 'You did send the ring deliberately to hurt me.'

His hands caressed her again, but not for passion now, more seeking understanding. 'Rhianna –' and it was the sigh. 'What I said about revenge was to hurt you, not the sending back of your ring. I'm sorry . . .' He suddenly seemed completely lost, extra vulnerable and bewildered. 'I wanted you to have it, to remember happier days. That was all. I didn't want revenge. I didn't want to hurt.'

She wanted to believe him. She understood split emotions, suffered them herself. She had wanted to belittle him that night, yell he was unfaithful, because she couldn't bear to see him with another woman, not even a drunken woman. She had wanted to possess him, utterly, relentlessly.

She sighed. 'Why do we keep being so cruel to each other?'

'What is one more question? I still don't know why you came back.'

She gazed up at him, searching what she could see of his face, longing for one endearment, one sign of love, so she could confess her own.

He went on, 'It's true you are getting a lot of publicity because you're here.'

She noticed a few grey hairs mingling with the black above his temples. Had the last years really brought those? How long would he continue in his mental hell?

She tried to laugh a little, 'I came because I wanted to. After all, when a friend is ill, it is usual to visit them. Isn't it?'

He nodded and released her. 'It is. Of course.'

She waited for his hands to rise again, but he pushed them into his trouser pockets and turned from her. He said, as if the last minutes had been completely erased. 'I hope to be out of here in a few days. You'll be able to return to your career then.'

'Yes,' she said bleakly.

'Carl tells me New York is at your feet.'

'Carl exaggerates.'

'Has he proposed to you yet?'

'No.'

'I wonder why.'

'He probably knows he would be wasting his time.'

'Ah yes, it isn't wise for stars to marry. I understand your predecessor lost her husband.'

'The nurses have kept you well informed.'

He smiled, gently ironic. 'I can no longer pick and choose my interests. I have to accept what others consider I want to hear.'

Rhianna took the sapphire ring off and moved to the bedside locker. Carefully she laid the ring there, as if her heart was being laid beside it. 'I had better be going,' she said, and he lifted his head quickly, as if he hadn't expected such a remark.

He said, 'You'll be staying with Mary?'

It was her turn to be startled. 'I don't suppose she knows I'm back. Carl booked me into a hotel near here.'

Rhodri nodded as if he understood. 'Is he staying there?'

'No,' she said wonderingly. 'I imagine he has left London. He didn't say where he was going.'

'You'll be returning to New York. When?'

'I haven't made any plans. Not yet.'

Again Rhodri nodded, his lips pursed as if his brain was working things out. He was standing tall and straight, proud, the bandage startlingly white against the black of his hair.

'If . . .' He hesitated. 'If I regain my sight, I may call on you. That is, if you are still in this country.'

'That will be nice,' she said mechanically, and realised he was telling her 'don't call me, I'll call you'. She crossed to him and stood on her toes. She kissed his jaw. 'Goodbye Rhodri. Best of luck.' And she went; walking out again, whilst wishing she was capable of staying, of truly putting things right.

She made for a leather chair in what she assumed was a waiting room, but looked more like an alcove, and she sat, dispirited. She told herself it was her own fault. She should have expected these things. Rhodri had been through hell and, in spite of his show of bravado, she should have known, right from the beginning of their friendship, when she was still a schoolgirl, that he had a deep well of sensitivity.

It was he who had rescued a wasp from the swimming pool, he who lay it carefully on the tiles, then blew on it, so it warmed and dried.

'There,' he had grinned with satisfaction as the insect flew off. 'Now you are free to go and sting people to your heart's content.'

Yet now, only minutes ago, that man had scorched into her with dreadful venom. Had she deserved it? She leaned back in the chair, telling herself it did no harm to analyse her actions. She had been trying to justify them to Rhodri for weeks.

A woman wearing a blue striped uniform caught about the middle by a wide white belt, a bust thrust out in front, came stalking along the corridor, self importance in every step. She stopped as she saw Rhianna and smiled the smile of the knowledgeable to the dim. 'Miss Morgan?'

'Yes.'

'Mr Dickens would like a word with you.' She made to stalk away, certain Rhianna would follow.

'Mr Dickens?' Rhianna queried.

'He's in charge of Mr Blackmore's case now. Mr Dotoytsky returned almost immediately to Russia.'

Rhianna got to her feet, clutching her handbag beneath her arm as the bust and belt marched forth.

'This way, then,' came the order. 'He is waiting for you.'

Rhianna drew a deep breath, her mouth dry. Was all about to be revealed? Was she about to hear secrets of Rhodri's blindness that Rhodri had not been told? Surely it wasn't usual for specialists to be in attendance at this time of day?

Mr Dickens stood as she was ushered into his presence. 'How kind of you to come,' he said in a tone he must have used to hundreds of people. 'Do sit down, won't you?'

He gave the impression of being a very busy man, anxious to get to the point. He sat as she did and rested his elbows on the wooden arms of his chair. He was a pompous man, his belly no doubt as solid as it appeared in the dark grey swell of his well-cut suit.

He lifted his brows. 'What did you think of our patient?'

Rhianna couldn't reply. It was not a good question at that particular moment.

He understood. 'You found him, shall we say, erratic?' He didn't wait for her to agree or disagree, and Rhianna wondered fleetingly if someone had overheard the discord coming from the little room. 'You mustn't let things like that disturb you too much.' Mr Dickens could have been discussing a secretary's day off. 'We understand he has been having an exceptionally bad time and, even if he hadn't, an operation such as he has undergone, brings about this attitude. Depression, you know. Dread of the outcome, especially for a man of Mr Blackmore's calibre. He needs to be out there, getting on with his business matters. You understand, Miss Morgan?'

'Completely.'

'Ah, yes.' It was if her concise reply knocked him off balance for a moment. 'Hm. Now we come to the crux of the matter.'

Rhianna waited, her knees crossed, her hands resting lightly on the handbag in her lap.

'I understand,' said Mr Dickens, and he sniffed. He was finding this a bit difficult, 'that Mr Blackmore has no relative in a position to care for him just now. That is, no one would be in a position to – er – help him in a personal way, as it were.'

187

Rhianna couldn't conceal a half smile. She said, more lazily than she felt. 'You are asking if I will take care of him.'

'Exactly.' Mr Dickens was delighted. He removed his elbows from the chair arms, sat back and patted his belly. 'How astute you are. Yes. You see, he is not in need of a nurse, as such. More of a – shall we say – companion with a light disposition?'

Rhianna said carefully, watching the man's pink fleshy face. 'Have you discussed this with Mr Blackmore?'

'Oh certainly. Certainly. Mr – er – Jurgan and I went over the matter, then we put it to Mr Blackmore.'

'And he agreed?' Rhianna was incredulous.

Mr Dickens coughed discreetly. 'Not as yet. No.'

'Then we are wasting our time.'

'I beg to differ,' Mr Dickens argued. 'I am used to blind people, Miss Morgan. I can read them like a book; the movement of the hand, the twitch of the jaw, and I can tell, nine times out of ten, which way the wind is blowing. They can be very cagey, the blind, but because they can't see faces they forget we can.'

Rhianna smiled. She had to admit that possibility had not occurred to her. 'So you are saying you believe he does want me to care for him?'

'I am saying we believe he *will* want you to, Miss Morgan –' Mr Dickens was near jubilant – 'once we assure him that no pressure was put upon you; that you, and you alone, had made the decision.'

Mr Dickens stopped talking so abruptly that Rhianna was startled. Was that the end?

Apparently it was. Mr Dickens beamed at her, his receding forehead gleaming all the way back to his strands of pure white hair. After a while, as if he needed time to recover from such an exuberant outburst, he said, 'So, when can we hand him over?'

'Hand him over?' She still hadn't quite understood what was being asked of her.

'Certainly. As soon as you are prepared to move into The Turrets, we can arrange for Mr Blackmore to return home.'

Rhianna felt her jaw drop. She hadn't contemplated

moving into The Turrets. She said, 'Mr Dickens. Mr Black-more and I are not the best of friends at this moment. My presence at The Turrets might disturb him still further.'

'Splendid!' said Mr Dickens, then he leaned forward. 'In confidence, Miss Morgan, you are the ideal person. You have known him a long time and, in spite of his moods — born of frustration, I assure you — you are the one person who can influence him.'

Rhianna wanted to laugh. 'Who ever told you that?'

'I had it on good authority, Miss Morgan. I assure you.' The man was peeved at her disbelief.

'Carl Jurgan.'

'Excellent gentleman. Excellent, with remarkable con-nections. He arranged for you to stay at the Alambra, I understand. Quiet. Just correct.'

'And now he has arranged for me to stay at The Turrets,' she replied drily.

'Not arranged,' Mr Dickens corrected quickly. 'Sug-gested. Your decision, Miss Morgan. Your decision entirely.'

Rhianna stared at him. Rhodri must be paying a bomb to be receiving so much individual attention.

'Of course,' Mr Dickens stunned her still further by saying. 'I shall remain in charge of the case.'

'Almost two hundred miles away?'

'A hundred and eighty,' Mr Dickens smiled. 'Not only do I have a relative in that area with whom I enjoy staying, but both Mr Blackmore and myself are capable of travelling. You see, Miss Morgan,' he went on. 'I am serious. My colleagues and I have gone into this matter most deeply. Mr Dotoytsky specialises in unusual cases, complicated cases and, although Mr Blackmore is unaware of the fact, he has been visited by a psychiatrist.'

'A psychiatrist!' She was gasping. 'Wasn't that going a bit far?'

'All for his own good, and it did prove one thing. There is nothing wrong with Mr Blackmore that surgery and a bit of thoughtful attention cannot put right.'

'You mean he is not off his head,' she said caustically.

'One does have to look into these things.' He smiled

directly into her eyes, an effort to disarm her. 'Of course, Mr Blackmore is bound to hear of it. It will go down on the bill eventually. But Mr Dotoytsky was emphatic. We treat the whole man, not just the eyes.' Mr Dickens swivelled sideways in his chair and managed to cross his knees. 'There is no doubt whatever that Mr Blackmore's corneas were badly damaged by the heat – I marvel his flesh wasn't. The basic question now is, does he want to see?'

Rhianna sighed, here was the basic thought she had so often pushed to the back of her mind. Rhodri's eyes were so tightly closed that he looked like a man determined not to see, yet, surely to heaven, no one could ever want to be blind!

'He's afraid –' she said quietly.

'Subconsciously, of course,' agreed Mr Dickens, and watched her speculatively. 'Here we have a man brought up with the proverbial silver spoon in his mouth, then the spoon unexpectedly snaps and, in a few split seconds, he not only has to see the worst horror of his life, he was also the only one there to deal with it.'

Rhianna's fingers clasped tightly together. She said, 'He's been trying; training his memory. I think he needed the last months as a sort of convalescent period.'

'Most certainly,' Mr Dickens agreed. 'You really do understand the man. But –' Mr Dickens held up a pink forefinger – 'He is lacking that old fashioned requisite, Miss Morgan. They call it love. It could be a reason for regaining his sight. Everyone does things for another; he needs someone to do things for.'

Mr Dickens let her think about it, let her consider, before he said, 'The greatest motivation in the world. Animals. Even fish, need it.'

Levelly her gaze met the questioning one of Mr Dickens, 'Thank you,' she said seriously. 'For speaking so plainly.'

'Then, shall we say Monday?' He drew a large leather bound pad towards him and, opening it, wrote quickly with a gold coloured pen, then he pressed the intercom. 'Sister? Arrange for Mr Blackmore to be discharged on Monday, will you, please?' Then, to Rhianna. 'You can arrange his transport? Make it seem as normal as possible.'

She nodded and all that was left was the hand shaking, the smiling and, for Rhianna, the bewilderment. She had taken on more than she had expected. Could she believe Mr Dickens when he said that Rhodri would agree?

Rhianna considered going back to Rhodri now, tell him of the interview, but the bust and white belt was waiting. 'This way, Miss Morgan,' and Miss Morgan was in the street with a lot to think about, and the future already beginning to conjure up a sort of dreaded excitement.

It was Friday afternoon and Rhodri was relaxing on his hospital bed. He touched the bandage about his eyes.

Rhianna, sitting by the window, saw his movement but said nothing. His stress was almost tangible. He had waited a week. He had another five days to go before he might know.

Might. His tension had permeated to her and she had spent last night sleepless, wondering what she would do if the operation was not successful. Would the experts try to put the failure down to psychological reasons? Was it possible a Russian genius would not be allowed to fail, and the blame put on the patient?

She looked at Rhodri now, in a turquoise shirt and thin tan slacks, his legs were crossed at the ankles and his mouth was down at the corners.

He said, 'What are you doing?'

'Looking through the window.'

'At what?'

'The park.'

'Is it worth seeing?' There was an undercurrent of vexation in his voice.

'That depends on what you want to see,' she answered carefully.

'Rhianna!' The name burst from him, and his hands became fists on his thighs. 'I want to see YOU!'

She left her chair quickly and sat on the bed beside him, as the telephone began to ring.

'You answer it,' he said wearily.

It was George Gubb. The cigar smoked voice of the little fat man came with a note of surprise. 'Miss Morgan? You still with him?'

She smiled. So many people seemed to know about her habit of walking out.

'Is he approachable?' the fat voice came humorously cautious.

'Yes, of course.' She put her hand over the mouth of the receiver and turned to Rhodri. 'It's George Gubb.'

Rhodri took the receiver from her, listened, then sat upright. The pale tenseness went from what she could see of his face. 'I told Carl. I don't want that lot shifted. The index will probably . . . Is it? Now that is interesting . . .'

Rhianna went back to the window. She knew of old that when business came through the Blackmore door, other relationships went out of the window. It was another of the things she had been jealous about.

The telephone conversation was long. It was amazing how Rhodri remembered facts and figures. Once he put his fingers through his hair, then grimaced. He lifted his head towards where Rhianna was sitting, 'I'll have to get a proper hair cut,' he said as an aside. 'I must look like Tarzan.'

'You do, rather,' she said smiling, thinking that he did, but a well clothed, civilised Tarzan, wide shouldered and strong necked.

She heard George Gubb say, 'Well, if that's what you want. All right, I'll stick with you on this . . .' Then the receiver was back in its cradle and Rhodri was leaving the bed. He held out a hand, feeling his way to her, his lips turned up in a smile.

She said, 'You look disgustingly smug.'

'I might be going into the media business.'

'Oh yes?' She had learned to always make a comment because he couldn't see any questioning motion.

'A newspaper,' he said. 'A new field. A new challenge.'

She preened slightly, pleased. He might have post operative depressions and doubts, but he was still planning his future.

'If it comes off,' he said, 'I might need a Woman's Page

editor, or a female columnist or something – to please the ladies.'

Rhianna's heart jumped, was he offering her a future association?

'It's a small paper,' he went on. 'The work wouldn't be arduous. Not for someone who has already made their name. And lost their job.' His hand found her shoulder and he stood beside her.

She said hopefully, 'I wonder what makes you think I would be interested in such information.'

Rhodri laughed knowingly, 'Because you rarely listen to a word I say. I told you not to come near me again, that I cannot possibly marry you, and that you must get on with your own career.'

'Yes,' she cut in, beginning to bridle.

'But you didn't. Miss Bossy Boots went ahead and did exactly as she wanted to do. She walked out. On the whole company.'

'The company will do fine. The show got a lot of publicity and Lynsey has another chance to become the star she wants to be.'

Rhodri bent, as if trying to press his words into her, and his hand slid to the back of her neck. 'Carl put it this way: she sacrificed everything to be with you, my friend.'

There was an embarrassing silence, then Rhianna scoffed, red-faced, 'Nonsense. The man's a silly sentimentalist sticking his nose into other people's affairs.'

'Do you have a job to go back to?' Rhodri demanded.

'I'll soon get another.'

'Producers have long memories, Rhianna. They are in business to make money, and you spoiled that, didn't you?'

'I'll be all right,' she argued, but she knew he was right.

His thumb moved gently against the skin at the nape of her neck. Her scalp prickled and shock waves of erotic need scudded through her. She jerked her head away, laughing unconvincingly. 'Don't do that!'

'Why?' His mouth was twisted, not knowing her reason for exclaiming.

'I don't like it!'

193

'But I do. Stand up, Rhianna.' His hands caught her upper arms and, firmly, he persuaded her to her feet.

She felt her breath tighten. He had made it clear he had no intention of divorcing Fay yet she, Rhianna, was here, throwing herself at him. Could she blame him for knowing it, and taking advantage of it?

He kissed her, his mouth moving to her as accurately as radar, and he teased, laughing softly, his lips playing with her, his hands now holding her like a soft vice.

She said between little kisses, 'I . . . know . . . what . . . you are . . . trying to do.'

'What?' He leaned back, as if attempting to see beneath the bandage, and she put her hands against his chest, pushing herself from him.

'You are trying to coax me into –' and she couldn't say 'bed'. It had been such a long time since he had loved her.

He released his hold and frowned. 'That would be a bonus, of course, but I was only trying to share my pleasure,' and immediately she was contrite.

She leaned to him with a little sigh, regretting her accusation even though she still believed it true. What Mr Dickens had said was so plainly right. Rhodri did need loving. She reflected that so did she.

He held her, one hand moving in caressing motions on her arm, the other on her back. 'I know,' he said softly. 'I understand.'

The sun glowed its heat on to the polished floor, and the only sound was of breathing. Rhodri and Rhianna were communicating without the need for words.

Then he said, 'Has there been anyone important since me?'

'No.'

'Not for me either.' He put his hand under her chin and kissed her again. There was no ardour now, just lips touching as if to seal their confessions.

'But you did get married,' she accused quietly, and he jerked, as if she had slapped him.

Rhianna looked up at him, startled. She could see so little. The bandage covering his eyes hid such a lot. His lips were apart and crease lines furrowed his brow, then he said slowly, 'You realise what you have just said.'

'The fact that you are married and that is why you can't marry me.'

He gave a small choked laugh then drew the edge of his hand across his mouth. 'The fact that you brazenly make up to a –' his lips quirked – 'married man.'

'At least I'm being honest!' she retorted. 'You have the nerve to stand there and infer you never slept with Fay.'

'Maybe I didn't,' he said, seriously tantalising. 'And maybe that's why she hit the bottle so much harder and turned to people like Will Pepper.'

Rhianna's mind was twirling, imagining more than thinking, of Fay wanting Rhodri so much, of Will being a wanderer anyway. 'She didn't get much of a bargain, did she?'

Rhodri moved from her, feeling his way to the arm chair. 'You know,' he mused 'she liked making love by candlelight. It was probably a candle that caused the fire. Will left her, sozzled, ready to become even more sozzled because the evening had not been a success, and he left her with eight candles burning; all around the bed, and her in that damn silly nylon négligé. No wonder the whole lot went up in flames. No wonder –'

'Sssh,' Rhianna said, and hurried to him, standing behind him. 'I love you, Rhodri Blackmore. Do you hear me? I love you.'

'It was my fault, Rhianna. I knew what she was. I knew what the pair of fools were up to. I should have made other arrangements.'

'Was the theatre good?' She had to get his mind from the actual fire.

'Theatre? What theatre?'

'You went to the theatre that night.'

'No.' He shook his head, remembering. 'Oh! That! They wanted me to back a play. I had some foolish notion that if I did –' Restlessly he left the chair. He went to the window and stood before it, his hands gripping the sill. 'I thought a certain young woman might come and be a star in Wales –'

Rhianna did nothing. Was this what Mr Dickens wanted of

her? That she should listen to Rhodri more and more, let him remember and, if necessary, discuss?

He talked now, as if the flood gates had opened, and there was so much coming through; about his father, the shambles at The Turrets that night, the confusion of the weeks following, his inability to cope with the solicitude – the mass of which he translated into pity – his desire to hide until he came to terms with his new way of life, then the difficulty of picking up the threads again whilst so alone.

Eventually he said wryly, 'So you see, the funeral of your step-father was something of an experiment that became a catalyst. I needed to meet Mary again. I owed her that, but I also needed to find out if I could, at least, make the effort and succeed.'

Rhianna waited until he became silent, then she said calmly, 'Has Mr Dickens said anything to you about Monday?'

'Monday?'

So the man hadn't. This was obviously something else the medics were expecting her to do.

'Well –' She found it easier than she had thought – 'I have news for you, Rhodri Blackmore, and the sooner you grow out of this state of self-pity the better.'

He half turned, 'Yes? What have you and Carl been conniving this time?'

'Not Carl; not me. Mr Dickens. He called me into his office. Tomorrow I return to The Turrets and get rid of that burned-out room. It should have gone long ago. On Monday Johnnie will be here to collect you. Then you will come home – to me – at The Turrets. D'you understand?'

He paused, as if shocked at the way her instructions had been given, then he combed his fingers through his hair again. 'If only I could *see*. Just *see*, instead of these damn pictures that are stuck in my mind.'

'Wednesday,' she promised. 'On Wednesday you will see.' She gazed at him for a while before adding, 'You have been right to the bottom of the pit, now you start rising to the top.'

His hands moved out, wanting her, but she avoided them.

196

In her present state she dare not risk a caress, a kiss. Her love for him was engulfing in its tenderness and longing to give, while the hospital bed was so close, so handy, if not entirely inviting.

She had told him she loved him and he had ignored it, pretended not to hear.

Her voice shook as she said, 'I'll be off then,' and he gave an indulgent laugh.

'You sound Welsh-Welsh.'

'And you sound as if you are coming back to yourself.'

He took a deep breath and moved his shoulders as if removing a great stiffness. 'Thank you, Rhianna. Will always said there was more to you than meets the eye.'

'Poor Will.'

'See you Wednesday,' he said facetiously.

'*I'll* see *you* Monday,' she pointed out. 'We'll open a bottle of wine. What do you have in that cellar? Anything special?'

'There's champagne,' he smiled.

'We'll keep that for Wednesday. Any ideas as to what you would like to eat?'

He thought about it, as if her question was of prime importance.

'Turkey?' she said, and her lips quivered with teasing. 'Turkey sandwiches?' It was a joke.

'So you remember that picnic?' He lifted his head, as if looking at her. 'I sat on the things.'

Both were laughing. Rhianna said, 'They were the finest squashed sandwiches I have *ever* tasted,' and, as she left the room, Rhodri followed her.

At the doorway he put out his right hand, 'Thank you,' he said solemnly, 'for your support and friendship.' Then he stood, obviously listening to her footsteps as she hurried away.

Chapter Thirteen

Mr Dickens stood outside his office door, whether by accident or design Rhianna didn't pause to wonder as he greeted her, then fell into step beside her. They exchanged pleasantries and reached the sunlit forecourt.

'You gave him the glad news I presume?' Mr Dickens asked, as he peered around.

'Yes. A few minutes ago.'

He nodded and looked at her happily. 'Better, coming from you. Of course, you do realise that allowing Mr Blackmore home on Monday is an exceedingly special concession?'

Rhianna waited, saying nothing. There was more to come.

'We don't usually like our patients to leave us before the results are conclusive. And sometimes not even then.' Mr Dickens squinted to where his black Mercedes, highly polished and sparkling, as if trying to see if it had been harmed in any way during his absence. 'But Mr Blackmore is a vastly different proposition. Strong personality. When he makes up his mind that a thing can, or cannot be done then, it can, or cannot, be done.'

Rhianna smiled. 'How true.'

Mr Dickens put one hand in his jacket pocket and transferred his squinting to Rhianna. 'That is why we hand him over to you. You, Miss Morgan, can convince him this operation was a success.'

Rhianna returned a trifle primly, 'I can't perform miracles.'

'How do you know?' Mr Dickens demanded. 'We believe he has been given the equipment, now it's up to you, young lady, to make sure he has the will to make it work. You do understand?'

'Perfectly,' Rhianna answered, 'But I –'

'But nothing,' came the tart reply, and Mr Dickens looked anxiously towards his car again. 'My wife promised to meet me here – ah!' He suddenly grinned in great satisfaction. 'There she is.' He waved like an overgrown schoolboy as a rather plain lady advanced.

Rhianna grinned with him; it was good to see two people so happy.

Mr Dickens' hand was extended. 'Well, cheerio, Miss Morgan. Thank you for your help.'

'You'll be removing the bandage?' She had to call as he hurried to his welcoming wife.

'What's that?' He spared the time to stop and turn.

'You will be removing the bandage?'

'Of course. Of course. We'll be down on Wednesday afternoon. Make a long weekend of it. Get some golf in.' Then he and his wife were packing themselves into the black Mercedes whilst Rhianna set off for the hotel.

She speculated on her lack of courage. She hadn't said anything to Rhodri about her actually moving into The Turrets, only that she would be there when he came home. She had told him that Mr Dickens invited her into his office, but not what Mr Dickens had inferred.

It did appear as if Carl and Mr Dickens, and probably every other person who had dealings with Blackmore interests, had decided that she, Rhianna Morgan, was the one to shoulder these last crucial days of Rhodri's waiting. Was it possible they did honestly believe that she, and she alone, could work this miracle? She prayed that it was so, because her faith in herself was at a very low ebb.

When Rhodri had kissed her in the garden last April she had believed he truly wanted her, not any woman, but her in particular, that he wanted to love and cherish her in the way that is fundamental to every normal man, but now she had so many theories that she preferred to consider none.

She moved into The Turrets on the Sunday afternoon. Mary had smiled and looked knowing. 'Oh yes,' was all she said, and Mrs Foster had smiled with her eyes and almost bent a knee in acquiescence. Rosie sniffed and said, 'Well, if it's all for the good of the master,' then succumbed to the general delight that Rhodri was coming home.

Johnnie was more cheeky, all wide grin and sticking out ears he quipped, 'Are we all set for the great celebration, then?'

'You can stop asking silly questions,' Rhianna scolded, but her heart thudded with hope. 'We'll have to wait and see what the specialist says.'

'It'll work,' Johnnie said confidently. 'Bound to.' And he carried her suitcase up to the room Mrs Foster had prepared.

It was a large, clean room, cream walls and light pink carpet, the double bed covered in cream bedding lightened still further with wide yellow stripes.

Rhianna had bought herself two navy blue, business dresses. She resolved to regard herself as a superior type of housekeeper-cum-nurse. That status would remain until Rhodri, or Fate, changed it.

She was in the burned-out room when she heard the fracas at the foot of the stairs.

'Rosie! Don't. Don't hit her with that!' Mrs Foster was crying.

Then there came another voice, composed, feminine, insolently superior. 'No, Rosie. Don't hit me with that, or Mr Rhodri will have you out on your ear. Unemployable.'

'Get out!' Rosie shouted, not even slightly intimidated, and Rhianna hurried to the top of the stairs.

Fay Hanson was coming up them.

She looked lovely, sophisticated, not remotely inebriated, in a white suit, her black hair thick and lustrous about her squared shoulders. She saw Rhianna, and her shock was as severe as Rhianna's.

They stared at each other, then Fay's eyelids lowered, hiding any expression in them, and her right hand beckoned someone from the depths of the hall. 'Come on, darling. Bring the bags.'

A delicate looking young man carrying two huge suitcases found his way between the fatly furious Rosie and the frantic Mrs Foster.

Rhianna gestured to them, 'It's all right. Leave it to me.'

Fay smiled, a flash of perfect white teeth in a perfectly made-up face. 'Don't make tea or anything, will you?' The sarcasm was thick.

Rosie snarled and lowered the heavily bristled handbrush she had been wielding, while Mrs Foster said regally, 'I shall fetch my son. He'll see she causes no more trouble in this house.'

Rhianna moved aside as Fay came up, then they stood, face to face. 'Hello Rhianna,' Fay said. 'The newspapers made a big thing of you coming back.'

'So Rhodri told me.' The brittleness was there.

'It was I who told him.'

Rhianna's mouth opened without a sound. She hadn't thought of Fay visiting the hospital, of Fay sitting there, reading to him, talking to him, yet what could be more natural?

She said unevenly, 'I did wonder how you are.'

'That was kind of you. I'm fine. Really fine.'

'I hoped you were –' But Fay didn't stop to listen to what Rhianna thought; she went straight to the burned-out room.

'God!' she gasped, and her hand flew to one side of her face. 'I had to have cosmetic surgery, you know. Grafts. I use a lot of make-up now.'

The young man came with the suitcases. He was expressionless, not looking at Rhianna, and she hated herself for wondering if he was a gigolo.

Fay went to the wardrobe, lifting out clothes, examining them, grimacing, dusting the shreds of burnt-out pieces that stuck to her white suit. Some clothes she flung to the bed, some she flung to the young man, and he packed them in the suitcases. The whole incident lasted no more than ten minutes.

Mrs Foster, Rosie and Johnnie waited between the corinthian pillars, their faces patient, as Fay, the young man and Rhianna came down the stairs. Fay swept past them, smiling, and led the way outside.

Heat shimmered in the valley. There was a silence born of no breeze, and the young man opened the boot of a white Jaguar and placed the suitcases inside. He got into the car, the windows open, and he waited.

Fay put out her hand to Rhianna. 'Wish me luck,' she said. 'I left the clinic a week ago and got married yesterday.'

'Married yesterday!'

'Maybe I'm being silly, risking things, but Damian knows I was a drunk. He was one of my doctors.'

'Really?' said Rhianna, and the whole of creation began to look different. 'I thought –' She heard a cuckoo call in the woods. The hot silence was easing.

'You thought?' Fay's hand waited, and Rhianna took it. 'Nothing.'

'It's best that way. Don't ever think. It spoils things. And you have so much. Damian loves me –' she jerked her head towards the delicate patient young man in the car – 'but not like Rhodri loves you.'

Rhianna couldn't even blink. This was the woman she had hated for over seven years. She laughed self-consciously, 'The last time I saw you was in a gown shop. You were trying on a bridal gown.'

'Was I?' Fay went pensive. 'Was I half-cut?'

'I have no idea.'

'I must have been. Living one of those dreams. Wishing I was sober, and wanted by someone.' Then she was in the car. 'Rhodri knows I'm taking the clothes. Some of them were his mother's. I used to spend hours in that room, dressing up, being Mrs Blackmore.'

Pity flooded from Rhianna; Carl had said Fay and the Colonel were the people Rhodri loved, and Rhodri had said Fay had returned the sapphire like a child trying to be good. Now Rhianna could believe all that, and wondered why she hadn't done so before. There are so many different kinds of love. She said quietly, 'Fay. I am sorry.'

'For what? Did you ever think I was serious competition? Don't worry. You did me a favour. He took charge of me, made me his housekeeper, gave me a chance. Then, when I let him down, he paid for me to go to this exclusive clinic. He paid the bills, and I met the man who cured me.' She smiled at the waiting, new husband. 'Ready?'

'Ready,' he nodded back, and in moments the white Jaguar was gliding away, leaving a cloud of dust in its wake.

Rhianna turned and saw Rhodri's staff. They reminded her of a disappointed lynch mob.

'Right!' She clapped her hands sharply. 'That burned-out room. I want everything shifted from it. Everything. Johnnie, can you find someone able to redecorate it? New window frames, a new door.' He nodded and she grinned, feeling better than she had for years.

So Rhodri Blackmore was so determined not to marry her that he had deliberately let her continue to believe he was already married. Tomorrow he would be home. And she would be waiting.

When the Daimler brought him she was at the door, under the portico, to greet him. Behind her was Rosie, then Mrs Foster, while in the hall stood the rest of the small staff engaged over the May period.

Rhodri left the car with the walking stick waving before him, as if afraid he had forgotten the way, but he was smiling, not objecting to holding Johnnie's arm.

He greeted everyone in turn, not seeing them, but acknowledging the direction of their voices as they each said, 'Welcome home, Mr Rhodri,' then he and Rhianna were alone in the room where the logs were prepared for the evening chill, and the french doors were open to the garden.

The settee was placed as Rhianna liked it, and she and Rhodri sat close together. It was warm. The sun was already sliding past this side of the house but the air had been heated, and the roses were lined up in vases on every bit of space, as if Rosie and Mrs Foster had prepared for the moment when Rhodri could see.

Rhodri sat in a long silence, and Rhianna didn't try to urge him out of it. When Carl phoned Rhianna didn't call Rhodri to speak to him.

'It is a bad time for him, yes?' Carl said.

'Yes.'

'I understand. I am going to Switzerland on Friday, but I would like to see you before I go.'

'Carl –'

'And Rhodri also. Naturally. You have made it so very clear, *chérie* – it is to be Rhodri or no one, heh?'

She laughed gently, then whispered, 'But I still haven't bagged him.'

'So, may I come on Thursday? In the afternoon, maybe?'

'Of course. Lovely.' She felt like the mistress of the house. She was in charge; the ghost of Fay Hanson had gone.

'*Chère amie,*' came the seductive voice over the wires and, when she made no reply, 'If you do not, as you say, bag him. Maybe I will bag you, heh?'

'Carl!'

'It is just the thought. A little insurance against your lonely old age.' He was laughing, and she had to laugh with him.

When he finally went off the line Rhianna returned to Rhodri.

'Was that Carl?' he asked lazily.

'Yes.'

'Have you seriously considered marrying him yet?'

'He hasn't asked me.'

'He will.'

Rhianna reflected that by Thursday the bandage should be off. By Thursday Rhodri would know if his sight was returning, his medical need of her might be over. Maybe she should give him a jolt now.

'If he does,' she said flippantly. 'I will certainly take your advice and consider the question seriously.'

He held out an arm of invitation. 'What time are you planning to leave this evening?'

'I'm not. Mr Dickens made me promise to live in, for a day or two.'

She sat close and his arm went about her shoulders. He said philosophically, 'People do take it upon themselves to try and run my life.'

She snuggled closer to him and said, 'Your wife was here yesterday.'

She felt the tremor run through him as the comment caught him off-guard, but immediately he rose to the occasion. His voice was casual. 'She said she would.'

'She collected her things. And some of your mother's.'

'Yes. I expected her to.' He stretched out his legs nonchalantly, a tiny smile about his mouth.

'Then she drove off with her new husband.'

The black marble clock between the two rearing horses ticked, the blackbird decided to go 'pop-pop-pop' outside the french doors, and Rhodri's hand tightened on her shoulder. 'It wasn't my fault,' he excused. 'I didn't say I was married,' and they giggled together, their heads turned so their noses were touching.

'Why did you let me believe you married her?'

'To pay you back for believing that I would.'

'So why can't you marry me?'

'Because I have no such plans. What did she take exactly? Can you remember?'

They talked quietly, then Johnnie came in, all ears and interest. He put a light to the logs and stood a moment, watching, to make sure they caught, then he grinned, automatically cocked his head in salute, and went. Rhianna wondered how Rhodri would feel, how he would react, when the bandage came off. What would he see first? Would fires be barred from the house for ever? Would it take much longer to draw a veil over the last months?

Rhodri's arm jerked her shoulders and he said impatiently, 'Did you hear me?'

'Yes,' she guessed. 'You said, yet again, that I should marry Carl, that you no longer have any desire to marry.'

He nodded, his fingers pressed into her upper arm. 'He is ideally suited to you. He laughs easily. He would take you to all sorts of places.'

She said, 'I thought I was going to apply for a job as Woman's Page Editor?' and he laughed, his chest heaving.

'That was one of my weak moments.' Then he shook his head and sobered. 'I have been advised against it. It would be foolish to try selling a commodity I could neither see nor feel.' He was facing her, his lips twitching as if she amused him, and she wanted to kiss him.

'One thing Carl would not do,' she chided, 'is tantalise the way you do.'

'Tantalise?' He made mock of being indignant.

She groaned loudly and turned from him with exaggerated exasperation. 'Well, anyway. As you have made it quite clear you have no intention of marrying me, I had better be nice to Carl. He'll be here on Thursday.'

'Thursday?' Rhodri's arm dropped from her. 'Why is he coming on Thursday?'

'To see me,' she said, but an unexpected spark had lit inside her. Rhodri was jealous of Carl! She had wondered about it before, but she had felt it now. She couldn't contain a self satisfied smirk; was Rhodri continually telling her to marry Carl in the hope she would say she could never, ever, do such a thing? The idea tickled her and she said, 'He's going to Switzerland on Friday, so he's making a quick trip to see me before he goes.'

Rhodri's mouth almost turned down, but then he scratched the top of his head quickly and said, 'Yes, that's right. George told me. They're going to Switzerland. Probably for the weekend. You know, Rhianna –' and she guessed instinctively what he was going to say.

'*If* my sight returns –' she pre-empted lightly.

'All right.' he agreed grudgingly, '*When* my sight returns. I'll have to get a good secretary. I suspect all my business matters are in a hell of a mess.'

'You'll soon straighten them out.'

'Not on my own, I won't.'

'Are you offering me another job?' She was lightly caustic.

'Well, Dad and I used to do it together. I'll need someone else . . .'

'Unless I decide to go off with Carl,' Rhianna said calmly. 'Although I would prefer to be your wife.' His face closed down, the stubborn lines coming about his mouth and Rhianna said impatiently, 'Rhodri. I am proposing to you!'

He took a deep breath and drew his legs up from their

stretched out position. He slapped his thigh, 'Rhianna. We are not suited. Life would be one long hell. You like a man to be chasing you all the time, and I am passed chasing anyone. I have had enough.'

'That's just because you've undergone a wearisome operation,' she said shortly. 'Because you still don't believe you'll see again. Sometimes I could shake you.'

She went to the cabinet and got the decanter of white wine. She said, 'You'll have a glass with me?' and he ignored her, his head slightly towards the fire, as if his bandaged gaze was transfixed by the orange and scarlet of the licking, flickering flames.

She put the glass in his hand. 'I shall say it again. I want to be your wife, Rhodri Blackmore, and it is I who am doing the chasing, or haven't you the good manners notice?'

He licked his wine wet lips then said, 'Get one thing straight, Rhianna. I am not marrying you. I never know where I am with you. Whether you are for me or against me . . .' He was going to say more, but Rhianna sat beside him and cut in.

'Rosie and Mrs Foster are arranging a special celebration for the end of the week. I think they've made an iced cake too.'

It was as if the talk of marriage was over, but Rhianna was deeply aware of emotion flowing between them. He loved her, she felt certain, especially after Fays' assertion, but he was afraid, afraid of what. Of saying yes, then being blind all the rest of his life?

After a while he said quietly, 'Rhianna, have you thought, that you caused the hell of the last years?'

'Me?' Her glass tipped and wine fell down her skirt. She dabbed at it, too unnerved to think.

'You hadn't thought about it?' he probed.

'I did,' she confessed. 'Once or twice.'

'You didn't trust me enough to ask what happened that night with Fay,' Rhodri said. 'Would you expect any man to marry you after that? Isn't marriage based on trust? On belief in each other?'

'All right,' she said wearily. 'I proposed and you rejected.

We can leave it at that. I shall say yes to Carl – if that is what you want.'

'You have a habit of making me feel a heel.'

'And you have a habit of making me feel guilty all the time. Go and marry someone else, you say, while your arm is about me. Go and marry a man who is so busy flying around the world you'll never see him.'

'You won't be able to quarrel, will you?'

'I don't quarrel with you, Rhodri. You quarrel with me.'

'Don't start again, Rhianna. I have been very patient, very easy going. You get into my car. You move into my house. One day you'll blame me for your lost career –'

By the time she went to the room that was temporarily hers, Rhianna had a headache. She should never have come here, never have given him a second thought. She would leave. Mr Dickens, Rosie, Mrs Foster, Johnnie, they could all get on with it. She, Rhianna Morgan, was fed up, up and up. She had stuck her pride on the line and the man had just steam-rollered all over it.

She fell back on the covers of the bed and sobbed; not stopping to realise that Rhodri's operation and leaving America, had all put her under terrific stress too. All she could think of was that ever since Mary first telephoned her saying Will was poorly, she, Rhianna, had nursed an odd sensation that this was Fate bringing her and Rhodri together again. For better or for worse. It had been for worse.

'Am I a big head?' she scolded herself. 'Deep down inside me I believed I could oust Fay Hanson yet, when it comes to it, there was no Fay Hanson, and I still can't have him.'

She lay and gazed at the ceiling, telling herself there is only a razor's edge between loving and hating. Hatred explained Rhodri's changes of mood when she first came home, smiling one moment, bawling her out the next. He had been acting, trying to be polite, trying to hide his hate. And everything he had said was true. It was her fault. She should have trusted him. She should have asked him what was happening on the terrace, even gone to his aid.

In an agony she rolled over onto her stomach and pulled

the pillow over her head. Did she really love Rhodri? In hopeful despair she wondered if it was possible she hated him. How much easier it would be if she could brain wash herself into fully despising him.

A long groan escaped her. Her body yearned for him, for his touch, for his dominance, yet her mind squirmed and said no, she didn't want him. He was right. It wouldn't work. They should both find kinder partners.

Next morning her face was still swollen, her eyes red, but Rhodri couldn't see and none of the staff commented. It was easy to eat at the same table as him and not speak. He had locked himself away again, and when he stumbled against a stool Mrs Foster had forgotten to replace, Rhianna did not rush to help.

In the middle of Wednesday afternoon Mr Dickens arrived with his entourage. He stepped from his car with all the pomposity of a visiting rajah, and entered the house rubbing his hands as if about to perform brain surgery.

The heavy curtains in Rhodri's room were drawn closed with a great swishing of rings on rails, and Rhianna was banished, the door closing after her. The whole house was stiff with tension.

She went to the burnt-out room, not knowing why, and stood in the centre of the new debris. The remains of the furniture had gone in a huge bonfire out in the fields, the walls were stripped of paper, but the place still smelled dankish of smoke and water and decay. She wondered what could be done with it once it was refurbished, and came up with no answer.

After a light tea Mr Dickens and his entourage went. The bandage had been removed. And replaced. Rhodri was still blind.

Rhianna walked to the group not knowing what to say, how to go back to Rhodri, how to cheer him when she and he hadn't exchanged a word since Monday evening.

Mr Dickens' soft pink hand took Rhianna's. 'There's still time,' he said unconvincingly. 'We'll see how things go. Ring me the moment you sense any change.' Then the black Mercedes was gliding away, followed by another carrying his colleagues. They left Rhianna bereft. Without hope.

What did she do now? Let Rhodri return to sitting alone in a room here, while she went and sat alone in a room in London?

She spent a while strolling around the garden. The sky was overcast. The sun hadn't even tried. She looked up at The Turrets and Rhodri was standing at an upstairs window. His arms were outstretched, supporting him against the inner framework. He looked like a man crucified, his head bent.

She ran in to him. 'Rhodri! My love!'

He didn't move, and she crossed the carpet to him. She put an arm about his waist, noticing that one tear had escaped the bandage and rested beside his lips. For what seemed years she stood and stared at it, unable to say anything, not wanting to say anything, her head against him, nuzzling, trying to comfort.

Neither he nor she ate anything later that day. He was tired, he said, as if their quarrel had never been. He would go to bed early.

She bathed and put on her white nightdress. She stood before the mirror and gazed at herself. A ribbon held back her mass of golden coloured hair, her face was devoid of cream. She smoothed her hands down over her hips and thighs, and she longed for Rhodri, then she got into bed and put out the light.

She couldn't sleep. She was in Rhodri's agony, his deepest, darkest hour of perdition. No matter how he had protested his sight would not return, she knew there was bound to have been the hidden hope that it would.

She heard the hall clock strike midnight, and she stared at the window. The moon was trying to appear, scudding fast, then disappearing.

The clock struck one, and an owl screeched. Rhianna left her bed and didn't pause to put on slippers. Quickly she sped to Rhodri's room and quietly opened the door. The place was pitch dark, the heavy curtains still closed.

'Rhianna?' he said, and her name was a sigh on his lips. 'Oh, Rhianna!'

210

She went to him and climbed into his bed. His naked body was warm against her. She snuggled to him, putting her arms about him, and he turned from his back to his side. He nestled his chin against her hair and whispered, 'I'm glad you came to me.'

'You could have come to me.'

'After what I said? And a blind man!'

'We have said worse, and being blind doesn't stop us loving.'

His hands moved over her and her blood began to heat. Her face lifted and her lips touched his jaw, pursuing then parting, little kisses across his chin, enticing, inviting.

He kept talking. 'I'm sorry. About everything. I've been pig-headed . . .'

The top of her tongue tasted the side of his throat, and his hands slid the cloth of her white nightdress up high and higher. His fingers touched her bare skin, finding her breast. His caress was like a match to dynamite. She sighed, then she gasped, and he brought his head down to hers.

She felt the bandage about his eyes and murmured, 'Will it matter if you don't wear this now? The room is quite dark.'

Gently she removed his bandage, then his mouth was tracing across her face, to the lobe of her ear. She pressed herself to him, to his nakedness, and scolded herself for wearing a nightdress on a night as warm as this.

His hands loved her and he groaned, 'Rhianna . . . Will you regret . . .?'

'Kiss me. All over.'

His lips took hers and their limbs became entwined. All the unhappiness of the last years became dissolved in a blur. Rhianna breathed only for now, for the ecstasy he was invoking, for the wonder of passionate hunger that filled her mind as well as her body. His hand trailed down the soft smooth silkiness of her, across the gentle swell of her belly, to where only a lover is welcome, and she curved to him with voluptuous rapture.

Rhodri didn't just take her that night. He gave and she took, and gave back, and they shared the recapturing of perfect blending.

Satiated he lay beside her, breathing deeply. 'I love you,' he said.

She put her head with its untidy mass of hair on his chest and echoed, 'I love you.'

She realised her nightgown had gone yet had no memory of it being removed. She laughed chokily, 'I came in because I couldn't sleep.'

'And I lay waiting because I couldn't sleep.'

They talked softly, secretly, each still caressing the other, then she said, 'My hair's a nuisance. I did have a ribbon in it.'

She sat up, her fingers probing the pillows in search of the ribbon, and she heard Rhodri gasp, then gurgle.

In panic she called, 'Rhodri! What's the matter?'

'Oh God!' he cried. 'Oh God!' and she flung herself against him, staring into his face, trying to see in the darkness. He was a faint pale outline.

'Darling,' she whispered urgently. 'Darling. What is it?' Her mind raced in panic. Did young men have heart attacks? Had the stress been too much? Was he dying?

He put his hands to her shoulders and eased her from him. 'Sit up,' he said thickly, and she did so.

He sat up beside her. 'Rhianna! Get out of bed. Quick. Stand there,' and he pointed to the foot of the bed.

There was awe in his voice and silently she did as he asked. She stood, naked, silent, not daring to think, the bandage from his eyes visible in its whiteness on the floor beside the glossy white of her nightdress.

'Rhianna. I think I can see.'

Even then Rhianna didn't move. 'Are you sure?' She was afraid to believe.

'There's a greyish cloud. Not a shape. Just a greyish in the blackness.' He began laughing, softly, frighteningly, then exhaustedly, and she climbed back into bed with him, shivering with shock.

'Put the lights on!' he urged, his arm groping for the bedsight lamp. 'God! Where is the bloody thing?'

'No! Rhodri, no!' She flung herself over him again, pushing the lamp so it fell to the carpet with a thud.

'No light. Not yet. Not yet.' She knelt above him and put

the bandage back about his eyes.

'I don't need it!' he urged. 'I can see!'

'You do need it. I'm going to phone Dickens.'

'This time of the morning?'

'I don't care what time it is.' She felt hysterical. Rhodri was lying back, laughing, his body wracked.

'Cover your eyes!' she commanded. 'Cover them properly. Put the sheet up over them. Don't let any light touch them. Don't do them any harm.'

She ran downstairs, stark naked, to the hall, forgetting there was a phone upstairs; only one object in mind: phone Mr Dickens.

The man sounded asleep. 'Yes, Miss Morgan. Yes.' He was earning his fee, no matter how high it was. 'Splendid. Well, we can't do anything tonight. We'll have him back in the hospital for a few days. I'll pop over tomorrow.'

Thank God he had stayed in the area to play golf. Had it really been to play golf, or to await the result? She didn't care either way. She wanted to scream, dance, waken the world, yell from the roof tops.

She ran back to Rhodri. He was lying on his side in the darkness. She had to feel her way to him after the light of the corridor.

'Come here,' he said. 'The bed is getting cold.'

She paused. 'Will you marry me then?' Still shivering with shock she waited for what seemed a hundred years, for his reply.

'If you still insist.'

'Of course I insist. I might be pregnant.'

'Already?'

'Well, next time.'

He gurgled, flung back the sheet that had been covering him and she crept in.

'Rhodri,' she whispered. 'Why didn't you agree to marry me before? I kept asking.'

'Tie you to a blind man? It would kill you.'

'It wouldn't. I promise.'

'You're a butterfly, my love. A blind man would be terrible for you.'

'But now you say yes?'

'On condition you remember it was your idea. You did the proposing. I did keep saying no.'

'All right,' Rhianna agreed placidly, while her arms went about him. 'It'll be my fault if it all goes wrong.'

He laughed, hugging her. 'Rhianna! I'll be able to see you. *See* you!'

'When shall we get married?'

'Tomorrow?' Happiness flowed from him as she cuddled closer.

'Next week,' she glowed. 'Give me a chance to get my hair done!' And her lips were pointed at his throat again, while his sensitive fingers found their way to the rose tips of her breasts.